# What readers said about *In the Vale*

... a must-read for anyone with a drive to explore the intersection between life and death, between faith and science, and between God and self... intelligent, mind-boggling concepts of the nature of God and the possibilities in the afterlife.... compels the reader to keep turning the page... Anyone who read and liked *The Shack* will love *In the Vale*.

—PATRICIA BURKETT in *The Southern Cross*

... truly an exciting attempt to give a new insight to the concept of Heaven.

—REV. ALFRED MONTALTO

... great story crafted in a very special way.

—SILAS AYER

... a religious theme and lots of action.... looking forward to the sequel.

—SANDRA BLAKER

A thought-provoking read.... a message of God's grace that touches the lives of all who come together in the Vale. For those who have read *90 Minutes in Heaven* and *Life after Life*... I look forward to a sequel.

—J. MCDONALD on Amazon

Good read for book clubs.... characters you can believe.... reminds me of C. S. Lewis' *The Great Divorce*.

—M. LEWIS on Amazon

# out of the VALE

# out of the
# VALE

*Merry Christmas, Pat*

## John Hamm

*John Hamm*
*& Linda too,*

**TATE PUBLISHING**
AND ENTERPRISES, LLC

*Out of the Vale*
Copyright © 2012 by John Hamm. All rights reserved.

No part of this publication may be reproduced, stored in a retrieval system or transmitted in any way by any means, electronic, mechanical, photocopy, recording or otherwise without the prior permission of the author except as provided by USA copyright law.

Scripture quotations are taken from the *Holy Bible, King James Version,* Cambridge, 1769. Used by permission. All rights reserved.

The opinions expressed by the author are not necessarily those of Tate Publishing, LLC.

This novel is a work of fiction. Names, descriptions, entities, and incidents included in the story are products of the author's imagination. Any resemblance to actual persons, events, and entities is entirely coincidental.

Published by Tate Publishing & Enterprises, LLC
127 E. Trade Center Terrace | Mustang, Oklahoma 73064 USA
1.888.361.9473 | www.tatepublishing.com

Tate Publishing is committed to excellence in the publishing industry. The company reflects the philosophy established by the founders, based on Psalm 68:11,
*"The Lord gave the word and great was the company of those who published it."*

Book design copyright © 2012 by Tate Publishing, LLC. All rights reserved.
*Cover design by Erin DeMoss*
*Interior design by April Marciszewski*

Published in the United States of America

ISBN: 978-1-62024-175-2
1. Fiction / Christian / Suspense
2. Fiction / Visionary & Metaphysical
12.05.24

# *Out of the Vale*

A Sequel Novel to *In the Vale*

# Dedication

This book is dedicated to my dear wife Linda for her faith, tolerance, and patient endurance while both books were being born.

# Acknowledgements

All characters in this book are entirely fictitious except for John Kepler Lea, who graciously consented to appear as himself. I am also grateful to Tate editor Doug Fraser for making me write a better book.

# Prologue

The Ministry of Interior major had stopped asking questions. His face was a mask of rage and contempt as he drew a small, semi-automatic pistol from the polished, black-leather holster at his belt and carefully aimed it between the prisoner's eyes. Then he pushed the muzzle slowly forward until it was only inches from the man's face. The target's cross-eyed focus now kept shifting between the gaping barrel and the slowly tightening trigger finger below.

"For heaven's sake, don't do this!" the victim cried in desperation with tears in his eyes. "What have I done wrong? I didn't mean to wind up in your country. It was all an accident—a huge mistake. I didn't know I was crossing the border. Why do you want to kill me? Please don't shoot!"

The closing plea burst out in a pitiful sob.

The interrogator was unaffected by his victim's frantic speech. Nothing changed but the measured squeeze of his left index finger against the steadily receding trigger.

"I'm no spy, I tell you. I'm just Jack Nolan from South Carolina. I sell furniture; that's all." The prisoner's voice crackled with fear, and his words tumbled forth so quickly they ran into each other.

At last both men heard a sharp, metallic click from the pistol's hammer falling harmlessly against its firing pin. The prisoner's legs went out from under him, and he fell limply to the floor.

"Dear me," the officer said in accented English. "I must have forgotten to load the chamber. Oh well. There may be another occasion. Just remember, Mr. Nolan. Your life belongs to us. We saved it, and we can take it back. You are being very foolish to withhold your cooperation from us."

Now the officer ordered him to his feet for more interrogation, and the prisoner resumed the same litany of lies and evasions as before. The major's patience with these whining excuses and flimsy fabrications was exhausted. The man had entered the People's Republic obviously intent on some act of espionage or other mischief. The major was sure of that.

Ministry of Interior troops patrolling a prohibited border area had discovered him and rescued him from certain death. Meanwhile, another man had gotten away. This one called himself Jack Nolan and carried a passport in that name. His claim to be an American furniture salesman on holiday was just another lie. Everything he said was a lie, and the major knew it.

The only truth he told was that he was an American. The major despised him all the more for that. Americans were all pampered, overfed, politically effeminate parasites.

This Nolan was a tall, well-built man. He must have weighed nearly two hundred pounds before his trek in the snow and days of captive starvation. He now pretended weakness, but the major found him strong enough to resist questioning. The birth date in his passport made him forty-eight, but he looked younger with a head of thick, brown hair that showed only scattered traces of gray. He groveled in panic when he thought he was going to be shot, but his story did not change. Confronted with evidence of the other man, he boldly denied there was one.

The major had enemies at Ministry of Interior headquarters. Even now some were complaining that he was not moving fast enough to break this prisoner. They would soon demand the man be transferred to the ministry itself. There, with the advantage of enhanced coercion, they would crush his spirit, make him talk, and humiliate the major.

The major thought more questioning was a waste of time. He had spent too much of that already. Had he been given authority to just shoot this nuisance, he would have already done it.

"I have no need to talk to fools!" the officer finally shouted, slapping the prisoner across the face and knocking him to the floor.

The man whimpered and spat blood, which the major pretended not to notice.

"I will be back, Nolan, and there will be others with me," he grumbled.

Going out, he noisily secured a lock on the door to the wire-mesh prison-hospital cell of the man called Nolan.

The prisoner pulled himself from the floor and sat on his bed, the only piece of furniture in his cage. His brown eyes were bloodshot from days of sleeplessness and harsh interrogation. His stomach no longer ached with emptiness; he had gotten past that. He absently rubbed the gauze-covered wound on the right side of his head, where one of his border-guard rescuers must have hit him with a shovel while digging him out.

Paul was up to his neck in the snow pit that was drawing him inch-by-inch to his death. He could no longer see the back of his partner Barney ahead of him in the moonlit, mountain meadow by the river. Unaware of Paul's trouble, Barney continued to run toward the woods and their covert rendezvous in the hostile territory of this East European country. Being caught here meant death or imprisonment.

Paul had no fear of being captured. He was going to die for sure. At last the surface beneath him gave way, and he fell into the hidden ravine below. Masses of snow rushed to embrace him in silent, airless, flesh-searing cold.

Paul died and woke up in a place called the Vale.

He was there for what seemed a long time, but time was different there.

He learned the truth about life and death from people out of his past.

He was on his way to heaven.

Then he was not.

Paul was dragged from the doorstep of heaven, snatched from his snow-covered grave, and forced back to life as a captive. He now resisted his holders and prayed to be liberated by some devious manipulation of his boss, Grogan. This Grogan was not yet the therapist who had taught Paul in the Vale, but the still-living director of Paul's shadowy organization on earth.

Paul's prayer was answered. Less than a day after his mock execution, he was freed and on his way back to the United States. There he gracelessly told Grogan, who met him at the airport, that he was quitting his job.

Later that day, Paul thought hard about his new life. Why was this happening to him? Was his premature visit to the Vale an accident or a purposeful act of God? What was he supposed to be—some kind of latter-day prophet?

Just before noon, Paul drove out to his organization's headquarters in southern Maryland. There he wrote and submitted a debriefing report of his final operation, turned in all organizational property and documents, surrendered his phony passports, gave administration a formal resignation, cleared himself through security, and was escorted out of the building complex that had long been the center of his life.

*Goodbye to twenty-six years of Cold War, covert service,* he thought. *I can never come back now.*

# 1

The day after Paul resigned, he called ahead and went out to see his priest at the Episcopal parish of St. Athanasius in Maryland. Long-time friends, they greeted each other with a firm handshake. Then the priest sat back behind his desk, and Paul took a straight chair facing him.

Father Don Richmond was a tall, blond man with pale-blue eyes and a healthy glow to his face. He was over forty, but his lighter hair betrayed very few of the gray strands that were getting easier to see on Paul's own head.

"You know, Paul," he said, emphasizing the name, "it's still hard for me to think of you as anyone but the Peter Goetz I knew in the Philippines so many years ago."

"I needed to maintain that identity then," Paul said, smiling. "I appreciate your discretion in not sharing that part of our history with others."

"Of course I spilled the beans when Petra first brought you here."

"She knew more about my work then than you ever found out."

They were talking about Petra March, the widow of Jason March, whose death had spiritually damaged both Paul and Petra. By divine coincidence, Don had been on hand when each of them, far apart in time and space, found their way back to God.

Years after Jason died, a chance encounter reunited Paul and Petra in a spirit of mutual respect. At first, Paul pretended he no longer did the work he had once shared with her husband. When Don's innocent slip with Paul's name resurfaced the question of Paul's current employment, Paul promptly confessed, and Petra generously forgave him.

Neither one spoke of it again, but Paul sensed he and Petra could be no more than good friends. Fond though he was of her, he spared her the discomfort of dealing with romantic advances from a man in the same business that had cruelly taken her husband.

Paul willingly accepted this constraint in return for her trust and a near family-member status in her household, which included a divorced, older sister named Katya Norris, Katya's children Bobby and Patty, and lots of small animals.

Now Paul was eager to learn Petra's reaction to the news that he was no longer doing what had formerly kept them at such an unnatural distance.

"I haven't seen Petra for weeks," Paul said. "Is she okay?"

"She seemed fine at Mass last Sunday."

"I need to look her up."

"I'm quite sure you will," the priest responded with a quick grin. "In the meantime, what brings you here on a weekday?"

"The whole story is too long to tell. You know I can't do that anyway."

"Just tell me what you can." Don was used to Paul's reticence in professional matters.

Paul paused a few seconds, trying to decide where to start.

"I have quit my job. I will be doing something different."

Don smiled and brought his hands together in a single, loud clap.

"That is good news. What's next?"

"That's tough. I don't know yet."

Don held onto his smile but remained silent.

"You know how carefully I have concealed my work from you and everyone. Now I must decide what to say about this other thing. So far, I've told nobody about it."

Again Paul paused, and Don waited. Long experience in human counseling had taught him the value of silence in helping people talk about themselves.

"Do you believe in near-death experiences?" Paul asked abruptly.

"I believe a lot of people have them, but I'm not convinced they tell us much about the afterlife. Many occur in hospitals and other places where subjects are already under stress and are sometimes influenced by drugs. That's pretty fertile ground for imagination. Some observations are contradictory, and those that coincide are often suspect. The prevalence of such stories is too great not to generate new ones."

Don hesitated, but Paul did not react.

"Have you had one?" Don asked.

"Not the way you put it, but I was dead to my life on earth for quite a while. Now I'm back."

"You don't seem delusional." Don looked more serious now.

"I didn't say I became a radish. I only said I died. If death bothers you, call it time in the afterlife. What do you think of that?"

"It is important, but why are you telling me? Do you want a pastor, a critic, or a cheerleader?"

Paul's face remained calm.

"I think I want a friend."

"That's easy. I already am one."

"Can I share my experience with you in confidence? You won't have to protect the substance—only the source. Prophets aren't so popular these days. They get sent for psychoanalysis or lynched on the spot."

"That's not much different from the way they were treated in biblical times—but what do you mean by prophets?"

"When I died—make no mistake—I did die in the snow in a place I can't tell you about."

Paul paused, so Don nodded for him to continue.

"I woke up in a different place called the Vale, where I learned a lot about life on earth and God's reality beyond. There was no doubt about my death. All four of the people I met there—three anyway—said my time on earth was over. The only thing ahead of me was heaven and the total reality that surrounds God forever. Meanwhile,

I experienced the complete freedom and happiness of my soul, my true identity as I never had or could have known it in the universe we inhabit."

Paul meaningfully tapped the surface of Don's desk as he spoke the last few words.

"What a blessing." Don was obviously impressed.

"So far, so good. Then, without warning, it was over. My body had been salvaged and restored to life on our ratty, little planet. Listen to me; the happiest moment here is misery when compared to the most common experience there."

"So you were only clinically dead," Don suggested.

"Not unless the afterlife is being scripted by cornball playwrights. One thing I learned in the Vale is that God and everything in his reality is *simultaneously infinite*. Where God is, everything is always *now*. Past and future don't exist. For God, *was* and *will be* have no meaning. Everything just always *is*. God knows when I really die, so I should not have turned up in the Vale just for being clinically dead. That would mean God makes mistakes and can't keep track of his creatures. Do you buy that, Don?"

"No." Don hesitated for a second. "Simultaneous infinity is not a very common term, but I have run across it in philosophy. Immanuel Kant wrote something about it in a piece we studied in seminary. Some critics call it impossible and say, therefore, God cannot be omniscient, omnipotent, or have other omni-powers."

"But you and I know God is omni-everything. Don't the skeptics just prove the case for simultaneous infinity? Wouldn't he have to be a simultaneously infinite being in a simultaneously infinite realm to possess omniscience?"

"I never thought of it that way, but it bears the test of logic. It has to be one way or the other."

"I can tell you with authority that at this very moment both of us are already doing God's will in the place where God dwells. Our created universe, from your office to the farthest galaxies, is mostly illusion. Everything here is linear and relative, but that changes when we leave here to be with God. That's why clinical death won't explain the purpose of my visit to the Vale."

"Purpose?"

"What else? Do you think God has accidents?"

"Okay," Don said slowly. "I'll buy that, but what did happen to you? Why did you go there—and since you did, why are you back?"

"Remember what I said about prophets?"

"Yes."

"What is most surprising about leaving the earth and coming back the way I did?"

"Souls do not normally make a return trip."

"Except?"

Don considered his answer before responding with measured care.

"Except for those who have been caught up by God and come back with some kind of prophetic vision."

"Say Isaiah, Daniel, St. Paul, and the apostle John to mention just a few."

"I hear you. So what was your vision?"

"The whole thing, I guess. I saw a lot of weird stuff that was explained to me as being the way life is around God. I had four conversations with people I had known here; some or all of them are still alive. I actually spoke to one of them yesterday when I gave him my resignation, but he had no inkling of our Vale encounter."

"Because he hasn't been there yet?" Don asked hesitantly.

"Or at least he doesn't know about it. Everyone I met told me important things about how God acts on earth and beyond. A lot of that depends on simultaneous infinity."

"How?"

"For one thing, God is not limited by cause-and-effect. He can answer today's prayer yesterday or last year. It is all *now* to him. He does not foreordain our spiritual outcomes. He just knows them, always and all at once."

"So much for predestination."

"Exactly. I also learned a lot about the identity of souls and how that relates to each one's search for happiness. That's why coming back here is such a disappointment. I recall what it's like to constantly know and be what God made me to be."

"How wonderful."

"Yes, I remember, but I can't really be like that here. Too much interference comes from being in the universe of earth. We know the pain so well it seems normal. Believe me; it is not. It is just the best we can do for now."

"What about being a prophet? Were you told what to prophesy?"

"No. Remember what I learned there? Those who spoke to me said I was done with earthly life and on my way to heaven."

"But here you are, back in the world."

"I may have figured that out. One of the things I was told about God's simultaneously infinite kingdom is that what goes on there is entirely disconnected from what happens on earth."

"Is it?"

"Time here is like a linear and relative racetrack. We move in only one direction from past to present to future, although that is not nearly as simple as it sounds. At any given instant, our personal existence is strictly relative to every other existence on the track. We are all moving in the same direction at the same speed. Nobody overtakes, passes, or falls any farther behind another. When you die, your own race ends, but new souls are always popping up to keep things moving."

"That is the linear part."

"Yes, but in simultaneous infinity, where God dwells, everything is always now. The linear and the relative do not exist. The temporal outlook for all who live with God is the same as God's. Everything is *now* for them too, and the limits of time and space disappear. Since everything is always happening now, the spirits and souls around God are always doing different things in different places all at once. The people I talked to said that whenever we die, wherever we are and however long it might take in earthly time, we all go together to meet God at the same time and place. Spending a day or an eon in the Vale doesn't keep us from joining that great convocation of souls before God. We all turn up at the same nanosecond to be with God and to go on serving him."

"That might resolve a few complications in scriptural accounts of the end times," Don injected.

"I think so. All my friends agreed I was out of earth and on my way to heaven, because I am. I may be here with you in the linear and relative time of earth, but I am also free of it in the Vale, heaven, and the boundless spaces of eternity. I cannot see that now, but I know how it will be—how it is. When I finally die, I will be back in the Vale doing what I was before I was so painfully dumped out of there."

Paul stopped talking, but Don took several seconds to react.

"This is very heavy stuff. There are so many questions I want to ask."

"I gave you only a fraction of the explanation I got, and I put most of that together back here."

"Now you believe you were given a prophetic vision, but you don't know what to prophesy or to whom."

"That is the only purpose I can see for what happened, but you're right. I don't know where it goes. I don't know what God wants from me, but I'm sure he does."

"I suppose a prophetic vision can have some outcome other than prophecy."

"Nothing like this happens without God willing it. God has something for me to do—something important enough to route me through the Vale out of order."

"It seems that way. I'll ask you again, Paul. What do you want from me?"

"God will tell me what to do when it is time, but I can't just wait. I left my job to free myself for what comes next. I will be praying, meditating, and studying Scripture, but is that enough?"

"Don't rush things, Paul. If you are right—and I see no alternative—the Lord will have his own timetable. Be patient."

"I hope I learned a little of that from my exposure to simultaneous infinity."

"Don't be so sure," Don said with a quick laugh. "I fully recommend the disciplines you mentioned; they are well-tested paths for seeking God's will. Maybe I can offer you one more lane to explore."

Don took a piece of parish stationary from a desk drawer, wrote a few lines with a ballpoint pen, folded the sheet, and put it into an envelope. Consulting an index file on his desk, he went on to address the envelope.

"I am referring you to a dear friend, who is one of the holiest people I know," Don said, handing the message across the desk to Paul. "He is a Franciscan brother who ministers to homeless men at this address in Baltimore. He is highly educated, widely traveled, and very wise. Just show him my note. You may rely on his discretion as you have on mine. Please let me know how things work out."

Taking the envelope, Paul stood, thanked the priest, shook hands, and turned to leave.

"Say hello to Petra for me," Don called as Paul neared the door. Paul did not have to look back to know the priest was grinning.

# 2

Father Don was right. Paul was impatient to see Petra, but it was not quite three in the afternoon. She would still be at the Columbia, Maryland high school where she taught English and French. Paul decided instead to try contacting Friar Arnold at the address Father Don had given him.

Paul's knowledge of Baltimore was limited, so he consulted a street map from his glove compartment. This brought him into an old, waterfront neighborhood of Baltimore's ubiquitous, stone-stooped row houses well east of the upscale commercial area around Harbor Place. The one he sought was distinguished only by a white pasteboard sign in the front window proclaiming it to be Frank's House.

The block looked rundown, and Paul could not help noticing several men just hanging around. He still felt safe parking his beat-up, fifteen-year-old, two-door, orange Volvo at the curb. It was not easy to break into, and he doubted that super-annuated Swedish tanks were on anyone's list of cars to steal.

Paul was hatless and thought his well-worn sweater, jeans, and scuffed-up shoes were a fair match to the gloomy street and the people around him. He was not dressed to inspire much envy, and his posture climbing the stoop deliberately mimicked the resignation of those he saw nearby.

The cracked-paint-coated door did not look as if it was meant to be knocked on, so he just depressed the latch and walked in. A small entry hall led straight to a set of cheaply carpeted stairs and also gave way to a large, open room on the right.

The front of the room was filled with racks and stacks of second-hand men's clothing. In the rear was a small kitchen with a table-mounted coffee urn, a refrigerator, and a stove topped with a steaming stewpot. A long table nearby held a random selection of cups, plates, bowls, and eating utensils. There was also a large basket on the table with several loaves of hard bread that looked to Paul like a day-old donation from some bakery.

The pot's aroma suggested a few scraps of fatty meat, dominated by a massive amount of cabbage. It was a hearty smell, and Paul's salivary glands reacted despite what he suspected of its source. Three days earlier, starving in his hospital prison, he might have fought for a bowl.

Between the kitchen and the clothing was a small desk and chair, near which a young, black man was trying on a sport jacket under the scrutiny of a much older black man. The second man was tall, thin, and probably in his sixties with patches of steel gray in his coal-colored, wiry hair. He had the evenly black complexion and unmixed features of a native African. Except for a rough-carved, dark-wooden cross that hung at his chest from a stained leather thong, he was dressed as poorly as the younger man. He looked up briefly to note Paul's presence, but continued attending to his current client.

Paul stood near enough to hear.

"Be sure it fits comfortably under the arms," the older man said. "You'll be wearing it a lot."

Paul detected the slight remainder of an accent.

*Somewhere in West Africa*, he thought.

Meanwhile, two white men came through the door. The older man broke away to welcome them and ladle out some soup, while they took seats at the table and helped themselves to a few chunks of bread. Then he returned to the man with the jacket.

"Are you sure it fits well?" he asked, and the other man nodded. "Do you remember where I told you to go and who you must ask for?"

"Yes, Brother." The younger man was now looking at the floor.

"This is very important, my friend. You must go back to work. Your family needs you." He had somehow drawn the young man's eyes to his own, and both of them were smiling.

"Whatever happens, come back and let me know. With God there is always a way."

"Thank you, Brother," the youngster said, making a slight bow.

The older man placed both hands on the other's head and leaned close to speak into his ear. Then the young man left.

The two at the table were still eating, so the old man walked over to Paul.

"Forgive me for making you wait," he said with a wide smile. "Somehow, you do not look like a man who came here to eat or be clothed."

"You have unmasked me, Friar Arnold," Paul said, smiling and handing him Don's envelope.

"Just call me Brother. Everyone does."

"Father Don at St. Athanasius's sent me to speak with you, Brother."

The friar continued to smile as he opened the envelope and removed its contents.

"I can see that," he said, waving the envelope with the church logo on it. Then he examined the note, and his expression became more serious.

"Father Don says you have some interesting things to talk about. I regret that my time is fully occupied during the day, but I should be finished by eight. I live upstairs, so if you could come around nine?"

Confirming the friar's busy state, another man had just come through the door.

"Certainly, Brother. Will it be all right for me to park here at night?"

Again the friar's face glowed with a smile. He stepped over to the window to look out at Paul's Volvo.

"Ah, my friend," he said jovially. "Satan can strike us anywhere at any time, but I think you will be safe here against our more common variety of mischief maker."

Paul pulled away from the row house after five o' clock, when darkness had already begun to fall. He thought about driving over to Harbor Place for dinner and killing time until nine o'clock but decided against it.

He needed to talk to Petra. They had been out of contact for nearly a month, so she knew nothing of the change in his life and occupation. Would he have time to explain all that before going back to Frank's House? No, but he burned to tell her what he could. He would not put that off for another day.

Headed west out of Baltimore on US 40, Paul pulled into a service station to use a payphone. The phone was answered after three rings, and he heard a throaty voice that always reminded him of Joan Crawford.

"Hello?" It was Petra's sister. Years earlier, while going through a divorce, she and her children had moved in with Petra and wound up staying.

"Hi, Katya."

"Well hello, stranger. Where have you been so long? We thought you'd gone to the woods and forgotten the way back."

"You were not far from the truth. Is Petra around?"

"At the moment she is hanging over my shoulder muttering murderous threats."

Paul heard what sounded like a real or pretended struggle. Then Petra's voice came on. She was a distinct soprano against Katya's contralto.

"What have you been up to? It's been weeks. Are you home now?"

"I was overseas for a while, but I'm back." Paul was smiling into the telephone mouthpiece.

"Are you coming over here? We would love to see you."

"Actually, I have an appointment with someone later tonight, but I thought we might meet first for a sandwich and some catching up at the Pub."

"Just in time; supper is still in the fridge. Katya can fix something for herself and the kids."

Paul could hear an objection from Katya in the background. Then Petra began speaking away from the mouthpiece.

"Okay. What if I spring for a pizza delivery?" This was immediately followed by cheering voices.

"How far away are you?" she asked, again speaking to Paul.

"I'm coming out of Baltimore during rush hour. I should be there by six anyway."

"Tell you what. Since you have business later, why don't I just meet you at the Pub? That way, you don't have to worry about bringing me home."

"I'll see you there."

# 3

J. K.'s Pub in the community of Wilde Lake was among Columbia's happier watering holes in the last quarter of the twentieth century. The owner, John Kepler Lea, had visited many distinctive English pubs up close and dreamed of transporting some of their warmth, comfort, and dignity back to Her Majesty's former colony of Maryland. Since he could not actually bring a pub home, he had commissioned the construction of a very convincing imitation. The heavy mahogany bar, stained-wood canopy, frosted-glass dividers, and other components looked so authentic the word spread that J. K. had actually brought them over from a dying English establishment. It was an advantageous rumor he rarely troubled himself to deny. His pub did not take up much space, but its dark-wood accessories were richly cozy, its atmosphere quaint, and its capacity for revelers on a good night amazing.

    J. K. himself was a balding, bearded man of diminutive, thick-waisted stature. He was a born actor and had actually taught drama before becoming an innkeeper. His projected persona modulated between Sir John Falstaff and Don Rickles with a voice like W. C. Fields. His speech was crisply precise, correct, and betrayed no regional accent.

Paul arrived before Petra. He was early enough to secure one of the three standing bars that ran parallel to the main bar. After a waiter brought him a glass of Bass ale and left a menu, J. K. strolled over to address him in stilted tones of mock propriety.

"Will the gentleman be dining alone this evening?" he asked.

"The gentleman certainly hopes not," Paul replied with equally stiff formality. Then he relaxed and added, "But you know women, J. K. I might be waiting all night."

"Me thinks not, my good man," J. K. announced, gesturing toward the door, "for hence cometh the beauteous Petra."

Looking up, Paul felt his body betray him by bringing a deeply warming flush to his face. To him Petra looked no older and even prettier than she had ten years before, when they first met in Okinawa.

She was now dressed for mid-winter Maryland, but there was the same smooth, olive skin and the short-trimmed, black hair that showed off her forehead so well. Her hazel eyes still gleamed with hidden mischief, and her deep-dimpled smile looked as puckish as ever.

Paul stood to take her green winter coat and white scarf, hanging them on the back of one of the standing-bar stools. A white turtleneck sweater-and-slacks combination with a wide, black belt and calf-length, high-heeled boots perfectly accented the lines of her petite figure.

"Are you running a fever?" Petra asked with concern while still standing. "Your face is so red."

"No. It's probably just the heat in here. I'm sure it will pass," he answered, waiting impatiently for the blood to drain from his cheeks.

"How odd," J. K. observed with a crafty leer. Gallantly bowing, he brought Petra's hand to his lips and added as he rose, "The poor fellow seemed quite cool and comfortable until just now." Then he sauntered away to visit some other guests.

Petra seated herself gracefully on one of the armed stools and looked earnestly into Paul's face. Her attention was immediately drawn to the bandage above his right eye.

"What happened to your head?" she asked with concern.

"It's nothing really. I just bumped into something."

"Like what, a hatchet?" she asked, not at all mollified.

"Actually, it was a shovel, but it's healing up fine. Don't worry."

Her expression said she was not buying his dismissive attitude, but after a few seconds she relaxed and changed the subject.

"I was glad to get your call tonight. You were out of touch so long this time; I had begun to worry."

*Now is the time. She is giving me the perfect opportunity to tell her I've quit.* At exactly that moment the waiter came to take her order for a glass of Merlot.

"Why don't we just order our food now?" she asked the waiter. "I'd like a hot pastrami sandwich with horseradish."

"I'll have the Reuben," Paul said.

When the waiter had taken their orders and moved away, she returned to the same issue. His left hand was resting, palm down, on the surface of the standing bar, and she laid her right hand gently on top of it.

"There are times—all the time to be truthful—when I really wish you were out of this business and not doing these things any more."

*This is it*, he thought, but then the waiter came back with her wine.

Even before the waiter had turned away, Paul placed his right hand on hers and said, "I am, and I won't."

Suddenly incredulous, she scanned his face for meaning.

"What are you saying?"

"I am telling you that, as of yesterday, I am no longer in that business or doing those things."

"Did you lose your job?"

"No. I quit."

Her expression was a mixture of joy and relief. She completed the pile of hands in the middle of the bar by clasping his right with her left.

"This is an answer to prayer," she said a little breathlessly.

"Maybe more than you think. Something totally out of this world—and I use that phrase literally—happened to me, and I want to tell you about it. My life is changing, and I will need all the help I can get from all the sources I can find. I hope you will be one of them. I recall you telling me about a transformation that overtook you one Saturday afternoon at St. Athanasius's. I think that memory may help you understand what is going on with me right now; at least I hope it will."

Her eyes told him she remembered what he was talking about, but she said nothing. She just smiled and nodded her head for him to continue.

"Even at that, you will find much of what I tell you hard to accept. Don't mind that. I lived it, but the details still confound me. Defining the purpose of it all is a work still very much in progress."

At almost the same instant, they became aware of the waiter standing over them with their sandwiches. He was evidently trying to decide how he might distribute the food he brought without dislodging the entwined hands that lay on the bar top obstructing his purpose.

Paul laughed as he disengaged his fingers.

"Maybe we ought to eat first," he said.

Paul thought it best to postpone his revelation during dinner, so they spoke primarily of what was going on in Petra's life.

Katya had recently left an office management job to become a fulltime real estate agent. Petra was happy to report her hard work and success. The two children were showing evidence of their transition into young teenagers. They were good students with lots of activities that demanded close support from the mom-and-aunt-Petra taxi service. So far, they showed little sign of rebellion, but who knew how long that would last?

Polishing off their sandwiches and small servings of potato chips and slaw, Paul and Petra declined a dessert and ordered black coffee that arrived so hot it could only be sipped with great care. It was not Friday, so the Pub offered no entertainment, but the room was nearly full, and four patrons occupied each of the standing bars on either side of them. Still, the pervasive hum of conversation and activity seemed to shelter them under a dome of quiet privacy within a forest of noise.

"I talked to Father Don this afternoon about some of the things I'll be telling you," Paul began. Petra folded her hands on the bar, except when drinking her coffee, and looked directly into his eyes. Her lips were slightly pursed, which Paul remembered as a sign of her complete attention.

"At first he seemed a little incredulous," Paul continued, "but I think he believed me in the end. At least he knew I was not lying or insane."

Paul saw no alteration in her attitude or expression, so he forged ahead.

"A little over a week ago in a place I cannot tell you about—I died."

"You were ill?" she asked anxiously.

"No. I was dead by an accident of nature. I was crushed and suffocated in a cave-in of snow. The next thing I knew, I had left this world for an entirely different and unearthly place called the Vale."

Seeing Petra about to interrupt again, Paul held up his right hand with the palm toward her.

"Please let me continue, and some of your questions will be answered. They may be ones I have already asked and answered myself."

She responded by remaining silent and attentive while he continued.

"Did I have a near-death experience? No. I was not just nearly dead. I was absolutely dead and totally out of this world in a place where, believe it or not, I still very much am."

Petra set back on her stool.

"Don't be shocked by that, because I'm sure you're there too. We both are, even as we sit here talking about it."

Her eyebrows arched themselves noticeably at this revelation.

"Was I clinically dead?" he asked rhetorically. "Yes, in the sense that everyone who dies becomes clinically dead first. That's just how we all get out of this world on our way to the next. Then I went right on out of the earth to be in the Vale, where every soul goes and wakes up or doesn't to the prospect of heaven."

"Doesn't?" she asked quietly.

"I was told about some souls who consciously resist awakening there, because they have become something different and are bound elsewhere."

Now Paul wondered if he was getting ahead of himself. Did he sound a little crazy? He deliberately slowed his speech rate.

"I need to tell you more about the Vale and what I learned there. Then you can understand what happened to me and why my future here has become so different."

"Okay," she said guardedly. Then she smiled and went on. "So far, I admit, this sounds a bit squirrelly, but…" She hesitated. "Look, Paul. You and I have been through a lot together. You know there was a time when I hated you. I didn't stop hating you for your sake, but for mine. Then we met again, and everything was different—we were different. We had both put those old times and our former selves behind us. That's why we have been so close ever since. It means a lot to me, and I am not about to forget it.

"What you've been saying sounds strange, complicated, and sort of scary. I think you need more time to explain it." Here she paused and seemed to look past him. Then she took his hand and went on.

"Somehow, I don't think now will be the time for that. Here come Hank and Ida."

# 4

On the way back to Frank's House, Paul thought about his after-dinner conversation with Petra and her reaction to what he had told her. He could see how poorly he handled it. What he said about still being in the Vale must have sounded like lunacy to Petra, who knew nothing about simultaneous infinity.

*I might have recovered from that if Hank and Ida Ridley hadn't showed up.*

The Ridleys were mutual friends and fellow parishioners from St. Athanasius's, so they casually greeted Paul and Petra and took the two remaining stools at their standing bar. Paul stayed long enough to be courteous. Then he pled a prior appointment and excused himself.

As he was leaving, Petra stood and walked with him to the door. He stopped and turned to face her in the dimly lit area between two sets of double doors that kept the January chill away from those inside. There she caught the sleeve of his sweater and stood close to him with her face tilted up to his.

"I want to go on with this," she said softly.

Paul smiled down at her. Her nearness and the fresh smell of her hair made him giddy.

"Me or my story?" he asked.

"Both," she told him firmly.

He bent to give her a quick kiss on the lips.

"I'll call you tomorrow," he said gently and went into the cold night, where a radiation of great warmth spread itself through every inch of his body.

Paul parked in front of Frank's House at a quarter past nine. The street showed no sign of life except for some lighted windows, one of which belonged to his destination. This time Paul knocked. Brother Arnold was quick to open the door and motion him inside. In the main room Paul still smelled cabbage soup. The indoor temperature was barely warmer than that of the street.

"Winter nights sometime bring visitors," the friar volunteered. "We can afford only a little gas heat, but there is always wealth for the inside and the out." Now he pointed to the stove and piles of clothing. "Would you like some soup?"

"No thank you, Brother. I've already eaten."

"So have I."

The Franciscan, Paul observed, drew rations and clothing from the same sources he offered to others. He was clearly following the example of his order's founder by embracing the treasures of Lady Poverty.

Leading Paul to a clean end of the kitchen table, Brother Arnold silently invited him to sit, taking a chair directly across from him.

"Now tell me about this thing of which Father Don has written."

"I died."

"And then?"

Paul hesitated. The friar seemed not a bit surprised that Paul had left the world and still come back. What happened between those events was as important to him as their sequential aberration.

Paul was encouraged and began telling the man of what he had seen and heard in the Vale. He easily fell into the crisp, lean format that had always characterized his covert operation reports.

First, Paul described what it felt and looked like to be in the Vale—seemingly suspended in endless space in each and every direction, thoroughly illuminated by radiant light from no apparent source, and surrounded by constantly moving shapes and shadows that suddenly vanished from one place and instantly reappeared in another. Yet, while he was there he had felt nothing but complete calm, serenity, and fulfillment.

Then he explained his counseling by four important people from his life. At least some of them, he knew, were still living on earth at the time of his death. Yet those who guided him in the Vale were themselves as they are for eternity. Each of them spoke with that kind of authority.

"One showed me the unique path of every soul through life. According to her, such differences were now over. Like all who pass through the Vale to reach God, I would come to see reality exactly as it is and in no other way. The notion of different points of view existed only in the world I had left behind.

"The Vale prepares souls-in-passage for the spiritual reality of heaven, but some failed souls do not wake up there. They are bound for a place called the terminal ward to be attended by demons. They rejected God and other people for so long that they changed themselves forever into something they are not."

"Something they are not?" Brother Arnold interrupted. "Isn't that a logical dead end? How can they be what they are not?"

"I asked that too, but it is not such a paradox. Didn't God make us to love him and each other? Aren't those commandments what count most? If we fully followed them, wouldn't we become all God created us to be?"

"Of course."

"So that isn't just what God wants for us. It is what we *are*. Right?"

"What an interesting thought."

"Suppose we spend a lifetime opposing that—rejecting the way God made us. Maybe we demand control of everything—especially ourselves."

"Yes?"

"Can't we thwart God's will by turning ourselves into something else? Isn't that one outcome of free will?"

"So it might seem."

"Then doesn't it follow that spending eternity alone with your own, self-made soul is a consequence of choice—not a punishment from God?"

"I need to think about that for a while, but please go on."

Now Paul spoke of what a former colleague had taught him about simultaneous infinity.

"It exists for and around God as the medium for his omnipresence, omniscience, and omnipotence."

"This is an interesting proposition," Brother Arnold commented. "It would explain a lot of questions and difficulties we find in Scripture. A few great thinkers have believed in something like that."

"I was also told about the importance of each soul's identity—the way God made it—to its survival. Happiness, I learned, is the key to finding and freeing that genuine self. 'Happy,' one therapist said, 'is what we are when we are being what we are.' This simply reflects our spiritual imperative to follow the primary commandments of love. Being our real selves makes us happy as nothing else can."

"Point taken; move on."

Without mentioning Grogan's name, Paul told Brother Arnold how his former boss had reordered his thinking about religious tradition, love, punishment, faith, happiness, and the universal human obsession with control that generates all sin.

"Original or otherwise, every sin is rooted in our common conviction that we can make ourselves happy all by ourselves—without God. True happiness comes only when we live the way God made us—being what we actually are. On earth we find it in occasional spasms of joy, but in eternity it is the total and constant state of every ransomed soul."

"How beautifully you tell it."

"That's easy. It was my perpetual condition in the Vale, but I barely noticed it there. Now I feel its absence every minute of every day."

"Knowing the experience, can't you recapture some of it?"

"If only I could," Paul said, bowing his head. "Our lives here are stifled by the linear and relative confusion of this universe. Perhaps God will grant me my Vale memories. He has so far, but maybe they will fade the way most memory does on earth."

"You must feel a terrible loss."

"I do, but I am blessed with the certainty that I will have it all again."

"Pray the memory lasts."

"Even that is only the beginning. I did not get to heaven. The Vale is just the first step toward the final gathering of all saved souls all at once around God. My journey had barely begun."

"Yet how marvelous it is for you," the old man said, his dark eyes flaring up and fixing themselves firmly on Paul's face. "Tell me what you make of it all."

The other man's gaze was so penetrating, his tone so commanding, that Paul hesitated for a few seconds.

"I believe I was given a prophetic vision," he finally said in well-measured words.

"What for?"

"I don't know. I hoped you could help me with that."

"Why me?"

"Father Don sent me to you. He said you are the holiest man he knows."

The brother made a brief coughing sound that may have been a dismissive laugh.

"Father Don is a worthy shepherd, but his experience is limited. Mere works do not make one holy."

Paul could think of nothing to say.

Brother Arnold was silent for a bit. Then he spoke with gravity.

"Your view may be limited, but I believe everything you have said. We must look at some troubling possibilities. Your soul could be at risk."

"I don't understand, Brother."

"Throughout time, God has summoned and directed his people through visions like the one you describe, but all visions are not necessarily sent by God. In the history of my own order there are legends of traps created by demons to delude the faithful. During the lifetime of St. Francis, the evil one himself was said to have appeared to a brother as Christ crucified. In that disguise he told the man to abandon his life of poverty and sacrifice because he had no hope for heaven. Satan's purpose was to destroy God's work in that holy man and tempt him to loathsome acts. Do you see what I mean?"

"Yes, Brother, but I don't think that fits my episode in the Vale. I was not being tempted to do anything but God's will. My faith was not challenged or denied. It was informed and reinforced by everything I learned. The very fact that I woke up in the Vale reassured me and affirmed my hope for heaven. As I told you, I came to know my own soul there and was enriched by it."

"I believe you, and I fear all the more for your sake and for those you love." The old man's voice had risen without increasing much in volume.

"Why?"

"Think again of what you were told about the attendants for lost souls in the terminal ward."

"Okay."

"Too many people today think Satan exists only in folklore and entertaining fantasies. The idea of personified evil does not fit easily into our modern, sophisticated world view. Believe me. The evil one and those who follow him go to great extremes to keep us in that diabolical ignorance. Heaven and apparently the Vale are free of their insidious influence, but earth is not.

"Demons, like angels, have access here, but demons come mainly to promote the confusion we see wherever we look. 'The prince of the power of the air,' as Paul the apostle called him, is not just some metaphor for the wickedness humans do. He is a spiritual reality, and his power today is greater than ever, because we dismiss him as a figment of imagination and myth. A few depraved souls worship him directly, but most of his servants are mere dupes seeking their own pleasure. Some even support his work under the foolish illusion that they are doing good for mankind by demystifying religion."

"But how does that affect me?"

Brother Arnold came slowly to his feet, and his voice betrayed deep emotion. Paul stood up with him.

"Do you think I'm talking about some engaging amusement like Goethe's witty portrayal of Mephistopheles? The devil, his demons, and their human puppets compose a malevolent force so great on this planet that it is exceeded only by the power of God.

"If God has so purposely reversed his own laws just to call you to some peculiar service, you may be sure it will be something the devil doesn't want to happen. Sooner or later, you will come under attack—maybe even before you know what God has for you to do."

"Are you sure of that?"

"Count on it; you will become a target for destruction. It may be something as simple as a temptation to distract you. On the other hand, it could be something ruinous—even lethal. Remember that Satan despises you to begin with, and he will do anything he can to thwart God's will. Earth is the only place he has the power to try that."

What Brother Arnold said was pulling a string in Paul's memory. He recalled what great desperation he had felt during his recent imprisonment. There he had been sustained by the hope that Grogan was working to free him. Was there a parallel here?

"Brother, you just said the only power on earth greater than Satan's is God's. Isn't that where I have to look for help? If God wants me to do something, won't he protect me until I've had a chance to do it?"

Suddenly the ceiling light reflected brilliantly from Brother Arnold's upturned, wide-open, tooth-filled smile. He laughed as he strode around the table to grasp Paul in an enthusiastic bear hug.

"God bless you as I know he will, Brother Paul," he said, at last releasing him. "I have been too long in the trenches and seen the enemy too close-up every day. I needed you to remind me who is in charge here."

Now he took a step back, and his tone became more serious.

"Still, you must be very careful. Remember how our Lord Jesus identified the devil as 'the father of lies.' He is a crafty opponent for whom we alone are no match. Our only resort—your only resort—is faith in God and your total reliance on him to direct and defend you. Isn't that what your preparation in the Vale was about?"

Paul was momentarily surprised by Brother Arnold's perceptive synthesis of what Paul had said without fully appreciating it.

"You're completely right, Brother. Why didn't I see it before? I was told plenty about the folly of self-reliance that excludes God.

You just put your finger on at least one reason I was sent to the Vale. I was getting advanced combat training for my own good."

"Don't forget!" the old monk bellowed sharply. "God is on your side, but that's no reason to get cocky. You are still not bulletproof, and you have Christ's own admonition not to tempt the Lord your God."

"I'm not afraid for myself, but there are some people I care about very much." Paul was thinking now of Petra, Katya, the children, and even Father Don. "You're suggesting they might be threatened just to intimidate or distract me."

"That is clearly possible—even probable. The devil, whatever you may have seen in the movies, is no gentleman. You should be alert to such perils and try to forestall them. Some degree of seclusion might help for now. You cannot diminish your own danger, but staying apart might limit the attention given to others by your cruel enemy. Do I need to tell you to keep God in your heart with continuous prayer? That will both protect you and guide you to find what God has in store."

"I learned something about that in the Vale too," Paul said, glancing at his watch.

"Where did the time go? It's nearly midnight, and I'm sure you need to get some sleep. God bless you for what you've done. I'm a long way from the end, but I think you have brought me several steps closer to it."

"Go with God," the old man said at the door as he closed it behind Paul.

He had taken only a few steps back into the main room when he heard a knock. Returning and opening the door, he saw Paul on the stoop.

"Do you have a telephone I can use?" Paul asked, coming back inside.

"Certainly. What is the problem?"

"Devil one, Paul zero. Somebody stole my car."

# 5

Two uniformed officers arrived in a patrol car. They had to make a report, but were ambivalent toward anyone stupid enough to leave his vehicle at night on a street where even residents would not park. Neither of them could recall a case involving the theft of an aging Volvo, but they held out little hope for its recovery.

The policemen provided Paul with a copy of their on-scene report for insurance purposes and gave him a ride to a taxi stand. Most taxi drivers, one told him, were reluctant to pick up passengers in that neighborhood after dark.

Hiring a cab back to the District of Columbia was an enormous expense, but it was almost three in the morning, and bus or train schedules would not be accommodating for a few more hours. Fortunately, Paul had traveler's checks left from those provided for his return trip from Europe. The cab driver was content to take them, and Paul knew the organization would deduct their value from his final pay. Signing the checks outside his door, Paul made another mental entry to his current standing.

*Devil two; Paul still zero.*

In his apartment while getting ready for bed, Paul began to recalculate his gloomy scorecard. He had learned a lot this night. That must count for something. He had spent all his adult life fighting the enemies of his country. That was over now, and he was already locked in combat with an opponent more powerful than any he had ever faced.

Was that true? As a human soul, he had always been abroad on the battleground between good and evil. Maybe the evil side just seemed more general than personal then. Now he was caught in the headlights of the devil himself, a spiritual titan with a very personal motive for destroying Paul. Wasn't that how Brother Arnold had put it?

Tonight the Franciscan had told Paul who he was up against and what the odds might be. Until then, Paul had not equated a service to God as a stick in the eye for Satan. Now he could contemplate some of the tactics his demonic foes might use against him.

How much of his training in the Vale had been aimed at what he must do now? What were his most repeated lessons? True happiness comes only from depending on God. Totally trusting God is how we do God's will in the interlocking triad of love that connects God, a soul, and all the other souls God created.

Thinking back on the scorecard, Paul reckoned tonight's problems might have risen as easily from coincidence as from enemy action.

*Either way, I'm calling tonight a draw.*

Before lying down, he knelt to pray for protection and discernment.

After his late night out, Paul slept until nine. He breakfasted lightly on orange juice, toast, and coffee, while working the telephone to file a claim with his automobile insurance company. Before noon, he had cleaned up, visited a branch office to exchange documents and sign forms, and picked up a rental car provided by the company while his claim was being settled. That, he was told, would take a few days. The insurance company and the rental agency must have been connected, because the papers he signed to get the car contained what Paul thought a discriminatory provision. He would be financially liable if anything bad happened to the rental in the area of Baltimore where the Volvo was taken.

Now Paul was thinking about what to do next. Besides prayer and meditation, Brother Arnold had recommended he temporarily avoid those who might become proxy targets. He hated the idea of not seeing Petra for a while, but he could think of no reasonable alternative. The last thing he wanted to do was draw her into a diabolical line of fire. He would call her later. He had promised to do that, but it would have to be their last contact until his position became clearer. He did not look forward to making that call.

On the way home, he pulled into the used-car lot where he previously purchased the Volvo. By now he had written off the old car. This time he was looking for something smaller and newer. He test-drove a low-mileage, year-old, gray Dodge Daytona and was satisfied with it. Giving the dealer an earnest-money check, Paul asked him to get the paperwork ready and prepare the car for delivery that afternoon.

Paul went directly from the car lot to his apartment. The midday sky had clouded over. The rental-car radio announced a typical, late-January drop in temperature, but did not forecast any kind of precipitation. It was just going to be a cold, gloomy afternoon.

Entering his second-floor dwelling, Paul had started toward the telephone when he stopped midstride. Slowly scanning the living room where he was, he put all his senses to work.

"Come on out, Barney," he called.

The familiar figure of Bernard Rice emerged casually from the bedroom into the short hallway that also gave access to the bathroom and the kitchen. He was grinning bashfully beneath his bushy, ginger mustache and blue eyes. He was dressed in dark slacks and a white turtleneck, carried a dun-colored duffle coat over his left arm, and was wearing the same green, snap-brim Tyrolean hat Paul had seen him with three days before at the Frankfurt International Airport.

"It was the pipe tobacco, wasn't it?" Barney asked, with the slight British accent he had long ago acquired.

"Like I told you at the *flughafen*, the distinctive aroma of Balkan Sobranije clings to everything you own. Your passage here will leave traces for days."

Barney had been Paul's partner in the fateful covert operation that sent Paul to the Vale and later landed him in Ministry of Interior custody. Barney, who had seen Paul being dug out of the snow, had gone on to complete the operation alone. Days later he met briefly with Paul, who was passing through the Frankfurt airport on his way back to the states.

"Didn't you tell me you had work to do in Wiesbaden, Munich, and Bonn?" Paul asked.

"Grogan cut it short and called me back."

"Now why would he do that?"

"I can't say."

"Can't or won't?"

"Whatever you think. It doesn't matter much."

"Enough idle chatter, Barney. What are you doing here?"

"Here?"

"Yeah, in my apartment."

"You know I can't talk to you about that—not now that you've left the organization."

"No? I find you black-bagging my home, and you don't expect me to ask why?" Paul's voice had risen.

"Ask anything you want. I just can't answer." Barney's voice remained calm, but his grin was gone.

"Grogan must have sent you. Is this related to your sudden recall from Germany?"

"If you say so."

"Would you like to sit down and talk about it?"

"No," Barney said, putting on his duffle coat.

"What if I call the police?" Paul asked in a lower tone.

"You can't do that. It would violate your secrecy oath by exposing operations of the organization."

Barney was headed for the door.

"Okay," Paul said slowly with more than a hint of menace, "but if you come here uninvited again, I may not be able to resist an urge to violate your nose. You wouldn't be able to tell the police about that either."

Barney went through the door without looking back and closed it softly behind him.

Paul walked into the bedroom and looked around, but was unable to find any sign of a search.

*Neat job, Barney. If not for the tobacco smell and my untimely return, I would never have known you were here.*

Now it was time to think very hard about what was happening. Whatever his past association with Paul, Barney was just doing a job. Grogan had given him that job. Why? What had he sent Barney to look for in the apartment?

This brought on one of the internal conversations Paul sometimes had with himself.

What did Grogan think Barney might find?

*Grogan never does anything without a reason, and yanking Barney out of the field to do something like this is a real attention getter. Grogan's calamity meter must be reading crisis.*

Why would he so suddenly suspect me of something?

*Well, abruptly quitting your job and refusing to tell him why might do it.*

Maybe, but there has to be something else. By the time I walked out on him at the airport, he seemed almost glad to see me go.

*That was only after you threw every sweet offer he could make you back in his face. What ingratitude.*

But I've always been loyal to the organization. He knows that.

*Until two days ago. Then you abruptly walked out for no apparent reason.*

It still doesn't make sense.

*Maybe you should broaden your perspective.*

How?

*Didn't you recently attract the attention of some very powerful enemies?*

I've had plenty of enemies before.

*This kind?*

I see where you're going, but how could they wreck my reputation so quickly?

*You started it the other day. You made it easy for Grogan to become suspicions.*

How?

*Aren't we dealing with the supernatural here? Isn't their CEO still the father of lies? If the scandal sticks, you could spend the rest of your life somewhere in solitary confinement. Now wouldn't that set back God's purpose for you—unless he wants you witnessing to prison guards?*

I get it, but if things are that bad, why hasn't someone been at the door with manacles by now? The situation is bad, but Grogan is still trying to answer questions.

*So what are you going to do?*

What else? I'm getting out of town.

# 6

If Grogan's concerns had advanced to the point of searching Paul's apartment, there would also be bugs, and the telephone was sure to be wired. It might be safe to call his car insurance people on it, but for now, he did not want to give away any information about his current situation or plans. For all the organization would know, he needed to sink quietly to the river bottom and merge with the silt.

He thought of packing a small bag but quickly discarded the idea. Someone was bound to be outside watching, and he did not want to set off any alarms just yet. He was already wearing the windbreaker jacket he had bought after his arrival at the airport. He went through the apartment, loading the inside jacket pockets with essentials like toothpaste, a toothbrush, and a thousand dollars in fifty-dollar bills he had hidden there. The cash would let him purchase clothing and other necessities along the way.

He was taking a checkbook and a credit card with him, but except for one big purchase, he did not plan to use them for a while. He also pocketed his authentic passport, knowing that its use could pinpoint his location for Grogan even quicker than a credit-card purchase. He just did not like being without it.

He recalled happily that he had not been to the post office to resume his mail delivery since returning from Europe. That spared him the need to stop there on his way out of town or worry about things piling up in his mailbox while he was away.

The same compartment from which he removed the money contained a snub-nosed, hammerless Smith & Wesson .38 revolver, which he chose to leave behind. The only opposition he would be willing to shoot could not be vanquished by so puny a weapon.

Now he spent a few minutes at the living room window, observing the street below. His rental car was parked nearly in front of the apartment, but he could not see it without opening the window and leaning out. Several other cars were parked in either direction on both sides of the street. Time would tell, but he expected to find his watcher down the street to his right and facing in the same direction as Paul's rental. The tail had probably been in place to observe his return from the morning's errands.

At the front door he paused to take a battered hounds-tooth hat from a peg on the wall. It was a comfortable old friend to protect his head from the cold. He locked the apartment behind him and went downstairs into the street. Walking to the driver's side of his car, he unlocked the door, got in, and turned on the engine. He spent a few minutes fiddling with the heater and the windshield defogger, while examining the street ahead of him.

His tracker would not be in the car directly in front of him. Paul was sure of that. He would most likely be in the second or third car down. The vehicle would be tricked out with some clever mirrors that allowed continuous observation of Paul's building entrance and car.

There are techniques for eluding a tracker with abrupt action, like a sudden U-turn and getaway in the opposite direction. That only works if there is no back-up car behind you. Paul figured there was. Barney would probably be in that one, waiting to return to his task of searching the apartment after Paul drove away.

For the moment, Paul was not interested in escaping surveillance, so he simply pulled into the roadway and drove on. He had been right about the second car. It was a dull-beige Chevrolet Impala. As he passed it, he looked directly into the driver's side. There he saw the somewhat chunky profile of a bespectacled man in a brown tweed overcoat, trying very self-consciously to keep his eyes straight ahead of him.

*He acts like an amateur. This may be easier than I expected.*

Paul watched the rearview mirror to see the tracker pull out behind him. He deliberately drove quite carefully through city traffic to be sure the following car did not lose him at a turn or a red light. Before long, he saw the used-car lot where he had been shopping that morning. He intentionally approached it from the direction that would require him to make a left-hand turn in the middle of the block. This forced the following driver, who was really too close, to grab a parking spot just ahead with a rather poor view of the lot. The pursuer might have gone around the block to find a better spot, but he could not take the risk that Paul would disappear before he got back.

Rolling uphill into the lot, Paul turned right to park behind the office, so that only the rear of his rental would be visible from the street.

In the office the dealer was surprised to see Paul back so soon.

"Your Daytona is ready for the road, but we haven't had time to wash it yet."

"That's okay," Paul told him. "Something's come up, and I'm in sort of a hurry. Let's just do the papers and close the deal now."

"What about transferring the registration?"

"I'll pay your fee to take care of that and mail me the papers. Your dealer tags and bill of sale should do me 'til then."

"You're the boss," the man said, taking a folder from one side of his desk and pulling out some documents.

Since Paul was paying in full by check, the procedure moved quickly. He would have preferred to avoid the paper trail through his bank account, but there was no alternative. The car would be his last traceable expense for a while.

Paul had noticed what seemed to be a young salesman in the office who was manifestly unoccupied. Taking refuge from the frigid temperature outside, he was anxiously watching the lot for the appearance of a potential customer. His hopes had probably been raised by the figure of a man in a tweed overcoat who was loitering across the street, but that had not worked out. The man did not cross into the lot.

As his business with the dealer neared completion, Paul introduced a question loudly enough to be heard by the young man.

"I said I was pressed for time, and I need to get moving, but I still have that rental car out back to return to a Quick Rent office. There is one not far from here, and it would be worth fifty bucks plus a five for taxi fare back, if you could have somebody take it in for me. My insurance company is picking up the tab."

The young man turned around eagerly to face them.

"I know where that office is," he volunteered.

The dealer looked first at the salesman and then at Paul.

"I think my associate will be able to help you with that. You can call the office from here to tell them he's coming."

Later, as the salesman backed up the rental to drive it into the street, Paul stood at the window and smiled. He could see the tweed overcoat scrambling to get in and start his Impala before the quarry was out of sight. The man had sacrificed any chance to identify who was driving.


Day was drawing into late afternoon when Paul called Father Don from a pay telephone in College Park, Maryland. Calling the priest or Petra from his apartment might make them targets for tapping, but payphones were clean. The organization could not possibly monitor all the people Paul might know.

Happy to find Don at his desk so late, Paul told him briefly about Brother Arnold's advice to duck out of sight. He was careful to say nothing about being shadowed by his former employer. He wanted Don's hands clean in case Paul was later classified as some kind of fugitive. Agreeing with Brother Arnold, Don suggested a week-or-two retreat at an obscure monastery in Virginia. He said he would telephone the place immediately to set one up. Paul thanked him and promised to call back shortly.

Dialing Petra's number, Paul knew she would be a tough sell, but he had to try.

The phone had barely rung twice when Petra answered.

"Hello?"

"Petra?"

"Yes, Paul." He could hear a combination of excitement and relief in her voice. "I was hoping you would call. I think you have a lot to tell me, and I'm ready to listen."

Paul's heart leaped at that prospect, but he was going to disappoint her.

"You're right. We have a ton of things to talk about. I wish we could do it now, but something urgent has come up."

"Urgent. What?"

"Believe me, Petra. I would explain it all right now if I could, but I've got to leave town in a hurry. Please wait for me to get back."

"Wait for what? Didn't you tell me you were through with your old business?"

"I told you the truth about that, but I was not expecting what's happened. You and I—everyone will be better off if I disappear for a while. I promise to tell you the whole story as soon as I return."

"When will that be?"

"I can't be sure right now."

"Then it's not much of a promise, is it? It sounds like the same deception and evasion I used to get from you and Jason. I trusted you both, and you both lied to me. If that's all you have going for you, just write me out of your plan. I'm done with it."

Paul understood her feelings. He betrayed her once, but she had forgiven him. This looked to her like the same story, and she was at least half right. He desperately wanted to give her something to hold on to, but there was no time. According to Brother Arnold, anything he said now might put her and the family at risk. She would be safer hating him for a while.

"Please, Petra. I would explain if I could, but right now…" He was speaking to an empty instrument. She had hung up.

He felt sadness and frustration but had no time to indulge either emotion.

He called Father Don back.

# 7

Darkness had fallen by the time Paul exited the D.C. beltway west onto Lee Highway going away from Falls Church. Engaging late rush-hour traffic near Warrington, Virginia, he drove bumper-to-bumper and detour-by-detour through what would someday be an interstate highway. Hours later he was back on a fairly open two-lane road that eventually narrowed as it wound sharply upward into the Appalachian mountain chain.

Paul's immediate goal had been to go west until he could turn south through the Shenandoah Valley on Interstate 81. He had taken the most direct route to do that, but had reckoned without the construction or the mountains. He now realized how much better it would have been to intersect the interstate from a northwestern route. That would have cost extra miles but taken him over much easier and faster roads.

Past midnight, Paul was probing his way over a lightless, winding mountain road, wrapped in heavy fog which, contrary to his expectation, did not thin out as he went to higher altitude. It might have helped to pull over and wait for daylight, but in the fog he could identify no safe place to do that. He reckoned it would be suicidal to just stop in the thick fog on the narrow, curving two-lane pavement.

Paul's only advantage at the moment was being in a lane with the mountain face to his right. Oncoming traffic, none of which he had noted, should be in the outside lane. He suspected that people who knew the territory stayed off this road at night. Holding his speed to a minimum, his only visual reference was an occasional glimpse in his mostly useless headlights of the stark, stone face that rose sharply beside him.

The road, Paul guessed, ran fairly close to the rock wall. He occasionally felt his right front wheel drop off the road. Then he would agonizingly inch it back onto the pavement, desperately trying to avoid any overcompensation that might throw him into oncoming traffic or even farther—over the side and into empty space.

The scraping noises he heard and felt around the fender were almost as frightening. He had to assume these were random contacts with unseen brush, stones, or other obstacles on the side of the road. Such tactile incidents were making his hands moist and much less certain on the steering wheel.

Paul hated feeling helpless. He had rarely known fear. Even his death in the snow did not reduce him to the uncontrollable anxiety that now threatened to consume him. Growing ever more confused, he was being trapped in an alien world of blind panic. His normal senses were blanking out. A lifetime of experience offered no frame of reference for this.

*Take over, Paul.*

How can I do that? I can't even think. What's going on?

*Do you mean this crazy, high-altitude game of blindfolded chicken you're playing? Pull over now, or you'll be dead again.*

Pull over where? Everything to my right is solid rock, and I can't see that most of the time. God knows what's on the left except for a steep drop down the mountain. My headlights are no good. They only reflect the water vapor in the fog. Visibility is zero. If I stop, I'll be knocked off the road. If I keep moving, I'll run into rocks or dive over the side. From what I know about dying, those options might not be so bad.

*Stop reacting and start thinking. Quit running away. The Vale may be attractive, but you have work to do.*

Like what?

*Whatever God wants—and how about Petra? Isn't she worth sticking around for?*

Okay. My stomach has deposed my brain. I'm running scared with my mind on empty. I can't stop that or change what I feel. This time I really am helpless.

*Don't quit now. What's become of your faith?*

My confidence is shot, and I'm out of choices. You know that makes me crazy.

*Not faith in yourself, stupid. Where is your faith in God?*

Right again. I've lost control.

*You bet you have, and you're running out of road.*

Now I get it. I need to pray.

*Just in time.*


Before Paul could act on his resolve, the brightly head-lighted fog across his windshield lost its brilliance. An envelope of darkest black suddenly consumed all light around and within the car. Even the dashboard lights were gone. Worse yet, this encroaching cloud brought Paul the suffocating sense of some malicious presence that embraced and tried to force itself into his body.

*It wants to suck me out of myself.*

Fear of the fog gave way to this new terror. Some hateful power was trying to eat Paul up and leave nothing behind. He thought he must be looking into the heart of hell.

How could he get away from this thing? Brother Arnold had warned him about the danger of demonic interference, but Paul never expected this. There were no corny symbols—no horns, hooves, tail, or pitchfork here. He knew intuitively that this hellish enemy was pitilessly driven to ingest and feed on his spirit. It was groping to do that now.

Paul's first reaction was to steer away from such evil. That would have sent the car off the road and thrown him to certain death. Now he remembered what he was about to do before this new horror loomed around him. He rejected the temptation to plunge into even greater panic. The beast wanted that. It wanted his fright to season its meal. Instead, he did the only thing that had ever made sense.

Did he shout it out loud or only in his mind?—he could never remember.

*Dear Lord, please help me,* Paul prayed. *For Jesus' sake, show me what to do, and grant me the will to do it. Save me, Lord!*

The prayer brought Paul immediate relief. Fear was gone, and his mind was clear. Now he was just curious; that was how he usually reacted to danger. His hands grew steady and dry on the steering wheel. The surrounding penumbra of blackness suddenly receded, and he could see farther into the scraps of remaining fog. In an instant, the air around him cleared, the fog vanished, and he saw a small clearing on the right where he could pull off the road.

"Oh Lord, I praise you and thank you," Paul professed softly, as he turned off his engine and opened the door. Then he stepped out of the car to look across the valley in front of him. The air around him was cold and crisp, and the sky overhead was filled with brightly glistening stars. The crisis was past, but he remained curious. This was a mystery he needed to solve.

Paul could see mists clinging to lower parts of the terrain, but where were the thick clouds he had been fighting for what seemed like an hour? He had been shrouded in a featureless fog that was now fully gone. Massive fog banks might move quickly, but could they appear and vanish in seconds this way? That was not natural. Neither was the mind-numbing menace and hate that had tried so hard to destroy him in the end.

*Is that the answer? Must whatever is not normal be supernatural?*

Was this what Brother Arnold so gravely warned him about? Had the whole mountain range been covered with fog the way it looked to him, or was it a cloud that only he could see? Was there fog at all, or had those mists risen in his mind alone? Had fear been the sole source of his uncharacteristic panic?

Real or imaginary, the fog had been a true threat. He nearly lost his life to it. Only the grace of God had saved him. It was a blessing and a lesson he would not forget. Now that he knew what demons were like, he would be taking the devil more seriously.

Paul was about to get back into his car when headlights from the opposite direction swept around the curve ahead of him. As the vehicle pulled into a parking overlook on the other side of the road, he thought it looked like a park ranger's pickup truck.

The ranger, who Paul could see by moonlight and the headlights she left on, was a slender young woman. Her long, blonde hair was braided and knotted behind her head under the stiff brim of the campaign hat she donned while dismounting from the cab. She turned her head slowly from side to side, taking a visual inventory of the scene. Then she strode purposefully across the road to where he stood.

"Is everything okay?" she asked in coolly modulated tones while looking toward his car.

"Yes, thanks, but I had quite a scare in the fog."

"Fog?" the officer asked, glancing behind her at the valley below. "I've been patrolling for an hour and I've seen nothing like that, except for a patch or two in the bottoms."

"Maybe I was oversensitive. I'm not used to driving in the mountains at night."

The ranger had now walked to the front of Paul's car and was looking down.

"How did these branches get caught in your front bumper?" she asked, pulling the fronds loose and tossing them to the ground. "Your right fender has taken a few taps too."

"I don't know," he replied. "I must have picked those up driving through the…"

"Fog?"

"That's what it seemed like at the time. It appears to be gone now."

"I advise you to be more careful with our local flora," she said pointing to the torn branches she had just thrown down. "I've written more than one citation for people who do this kind of damage to the park."

"Thank you for understanding, officer," Paul said, climbing into his car. "Have a good night."

She shook her head, seemingly puzzled, as she watched him drive away. At first, her receding figure was clearly silhouetted in Paul's rearview mirror against the headlights from her own vehicle.

Then, before he rounded any curve in the road, she and her truck disappeared. All that remained were the stars he saw behind him shining through the dark and empty mountain air.

*Am I imagining things?*

*Perhaps, but in a world where demons prowl, might there not be angels too? Brother Arnold said there are.*

Idly, Paul wondered if the Forest Service patrolled this patch of mountains at all.

Paul enjoyed perfect visibility for the remainder of his mountain transit. With no more unusual incidents, he found his way into the southbound lanes of Interstate 81 well before dawn.

Soon after sunrise, he left the interstate near Salem and continued west beyond the crest of Catawba Mountain. On the lower west slope he found a narrow mountain road that led north to the Abbey of Saints and Angels, where Father Don had set up his two-week spiritual retreat.

Paul knew he needed time for prayer and meditation. He was no less grateful to discover that this ancient refuge for the soul also looked like a good place to hide out.

# 8

The little graveyard reminded Paul of the Vale.

He was free to roam the monastery grounds and surrounding area. He went to chapel each day for morning and evening prayer, but he was not invited to join the monks for meals. The sole tenant of a small guest house near the gate, he slept in a stoically furnished bedroom upstairs. Plain-but-flavorful meals appeared on a first-floor table at exactly eight o'clock, noon, and six with no sign of human agency. Used dishes vanished as soon as he left the room. He deliberately avoided confronting his elusive server.

There was no rule of silence here. Monks he met in the grounds might briefly exchange words with him. Yet, they were taciturn, thoughtful men, not much given to conversation—at least not with outsiders.

Most days he studied Scripture, read about the lives of saints from two books he found in the guest house, meditated, kept a journal, and explored the feral mountain surroundings.

The main abbey structures were built on a mountainside that sloped gradually toward a rocky, running stream at the property's lower edge. Most of the trees were seasonally bare, but wild life was visible from a respectful distance. At this altitude only a few patches of snow remained in shaded areas. The winter cold was offset by mostly clear skies and an absence of wind. Paul roamed with just his windbreaker and hounds-tooth hat for added warmth. Gloves might have helped, but his jacket pockets were adequate.

Paul discovered the graveyard on his second day at the abbey and made it a regular stop when he went out. It lay in a flat glade, sunk on one side of the road that led up to the monastery. An absence of worn paths from the road made it look empty. The anomalies of its flatness and apparent vacancy aroused Paul's curiosity and led him to investigate.

At first he found the earth and groundcover dry and firm enough for easy passage without leaving tracks. Then he discovered the verdantly tinted, metal tablets planted face up in the soil. He supposed them to mark the graves of monks who died in service to the abbey.

The plots were arranged in a rectangular field with a concrete bench, big enough for two people, positioned at each end. Paul visited daily, except once when rainfall kept him indoors. It was a peaceful place to rest and meditate. He could almost recreate the freedom from distraction he once felt in the Vale. It was not the same of course, but at times he could nearly grasp the oneness and wholeness of his soul's true identity.

Paul was thinking about this one afternoon a week-and-half after his arrival, when he saw a figure in a gray monk's habit coming toward him from the other end of the cemetery. This was the only person Paul had seen among the graves. He thought at first it must be one of the younger brothers, because the man stepped so briskly. His only concession to the cold seemed to be the cowl of his habit worn up and forward on his head.

*Maybe he is wearing long underwear*, Paul thought, but he instantly reasoned that such a provision would violate the ascetic self-denial practiced by this order.

As the man came near, Paul got a clear look under the cowl and realized he must be over sixty. All his wrinkles could not hide the vigor and interest in this face. Had Paul at last found the garrulous monk he was looking for?

"Good afternoon," the newcomer said, smiling and pulling the cowl slightly back. "I see you have uncovered our secret little treasure."

"It hardly seems a secret," Paul said, looking up from his bench, "but it has been very much a treasure to me."

"Those who leave the road to visit seem to agree. It projects a rather timeless quality, don't you think?"

"I am surprised to hear you put it that way, but yes, and that means a lot to me."

"Surprised? Surely you don't believe God is trapped in time like we are."

"No, I don't, but most people seem to." Paul recalled how Matt Harriford had used similar words in the Vale to tell Paul about simultaneous infinity.

"But are they thinking at all?" the monk asked, seating himself beside Paul. Now he gestured toward the graves in front of them. "Wouldn't you say that, if God is free in time, then so must his servants be when they have left the world to join him—souls like these?"

"Yes, Brother, but what would you say?" Paul knew the answer, but he wanted to hear what his companion thought.

The monk's expression became serious, and he paused before answering.

"It is one way I think things might be. It brings order to some of God's great mysteries. But who can be sure?"

"I am," Paul replied, instantly wondering why he did.

Now the monk turned to look directly at Paul and questioned him incredulously.

"How can you be? Have you seen God?"

"No," Paul said, knowing he could not back out now, "but I have seen a place few humans have come back to talk about."

"Who are you?" His doubt was gone. The monk was now asking for information.

"My name is Paul," he said, exposing minimal data out of occupational habit. "I am here on retreat as a guest of the abbey."

The monk hesitated, waiting for a last name.

"Just call me James," he said, when nothing followed.

"Very well, James."

"Were you given a vision?" James asked. His eyes probed Paul's face in wonder.

"I lived through one."

"Will you tell me about it?" The monk's eyes now sparkled with excitement.

"Only a little, but I can say you are right about God's time." Paul gestured to the graves. "The same is true for those who lie here. I will tell you about that, if you promise to keep your source a secret."

"I do," James said eagerly.

So Paul told him quietly about the simultaneous infinity of the dimension where God dwells, always surrounded by all the souls who serve him. He explained, as Matt Harriford had for him, how God's eternal time is always now.

"It is the same," Paul added, "for every soul who leaves this universe to meet God. Isn't that what Jesus must have meant when he told the penitent thief, 'Today shalt thou be with me in paradise'? Jesus was entombed by the end of that day. Does that matter? Not if 'today' means God's simultaneously infinite now."

"Or when Jesus and the apostles say 'the kingdom of God is at hand,'" James interjected. "Of course that is also taken to mean the person, sacrifice, and resurrection of the Lord."

"Yes, but don't you see how appropriate it might be to think of it as Kingdom Standard Time and to translate that as *now*? Of course the early Christians expected Jesus to come back right away. Maybe they were thinking only in terms of earthly time. Couldn't they have been overlooking what Jesus told Nicodemus about the difference between 'earthly' and 'heavenly' things?"

"Of course, and I can see how God's time has to be so very different from ours. You noticed, I'm sure, how sympathetic I already was to that opinion."

"Now compare that," Paul said, "to the way you, I, and the rest of humanity are stuck here in this numbingly linear and relative universe, where nothing is really permanent or dependable. Was and now are always turning into something else, and tomorrow never really comes. It is only the next today. Just try to imagine what it will be like when every soul stands all at once before God as part of his never-ending now."

"Wouldn't that get boring after a while?"

Paul smiled and put his arm around the older man's shoulders.

"I have only been part of the way—to heaven I mean. I still have this on the authority of souls who are already there. Our great coming together before God is just the magnificent opening act of the work that awaits. There we are already joyful and busy forever in ways we cannot even imagine here."

Now Paul released the monk's shoulders. James looked across the quiet graves for nearly a minute before speaking.

"I am indebted to you for this. You have confirmed things I only thought possible."

"You may want to be more wary. I am not an angel. I could very well be a lunatic or a liar."

"You may not be an angel, but I am convinced you have brought me a message from heaven. I will respect my promise and your confidence, but I will study, search, and share what I find, as I would any gift from the Holy Spirit."

"I am definitely not him, but maybe—just maybe—he inspired me to tell you what I have."

"Thank you, again. Now I must go." Rising from the bench, James shook Paul's hand. Then he walked thoughtfully out of the graveyard and up the road to the abbey.

The afternoon was almost gone. It would soon be dark. Paul sat quietly on the bench, thinking about what he had done. Had he been too impulsive, confiding what he knew to Brother James? Impulsive behavior was a weakness he rarely indulged in his former work.

When the monk spoke about God and time, Paul had felt a need to tell what he knew. Had he been moved by the Holy Spirit to reveal these things? Nothing could bring Paul to think himself part of a visitation.

Was he sent to James, or was James sent to him? Was it both, or was it neither? Was this the calling for which he visited the Vale, or was it even a beginning? Maybe it was only a coincidence.

Paul's mind was full of questions as he walked out of the graveyard back to the guest house. Supper had been laid out by his unseen caterer. This, he decided, was not the only invisible power at work here. Was he back on earth to spread the truth about simultaneous infinity?

*Maybe not, but today with Brother James it was right—the only thing to do.*

After Morning Prayer the next day and before breakfast time, Paul pushed fifteen fifty-dollar bills through the slot in the guesthouse alms box, got into his car, and drove slowly out the monastery gate with the sun coming up.

He still did not know what was going on or what to do about it, but his talk with Brother James had brought him peace and clarity. Whatever lay ahead, he was through running.

# 9

Paul's drive home was longer but faster than the trip out, so he got back by mid afternoon. The apartment was free of tobacco odor, so Barney must not have been there for at least a week. Maybe he had just been considerate enough to spray some deodorant around.

On the surface everything looked the way Paul had left it, but he was sure there were bugs in the rooms and a tap on the phone. He could find most of the bugs if he looked, but why bother? If he wanted to go on avoiding Grogan, he would not have come back at all. Instead of wasting time with a sweep, he simply faced the center of the living room and spoke slowly at a normal volume.

"Hello, Barney. Do me a favor and tell Grogan I'm ready to talk to him. *Muchas gracias, amigo.*"

Then he went to the small kitchen to make himself a late lunch of summer sausage and Swiss cheese with hot German mustard, thin pretzels, and a cold bottle of beer. After eating, he went back to the living room, sat down in the comfortable chair, and began browsing through a late edition of the *Washington Post* he had picked up on the way home.

Paul dozed off halfway through the first section of the paper. When he was awakened by the ringing telephone, it was already dark outside. The voice on the phone was Barney's.

"Where have you been, old chum? Your mobile tail caught a real ripping for losing you back there."

"Run the guy in the tweed coat back through surveillance school. Tails should always be suspicious of automotive subjects that pull into car-sales lots."

"That's axiomatic. Still, we checked all the usual places, and you were not there."

"I was on religious retreat."

"Spare me the humor," Barney said with a chuckle.

"Your cynicism crushes me, old friend."

"So don't tell me. I'm okay with that. Are you really ready to see Grogan?"

"That is what you heard me say through one more miracle of modern snoopery."

"Grogan's working late tonight. He'll be expecting you."

"At headquarters?" Paul asked archly. "Should I bring my own chains and blindfold, or will they be provided?"

"Calm your heart. This is strictly a parley."

"Like you really know or would tell me if you did."

"You're the one who wanted an appointment, Paul. Make up your mind."

"I'll be there. Just give me time to clean up."

"An hour?"

"Make it one-and-a-half."

"Someone will meet you at the security post."

The organization's headquarters looked from the outside like an insignificant but fairly isolated office park. All visible signs of occupancy suggested that it provided space to a variety of high-tech companies supposed to be associated with government research-and-development contracts. The companies were actually organizational proprietaries, but the appearance of things gave some justification for the non-concealable evidence of a thoroughly modern security perimeter around the place.

No longer possessing a car pass, Paul had to show identification and be confirmed by telephone just to get into the parking lot.

The escort who met him at the gate was Barney. First the guard on duty ran Paul through a metal detector. Then Barney clipped a visitor's pass to Paul's shirt and led him through familiar corridors that led to Grogan's office, a path Paul had thought never to walk again. Barney's main task was not to guide him but to make sure he went nowhere else.

As usual, Barney was neatly dressed. Tonight he was wearing a blue wool blazer with gray slacks and a maroon tie. Paul was more casually clad in a tieless, white dress shirt tucked into black wash pants with a red cardigan sweater worn over them. He had removed a light, gabardine overcoat that he now carried over his left arm.

It was late, so the anteroom to Grogan's office, where his secretary performed clerical and gate-keeping functions, was empty and dark. Grogan's door was closed, but light escaped at the bottom and spread over the carpet in front.

"I'll wait here," Barney said, taking a seat at the secretary's empty desk, turning on her desk lamp, and pulling a paperback book from his well-tailored jacket pocket. "You're the one he wants to talk to."

Paul knocked twice and went in at Grogan's response. He closed the door softly behind him.

Phil Grogan was now director of operations. That was the highest position in the organization, but he had been in and out of Paul's professional life almost from its beginning. He had directed Paul and a small team on a tricky operation during the Hungarian Revolution of 1956. Later on, Paul had been an instructor at a sensitive training school Grogan was running for the organization in West Texas. Their paths crossed many times after that.

Paul and Jason March were working for Grogan during the operation that took Jason's life, filled Paul with guilt, and embittered Petra for many years.

Most recently, Grogan had sent Paul and Barney on the East European operation that killed Paul and took him to the Vale. That was the last time Paul had been in this office, but not the last time he had seen Grogan. His old boss had been with him even in the Vale, but of course, the Grogan Paul saw across the desk knew nothing about that.

Paul looked up to Grogan like no one else in his professional life. That had made it very hard to give Grogan his unexplained resignation when Grogan had just saved his life.

Grogan was a notorious manipulator, but he had always treated Paul with his own version of generosity. He would have seen Paul's precipitous departure as an act of personal disloyalty. That should have buried their relationship, but apparently it had not.

Here was Paul, again facing the boss he remembered so well. The director's office was more imposing than ones of days gone by, but Grogan filled it no less impressively. It was the same Grogan, sitting behind his desk in a tieless, white, dress shirt with the sleeves rolled up below the elbow over his massive forearms. More than ten years Paul's senior, he continued to wear his now fully gray hair in a crew-cut style.

This desk was larger than those of the past, but he still sat in the black executive swivel chair he had retained longer than Paul had known him. Like Grogan, that chair never seemed to age as it followed him from one place to another throughout his service. A symbol of legendary power, it was inseparably associated with the man himself. He had even appeared to be sitting in it while he tutored Paul in the Vale about God, happiness, and the life of the soul.

This Grogan closed a folder he seemed to have been reading and placed it on one of several piles in the middle his desk. Silently, he motioned Paul toward a polished, wooden armchair that sat to his left in front of the desk.

Paul hung his overcoat loosely over the back of the chair and sat down. Then Grogan swiveled his own seat about forty-five degrees to face him but said nothing.

Paul was used to this kind of opening. Unless he was delivering a reprimand, Grogan did not like to start conversations. In this case, Paul was determined to outwait him. He smiled but kept silent, while looking directly into Grogan's hard, black eyes.

"Okay, Paul," he said after thirty seconds or so. "Why do you want to see me?"

Even if Grogan spoke first, Paul would have to define the content. Paul gave in.

"Why have you set the dogs on me, Grogan?"

"What dogs?" Grogan asked, lifting his eyebrows.

"Cut the kidding. Two days after I resigned, you had Barney searching my apartment and planting bugs. Some other clown was pretending to tail me in traffic. That's what I mean."

"I call that taking precautions." His face was blank as an unminted coin.

"Precautions? Have you forgotten? I don't work here any more."

"Some things did not terminate with your employment."

"Like what?"

"Think of your behavior after the last operation."

"What are you getting at?"

"Let's just say you have not been yourself since you came back. Our security people call that a sudden behavioral anomaly. You know how we react to such indicators."

"I can't respond to a riddle like that. How did I become a security risk by leaving the organization?"

"You tell me," Grogan said in a tone as blank as his face.

"It's not just my resignation, is it?"

"No. It's more than that."

"What then?"

"Do you really expect me to give that away?"

"Why not? If I'm guilty of something, wouldn't I already know it?"

"You make a good point. Let's explore that."

Grogan paused, but when Paul did not speak, he went on.

"Your final debriefing report made no mention of certain revelations you may have made to your Ministry of Interior captors. Why?"

"Because I did not make any. Who says I did?"

"You know I can't tell you that. You're not cleared for it any more."

"What am I supposed to have given them?"

"I can't tell you that either."

"Why do I feel like a character in a Kafka novel?"

"I'm doing my best."

"I am too, and I tell you I never went one syllable beyond my cover story. They knocked me around a little—that's in my report—but even that was halfhearted and incompetent. Why would I have told them anything?"

"That's one of the things I'm trying to find out. I have a polygraph operator standing by. Are you willing to strap on the cords and give us a reading?"

Paul's first inclination was to say yes, but he instantly had second thoughts.

"What would the boundaries of your questioning be?"

"Your accident, capture, and interrogation."

Paul had been afraid of that. The yes-or-no questions of a lie-detector test would bracket his Vale experience. Even if he registered truthful responses for anything important, his Vale memories were apt to create positive reactions elsewhere that would look like lies. That would do the one thing a polygraph is really good at. It would correctly infer that he was holding something back. Doubt would be cast over the whole business, and he would look like a liar anyway.

"Can you narrow the range of questioning some?" Paul asked.

"What do you mean?"

"Can you limit the questions to only those which apply directly to your concerns?"

"Not without leaving possibilities unexamined. I can't see setting the bounds any closer without telegraphing to you what the actual suspicions are. I think you will see them when you hear the questions, but the price of that knowledge is to take the test."

Go ahead and take it. What have I got to lose? If I know what Grogan is worried about, maybe I can challenge it.

*Not so fast. Once the polygraph calls you a liar, nothing you say will count with Grogan. Better to let him think you're holding out than take the test and prove it.*

What's wrong with telling him about the Vale anyway? I've already told Father Don, Brother Arnold, and Brother James. I was even trying to tell Petra.

*The three clerics were ready to hear and understand. So was Petra. Grogan is not. He'll have a spring-loaded excuse to put you away in a psychiatric ward.*

How could he do that? I don't work here any more.

*Have you forgotten what extra-legal tools Grogan carries in his backpack?*

"Sorry, Grogan, I cannot take the polygraph test for the same reason I didn't explain my resignation to you before. That has nothing to do with my conduct in captivity. You have the story on that in my debriefing. I want to respond specifically to your suspicions about my loyalty—with or without benefit of a polygraph. If we can do that, I will answer you right now. Where does that leave us?"

Grogan leaned back in his chair for a few seconds, stroking his chin with the fingers of his right hand. His face softened a bit, but his penetrating gaze held Paul transfixed. Then he leaned forward, palms flat on the desk, to speak slowly and precisely.

"My dear friend, you are making this very hard for me. Before last week, I would not have thought this possible. But here it is, and I have to deal with it. Your record is in question, and the investigation will continue until I know the truth. The polygraph might have helped, but I cannot force you to take it without making its readings worthless."

Grogan paused a few seconds. Then he placed his palms together, with his elbows still on the desk, and continued speaking.

"By the time you get home tonight your apartment will have been fumigated. If I left the bugs in place, I suspect you would just do that job yourself and maybe smash up some expensive equipment. Other forms of surveillance will continue, so be careful not to step on somebody if you turn around too fast. If you change your mind about cooperating, I am sure you will find a way to let me know."

Now Grogan turned his chair back to face his desk and reached for one of the folders in front of him.

"Since you have nothing else to ask me, good night Paul."

# 10

Paul was back in the Vale and just as overwhelmed as before. Memory alone could not be recreating what he saw and felt.

*Am I dreaming?*

No. He was there, and his spirit soared with God-given freedom.

He hung in limitless space among changing forms of color, light, and shadow that darted about, randomly disappeared, and popped up somewhere else. Paul knew these were souls doing God's work in the pervasive light of his simultaneously infinite reality. Paul alone, sitting as before, seemed not to be in motion.

"How do you feel, partner?"

"Never better," Paul told Jason March, who had just appeared in front of him.

It was Jason, all right—Petra's husband and Paul's former teammate. He was dressed in the same kind of garment Paul again wore. Its transcendent whiteness accented Jason's dark, Italian complexion, black eyes, and curly brown hair. Paul knew this was no longer the way Jason looked. It was only a façade to make Paul comfortable while he transitioned through the Vale and graduated to truly heavenly forms.

"Am I in the Vale?" Paul asked.

"Sort of, but not exactly," Jason responded.

"Have I died?"

"No. That's the 'not exactly' part."

"Then what's going on? Everything I see and feel says I am really in the Vale."

"Incredible isn't it? Your body on earth is asleep and dreaming, but your soul is being translated here. I'm no celestial technician, but I think that works only because you are already here. Your presence here is not being interrupted. I am your next therapist, and here I am. When we are done though, you'll have to go back."

"That's a letdown, but didn't you just say I'm really here?"

"Yes, but you are still on earth too. That won't change until you die."

"Again?"

"Yes."

"So what's going on right now?"

"This is a special setup. You were called."

"Wasn't I called before?"

"You were, but this time there is none of the violent stuff."

"Thank God for that."

"Of course you do." Jason smiled beatifically.

Paul paused and looked closely at Jason.

"I need to thank you too, Jason. You saved my life in Laos. I saw your body dragged through the jungle, and that ruined me for a long time."

"I know that. You and I are talking now, so I've known all along. We don't watch earth from here, but souls come through the Vale and tell us things."

"Sorry. I've been back on earth less than a month, but I'm forgetting how God works. It is all now. Past and future don't happen here."

"No problem. Your therapy is barely begun. I also know about Petra's despair and her journey back to God after you told her I was dead."

"I haven't mentioned that."

"Not yet, but you do, and she does. In fact, you just did."

Out of the Vale

75

"I thought I had mastered simultaneous infinity," Paul said, shrugging his shoulders and raising the palms of his hands, "but you're making me feel pretty dumb."

"Ironically, that takes *time* to master," Jason said, smiling at his own wordplay. "It is one of the more important things you do here before moving on to heaven."

"Did Petra also tell you I quit the organization and was trying to get closer to her? Sorry, old friend. I never thought about you waiting for her here."

"Someone must have told you that apologies don't count any more. We're not sorry for anything here except those poor souls lost to the terminal ward."

"Actually, someone did tell me that. Thanks for the reminder, but I still feel awkward. How do I tell a man who gave his life for me that I've been romancing his wife?"

Jason laughed gently before replying.

"Please don't bother. We no longer care what happens on earth— before or after we left it. Marriage is a holy sacrament there, but it is meaningless here. Didn't Jesus say there is no marriage in heaven? Here everyone loves God and everybody else all the time. That's all."

"I guess you already know how my earth-side love making turns out."

"So what if I do?"

"You're not going to tell me, are you?"

"Sweat it out yourself."

They both laughed.

"Okay, Jason. If you're not going to give me any clues, at least tell me why I'm here now."

"You're still trying to figure out your mission back on earth, aren't you?"

"You bet I am."

"Sorry. I can't help."

"You mean you won't."

"Nope, I just don't know. Even God can operate on a need-to-know basis."

"So why are we talking at all?"

"Haven't you been getting some demonic attention lately?"

"Okay, I have," Paul replied. "How am I doing?"

"You're still alive on earth, aren't you? You must have done something right."

"I learned to call on the Lord when things looked fatal. That worked, but something else is happening now."

"What?"

"I'm in some kind of trouble with the organization."

"I thought you quit."

"I did, but two days later, I was being bugged and shadowed."

Paul recounted some details of his flight to the monastery and recent interview with Grogan.

"Good old Grogan," Jason said, clapping his hands together. "Why didn't you stay at the abbey?"

"I wasn't fooling the devil, and I couldn't answer Grogan without facing him."

"Do you think you might be opposed by satanic forces in the organization too?"

"Come on. You can't believe Grogan is a servant of Satan. He is one of my therapists here in the Vale."

"Think about it, Paul. Nobody has to sell their soul to the devil to be duped by him. Now you are only under suspicion. If Grogan had more, you would be in irons. Grogan wants you to prove him wrong."

"You think Satan is behind this too?"

"He has always been the foremost master of deception. Suspicion is abroad in the organization. You don't know what it is, but it isn't true. Who else hates you so much?"

"No one I know of."

"Then what's left?"

"Maybe you've got it—something close anyway."

"Think it over."

"I suppose you're right. But how does knowing that help me? I can't just tell people the devil did it."

"Why not go see Grogan again?"

"There's no hope there. He just wants me to take a polygraph."

"Then tell him you will."

"Are you crazy?"

"You talk like someone who has never had a lie-detector test."

"What are you getting at?" Paul asked quietly.

"Aren't you forgetting the sin-and-tell session that usually precedes the test?"

"You mean the introduction phase, where the polygraph operator specifies each question he's going to ask. You get to talk about anything in your life that might cause a false positive. Then the operator gives you sort of an absolution. He rephrases questions or simply assures you that none of them refers to the event you've already confessed."

"Exactly."

"But I can't tell him about the Vale."

"Why can't you?"

"Grogan will send me to some psycho ward."

"Why would he do that? You don't work for him now. He only wants the truth, so give it to him. Between the time you slipped in the snow and were pulled out you had an afterlife experience. Go ahead and describe it. Who's going to care?"

"Don't you think I'll be asked if I believe it?"

"Just say you do. That's the truth, and you can prove it with a lie detector strapped on. Then you can answer questions about your captivity and dispel any suspicion that may be abroad."

Paul sighed.

"Why didn't I think of that?"

"Don't forget. You're up against demons. On earth they break into our minds all the time to sow doubt, trouble, and confusion."

"And I really fell for it, didn't I?"

"Maybe, but remember this, Paul. The only defense against lies is the truth."

"You're right of course. I know the devil is out to get me. He tried to kill me once. I should have anticipated more subtle things."

"What saved you from the direct attack?" Jason asked with a smile.

"Prayer."

"You'll find no better help on earth than that. Keep it up, as your namesake apostle says, 'without ceasing'."

Now Jason vanished, as Paul's Vale therapists always did, and Paul came suddenly awake in his bed.

Again Paul felt the burden of being a soul still trapped on earth. Its absence while he dreamed of the Vale now made him even more aware of its constant and oppressive presence.

Paul woke up from his latest Vale adventure after six in the morning. He had a lot of thinking to do, so he got up, showered, dressed, and made himself a soft-boiled egg. He believed what Grogan had said about pulling out the bugs last night, but he was sure the telephone would still be tapped. After eating, he picked up the handset.

"I'm ready, Grogan," was all he said before hanging up. Then he turned on the television set and tried to interest himself in the morning news shows.

The phone rang just before nine o' clock, and Paul answered it.

"Is it you, Barney?"

"Who else would I be? Come on out."

# 11

The polygraph readout machinery was not visible in the testing room, which was small and furnished with only a desk, two chairs, a filing cabinet, and a three-drawer safe. Paul thought the graphing readout was probably in the next room behind the two-way mirror he was facing. Someone, he suspected, would be in there to monitor the equipment and watch what was going on out front.

A blood-pressure cuff, chest strap, and finger-and-hand electrodes lay on the desk in front of the polygraph technician, who sat across from Paul in front of the mirror. The operator was a small, thin, balding man who introduced himself as Ralph and was dressed like an old-school college professor. He had a deep, soothing voice that seemed bigger than his body, and he wore a perpetual smile to inspire confidence. Paul had never met him, but he thought Ralph might make a good dentist.

"As you know," Ralph said, smiling, "I would normally go through the questions to be asked before beginning the test, but I have been told not to do that in your case. The reason, quite frankly, is that if you knew what I will be asking about before hand, you might refuse to go ahead with the procedure."

"Isn't it rather bold of you to tell me that?"

"Not really. I'm here to look for the truth, not take trophies. You know how this machine works. I cannot tell you the questions up front this time, but you have a chance right now to purge your mind of any internal doubt or conflict that might hang you up later. What do you say?"

"I am grateful for your fairness, but let's be sure I understand the timeframe we are talking about."

"That covers just about everything that happened to you from the time you entered the People's Republic to your release and departure from the country."

"In that case, I'll have to tell you something about the period when I was trapped in the snow pit, before I was rescued by the MI troops."

"I suppose you were unconscious most of that time."

"Yes and no."

"I'm afraid the polygraph cannot deal with that kind of dichotomy," Ralph said with a subdued laugh.

"I know, and that's why I'm telling you about it now."

Ralph said nothing, but appeared very attentive, waiting for Paul to continue.

"You might say my body was unconscious at least for a while, but I was quite dead before I was pulled out."

"I remember the account you gave in your debriefing report. It said you thought you were given cardiopulmonary resuscitation by the troops that dug you up."

"Yes, but I assure you I actually died in that snow."

"How could you know that for certain?"

"That, Ralph, is the other half of the dichotomy. The real me—not this flimsy body you see before you—was somewhere else entirely. By earthly standards, it was gone much longer than the moments this crummy sack of skin lay buried under the snow."

Ralph lapsed into a few seconds of silence looking directly into Paul's eyes.

"That is a long and complex description," he said, jotting on a notepad in front of him. "Do you mean some sort of out-of-body experience?"

"No. It was an afterlife experience."

"You are serious about this, aren't you?"

"Indeed I am, and I'll be glad to respond to that question with the polygraph running."

"Don't worry. You may be confident that none of my questions has anything to do with your...your afterlife episode while your body was caught in the snow. They will relate only to things that happened before or after that time. Is that good enough?"

"I'm ready when you are."

"Then let's get started," Ralph said, standing up and coming around the desk to attach the necessary devices to Paul's body.

Paul made himself loose and comfortable in his chair while Ralph went back to his own seat to activate the equipment. The machinery next door would monitor Paul's blood pressure, breathing, and perspiration for any reaction to the questions asked. Paul's job was to stay calm and still, so as not to confuse the graphing pens.

"Are you comfortable?" Ralph asked.

"Yes." Paul suspected this was a benchmark question to establish a mean for how he reacted to the stress of his current situation.

"I am going to begin the main questions now. Please try not to react emotionally to the nature of a question, and don't try to solve the mystery of what this is all about. You can do that later. For now, simply consider each question by itself and respond with a yes or a no." Ralph paused for about ten seconds and then began.

"Were you and Bernard Rice together from the time you entered prohibited territory until you became separated by your fall in the snow?" Ralph asked in a voice that had consciously shifted into a steady, level monotone.

"Yes."

"From the time of entry until you fell into the snow pit, were you and Mr. Rice ever separated from each other for more than a few minutes?"

"No."

*That sounds like the same question to me,* Paul thought.

"Did you know the coordinates for the rendezvous that you and Mr. Rice were supposed to make?"

"Yes."

"Was your fall in the snow completely an accident?"

"Yes."

"Were you in any way complicit in your capture by the MI troops?"

"No."

"While you were in Ministry of Interior custody, did you cooperate with your captors in any manner contrary to the purpose or integrity of your operation?"

"No."

"Did you ever reveal in any way to an unauthorized person the true purpose of your presence in the People's Republic?"

"No."

"While or before you were in the People's Republic, did you reveal in any way to an unauthorized person the existence of your assigned rendezvous?"

"No."

"While or before you were in the People's Republic, did you reveal in any way to an unauthorized person the location or timing of your assigned rendezvous?"

"No," Paul could not help finding an arc in the course the questions were taking.

*Probably not a good thing to think about that while you're strapped up for a polygraph exam*, he thought.

"I have one question of my own to add, even though I told you I would not," Ralph said, lifting his eyes from the written questions he had been asking. "Did you really enter the afterlife while your body was caught in that snow pit?"

"Yes, I did," Paul said with a happy smile.

Ralph stood and came around the desk to remove Paul's polygraph sensors.

"Relax, Paul. I'll be back in a minute," he said, leaving the room and closing the door behind him. Paul was quite sure he remained under observation through the mirror.

*What*, Paul wondered, *could have happened to the rendezvous or the people we were supposed to meet there?*

While Paul was waiting at the Frankfurt Flughafen to board his flight back to the states, Barney had told him the operation—the rendezvous—went off all right. The questions Ralph just asked Paul suggested something else. Had Barney lied to him about the rendezvous?

Had something bad happened there after Barney left? How come Barney was not the one being grilled with a polygraph?

Paul saw his chance to get at least one answer when Barney walked into the little office, closing the door behind him. This time he was moderately dressed in a long-sleeved red shirt, open at the neck and tucked into pressed black slacks.

"Why aren't you the one hooked up to this thing, Barney?" Paul asked, gesturing toward the polygraph paraphernalia.

"I already was, chum. Why do you think Grogan called me out of Europe so early? I may have broken a speed record getting back. You had already walked out on him, so he went for me first. I was tested the day after you quit. When I showed up negative, you were still in the line of fire, and you know how a moving target attracts the hunter's eye. You had suddenly resigned under peculiar circumstances and without explanation. When we applied a little discreet surveillance, you—"

"You call that discreet? You were leaving footprints on my bathmat."

"Okay, so I got careless and you caught me. Don't you think it looked just a teensy bit suspicious when you ditched your tail and blew out of town?"

"I told you I went on a religious retreat."

"I thought you were joking about that," Barney said lightly. His change in mood sparked a similar one in Paul.

"I don't think the monastery gives receipts, but if I needed to, I could prove I was there. You are right though; I was getting out of the way for several reasons. One was definitely the impression that Grogan might decide to pull me in for something. What you've told me kind of explains that."

"I hope you've noticed that Grogan did not jerk your chain when he could have. You wound up here on your own. I think the old man still has a soft spot for you. Maybe you ought to come back to work."

"I can't do that, Barney."

"Because of what happened to you in the snow?"

"What do you know about that?"

"No more than Ralph. Where do you think I was while you were in here itemizing your sins?" Barney asked, glancing at the two-way mirror. "We have an audio hookup back there too, you know."

"So much for the sanctity of the confessional," Paul remarked, shrugging his shoulders.

"Anyway, Ralph says you wrote a good read on his perceptive equipment—even about the afterlife thing."

"Are you going to tell Grogan about that too?"

"He'll get Ralph's report anyway. Does that bother you?"

"Oddly enough, I don't think it does any more."

"That's good, because I've put us on his calendar in fifteen minutes."

# 12

Darlene Parker had served off and on as Grogan's secretary during his assignments at the headquarters. She had quite naturally moved up with him when he took over as director of operations. Paul remembered her from earlier days as something of a pinup beauty. She was thoroughly devoted to her boss and made everything around him run smoothly.

Paul thought she had aged gracefully, maintaining a trim figure and a still wrinkle-free face. Artfully, she was not afraid to display a few streaks of gray in her thick, well-coifed, auburn hair. Grogan's move to the front office even led her to moderate a style of dress that had once bordered on daring. The well-tailored suits she now favored bore no trace of the dowdy or mannish, but they perfectly complemented the dignity that went with her old boss's current position.

Darlene stood and came around her desk when Paul and Barney entered her outer-office domain. Paul recalled how feminine she still was as he watched her approach. Ignoring Barney, she stopped a foot away to place her right hand gently on Paul's upper-left arm and look earnestly into his face. Her hair gave off a faint, but alluring scent of honeysuckle.

"Paul, I am so glad to see you. I heard—well, I read in your report—about your close call last time. I would be very sad if you had not made it." Her voice was soft, and her clear blue eyes seemed near to tearing up.

Paul could feel the honesty and warmth of this impressive female in the pit of his stomach. Then her expression changed, her look hardened, and her fingers tightened like talons around his arm.

"Now what is this drivel," she rasped in a voice turned instantly from tender concern to harsh reprimand, "about you leaving the organization and turning your back on the man who treated you like a son?"

Barney broke her passionate spell of rebuke by speaking up.

"I'm sorry, Darlene. Is Grogan ready to see us? I asked you to put us down for eleven fifteen."

She broke her hold on Paul, moved gracefully back to her desk, picked up her telephone, and spoke into it with her back to them. Hanging up the handset, she turned around with a full-lipped smile and pointed to the inner office.

Barney led the way this time, knocking before opening the door. Inside, Paul closed it behind them. Grogan looked to Paul as if he had not moved since their discussion the night before. The main change Paul saw was that two polished wooden chairs like the one he occupied the night before now sat a few feet in front of the desk. Of course the documents piled on the desktop had disappeared, been augmented, or migrated from one stack to another.

Behind the desk Grogan leaned back in his majestic executive chair and beckoned them to sit down. His face gave nothing away.

*How many times have I played this scene?* Paul asked himself. *Not all of them ended happily.*

Now Paul again faced Grogan with a close associate—a former one anyway—to talk about grave matters of dire consequence. Grogan so rarely initiated conversation that Paul decided to force the issue and move ahead.

"Did you get the polygraph results from Ralph yet?"

"Yes, I have them right here," Grogan replied, lifting a thin folder that lay in front of him. It could not have held the broad graph-paper roll the polygraph machine produced. It would be only a summary of the test results.

"How'd I do, coach?"

"I think you already know that." Grogan's face remained impassive. "Then I can go?"

Grogan leaned forward with his elbows on the desk and his hands clasped in front of him. He was giving Paul a curious, lopsided grin.

*This,* Paul thought, *is not a good sign.*

"Wouldn't you like to know more about what is going on here—why for example you were followed, harassed, and roped into a lie-detector test?"

"I can do without it. Information comes at a high price these days. Besides, I'm not cleared for such things any more."

Grogan's grin disappeared and his jaws tightened so visibly that Paul imagined an ache behind his own cheeks.

"I decide who is cleared for what around here," Grogan spat through barely unclenched teeth. "I am about to tell you some things with the provision that the full extent of the law will apply should you improperly reveal any one of them."

"What choice do I have? I can't get out the gate without your okay, so I remain your reluctant audience."

Grogan sat back in his chair, his face now relaxed into what Paul recognized as a mode of moderate conviviality. This was the mask of magnanimity he wore to persuade, rather than command.

"From the questions you were asked, I presume you know that something went very wrong with the rendezvous from your last operation."

"You're right, but Barney told me on the way home that the operation went well without me. That doesn't seem compatible with the focus of Ralph's questions today."

"We put Barney through the lie detector before we even thought about you. Of course we questioned him more thoroughly, because he had actually gone to the meeting place."

"He told me that."

"Barney successfully transferred the funding instruments he carried into the country to the representatives with whom he met. Fortunately, none of those things were in your pack, or the People's Republic might have treated you much differently."

"I'm grateful."

"Anyway, Barney must have been well into his egress phase before anything went wrong. He did not find out what happened until we brought him back here and started grilling him."

Barney nodded his head in silent agreement.

"According to our sources," Grogan went on, "those who received the funds were ambushed after the rendezvous by a band of what looked to be Ministry of Interior border guards. Some of the couriers were killed or wounded; others got away. None of the survivors claim to have any idea what became of the money. One thing we know is that it never got to the political faction of the disloyal opposition we were trying to help."

Grogan had gradually leaned forward until his palms and forearms were again flat on the desk.

"There was a leak somewhere. It may have been on the other side, but we are checking our own bases to be safe. At least we now know that neither of you played a part in what happened."

"That's fascinating, Grogan. May I go now?"

"Aren't you at all interested in finding out what happened to your final operation?" Grogan was no longer grinding his teeth, but Paul remained apprehensive.

"If I still worked here, I might be. As things are, it's not one of my priorities."

"What if I offered you a one-time contract to dig up the answer to that question?"

"I would say no. Besides, you need a cop, not an over-the-hill covert operator."

"I'll decide who I need and for what," Grogan replied, his tone again turning forceful. "Anyway, our security and counterintelligence people lack the operations background you can bring to the investigation. You'll have access to them if you need it."

Now Grogan paused and tapped the fingers of his right hand thoughtfully on the top of his desk. Then he leaned toward Paul and spoke softly.

"Would your refusal, like your original resignation, be related to what you seem to think was a vision of the afterlife?"

"That could be."

"I know you got a pretty solid smack in the head when you were being rescued. I see it took more than a few stitches to close the hole it made."

Grogan pointed to the gradually healing scar on Paul's scalp. Paul had not gotten around to having the stitches removed, but he no longer wore a bandage over it.

"Might not that blow have scrambled your memory of events a little?" Grogan's hands were once more flat on the desk.

"I suppose."

"You believe very strongly in this afterlife episode, don't you? I'll bet you think you've received some kind of message from God. That's why you left the organization so abruptly, isn't it?"

"You're getting warmer."

"Don't your accident and injuries throw any doubt on the reality of this spiritual safari? Wouldn't it be wise to give my contract a little more consideration?"

"I don't think so. Besides, if you believe I've gone loony, why do you want me back working for you?"

"I'm the one who makes those decisions. I never called you crazy, and I don't think you are."

"Thanks, but whatever you've decided, I'm not coming back."

"Don't make up your mind too fast. I may have an alternative proposal."

"Maybe you do, but it's not going to sell."

"Listen up, and see what you think," Grogan said, again planting his elbows on the desk. This time he raised his hands to make a steeple and rested his chin on top of the spire.

"Because of your sudden resignation, flight from surveillance, and initial refusal to take a polygraph, I have been going back over your personnel record. I think I discovered something pretty interesting."

Grogan paused here, but Paul remained silent. Barney sat still; he had said nothing since coming into the office.

"I had forgotten," Grogan said, "that you were once in the navy reserve."

"Yes, but the organization arranged for me to be released from that obligation on the grounds that my duties here were more important to national security."

"Released, yes, but never actually discharged."

"Come to the point."

"I also happened to notice that, because of your pressing duties here, you never fulfilled the three years of active duty service you owed the navy."

Grogan paused, but Paul said nothing.

"Well, you no longer have any duties here, do you?"

"What are you cooking up, Grogan?" Paul had stiffened visibly in his seat.

"Don't worry, Paul. I don't really imagine the navy would be interested in calling back somebody your age over a technicality like this." Grogan's voice had taken on an eerie quality, at once unctuous and menacing. "Not unless I call an old shipmate of mine at the pentagon and ask him to make that happen."

"You wouldn't," Paul said, coming to his feet.

Grogan held his position, but his voice turned thoroughly cold.

"Sit in a corner and watch, Paul. Have you ever known me to bluff? You're going to play ball with me, or I'll ram the bat up your nose. Walk out of here now, and you'll be packing your sea bag in less than a week. Then I'll get you transferred here, and you'll do what I tell you in the grade of—what was your former navy rank?—seaman? You weren't even in long enough to be rated."

Paul sat back down, hung his head, and looked at his feet.

*Does God want me back working for Grogan? Maybe God just wants me in the navy.*

*No. Either way, I will still be working for Grogan. Perhaps I am trying too hard to take control of things. Didn't I learn better than that in the Vale?*

"I'll take the contract," he said, raising his eyes to look at Grogan once more.

"I thought you would see it my way."

Grogan beamed as he handed Paul a bundle of papers across the desk. He also handed over the plastic-laminated photo credential Paul had turned in two weeks earlier. Paul had thought then that he was leaving the headquarters for the last time.

"You will sign the contract now and bring the security and payroll forms back to Darlene when you have filled them out. Your contract fees will be identical to what you were getting in your former pay grade. Double up with Barney for desk and filing space. He has an oversized cubicle, and your old one has already been reassigned. Call on Barney for backup; you are both working the same problem. Brief me at least twice a week until the job is done. I hope that doesn't take too long, because I know you are eager to put all this behind you. Any questions?"

Paul had no questions for Grogan, but as he stood to go, he was asking himself one.

*What if Petra finds out?*

# 13

When Paul had settled back into the organization and made himself at home in Barney's less-than-roomy cubicle, he went to visit Dr. Wendell Bythington.

Bythington was the headquarters' sole credentialed historian. He seemed to have been there forever and knew more about the organization than any employee, past or present. He looked more like an aging NFL lineman than the gray-bearded academic he was. He usually wore a coat and tie, but they rarely matched. His oversized office looked like a library or a document storage vault, because it was both. Several years earlier he had talked Paul into becoming a part-time archivist for the organization.

The old historian was sitting at his typewriter when Paul came in. He rose immediately and came around the desk to grasp Paul's hand and pat him heartily on the shoulder.

"It's so good to see you, Paul. Grogan told me you quit your job a few weeks ago, but now it looks like you're back. Does this mean I can count on you to help with the archives again? I haven't found anyone to take your place."

"Sorry, but I'm only back for a one-time, sole-purpose contract job. When that is done, I'll be gone again."

"That's too bad for me. You are the first additional-duty archivist I've seen take the job seriously. I'm going to miss you."

"I like your work too. That's why I'm here."

"What can I do for you?"

"I need to see everything we have on the *Bung Tick* operation Barney Rice and I went out for in January."

"That's easy enough. Neither of your debriefing reports has been filed, and I don't think the after-action report has come in yet."

"I'll want those of course, but that won't be enough. Barney and I need every shred of anything that relates to the preparation and execution of that operation: background studies, contingency plans, input to the operation plan, the OpPlan itself, progress reports, line-item reviews, and every syllable on record that affected the overall project in any way. Can you pull all that together for me?"

"That's quite an order, Paul, but I can get a package ready by next week. Once you have that, you may recall other sources you did not think of or forgot to ask about. Then I can look for them too."

"Great," Paul replied. "By the way, you can forget the *Bung Tick* after-action report for now. The action on that operation is not yet complete."

"I see," Bythington said in an interested tone. Then he cocked his head back as if to ask a question.

"Not now, doc, but you can read about it when we're done."

"I look forward to that, my friend." The historian smiled with an air of confidence Paul wished he shared.


"Who is Dollop?" Paul asked from behind the wall of file folders, loosely bound programmed-action plans, and related correspondence that covered his desk.

"Sounds like a codename to me," Barney responded from his desk across the cubicle.

"Brilliant, Sherlock, but a codename for whom?"

"We didn't pay much attention to things like that when we were working up the operation. We had no need to know true identities to do the job. Besides, not knowing them gave us a safety net if something dropped and the operation went south. Isn't that what codenames are for?"

"That's one purpose," Paul said, "but now the show has flopped, and we need to know who the real actors were. We're not going to sort this puzzle out any other way."

"You're right of course. Try going through this background study," Barney replied, tossing a fair-sized, conspicuously classified, spiral-bound document onto Paul's desk. "Things like this were off-limits to us when we planned the operation. The main man we went in to meet was just Dollop to us."

"No longer," Paul said. He opened the book and began scanning pages until something caught his eye. Then he slowed his pace and kept on reading.

Paul and Barney had taken days just to sort and organize the material Bythington kept feeding them. The historian had correctly predicted they would identify new sources as the process continued.

This kind of analysis was different from the way they usually worked up an operation. What the organization asked operators to do did not call for much depth. Operators were just supposed to operate and move on to the next job. Over his career, Paul had accepted the luxury of that ignorance. He did his part, but ultimate goals rarely mattered. He liked it that way.

Now he was forced to look directly at what he and Barney had been up to and ask why. He had to correlate and analyze how it all turned out and what that might mean.

"Barney," Paul said, looking up from his reading, "does the name Andrei Plavin ring a bell?"

"No, but I'm sure you will tell me why it should."

"Andrei Plavin is Dollop."

"That leaves more than one question about Dollop unanswered. I met him only once, and that was a hurried affair. You were in trouble, so I had to make an exit promptly. That probably saved my life and yours too."

"I appreciate that," Paul said hesitantly.

"Well?"

"According to this," Paul went on, holding up the document Barney had given him, "Mr. Plavin was a major figure—maybe the top man—of an underground opposition group in the People's Republic."

"Why am I not surprised?"

"What were we supposed to be delivering, Barney?"

"You know that. We were bringing in funds to prop up the opposition."

"Yes, but what kind of funds? It couldn't be precious metals like gold or silver. That would have taken a truck. Diamonds are transportable, but not very negotiable."

"Isn't the funding medium mentioned in your document?" Barney asked.

"I don't see it. I'm sure Grogan knows."

"The package I carried in was shaped like ordinary paper—maybe a bit heavier."

"Currency?"

"I doubt it. That much local currency would not be worth much, and dollars don't work there. Most other currencies would pose the same problem."

"So negotiability is the question," Paul said.

"Yes, something like bearer bonds on a foreign bank or business might do."

"Wouldn't negotiability be a problem with those too? If Dollop planned to start clipping coupons on an instrument like that, he would need a bank to process them. The People's Republic has only one bank, and that belongs to the state."

"I am shocked at your naiveté." Barney was exaggerating the slight British accent he affected. "Do you have no respect for the power of greed and bribery in a typically stifling, socialist paradise? For all we know, Dollop may have been a banker."

"Brilliant, Barney!" Paul shouted. "That just might be it."

They laughed together.

"Whatever the instruments were," Paul went on, "they were compact, transportable, and transferable. Did you give them directly to Dollop?"

"That's who he said he was, and he was where we were told to deliver the package. Besides, he gave me the correct secondary authentication phrase for Dollop."

"Now Grogan tells us there was an ambush; some people were killed, and some got away," Paul said. "How does he know that? Did it come from a survivor still in the country or from someone no longer there?"

"I have no idea."

"Let's ask a man who does."

Paul picked up the secure interior telephone on his desk and punched in Grogan's office extension.

# 14

Whenever Paul visited the IG Farben Building in Frankfurt, Germany, he was struck with contradictory impressions of awe and sadness. By any standard, the place was a triumph of early twentieth-century functional architecture. Yet its early history was awash with blood and full of evil memories.

Completed in 1931, the seven-story structure is joined by a long bow of central corridors that connect six wings, spaced equally between one end of the bow and the other. It was built to house the corporate operations of Germany's IG Farben cartel, the largest chemical manufacturer in the world at the beginning of World War II.

Before and during the war, this industrial giant was the heart of Wehrmacht munitions manufacturing. It was even reputed to have provided funding and influence that helped bring Hitler to power in 1933. Supplying the war effort brought huge profits.

The same combine produced and distributed the deadly Zyklon-B gas used to slaughter helpless prisoners, mostly Jews, at the Auschwitz extermination camp. That special connection involved the company even more deeply in the Nazi murder machine.

Near the end of the war, Paul had heard, General Eisenhower ordered the IG Farben Building spared from the aerial bombardment being visited on everything around it. He wanted to make it a headquarters for American forces in Europe after the war.

At the end of Allied occupation in West Germany, the compound came to house headquarters for the US Army Fifth Corps, the Northern Area Command, and a variety of lesser military tenants. It also made space available to obscure government functions that were much less public than the uniformed services.

In the mid-seventies, it was formally designated the General Creighton W. Abrams Building or simply the Abrams Building. More than six years later, the structure was still identified by its pre-war name. Everyone called it the IG Farben Building.

Passing through the central entry hall, Paul knew where to go. He went straight to one of the quaint, *paternoster* lift banks located in each wing of the building. He stepped smoothly into a doorless wooden capsule moving upward while the line of returning cars next to it went down. The *paternoster*, probably so-called because of its resemblance to a string of rosary beads, forms a continuous loop of constantly moving compartments-for-two that transport passengers from one floor to another. People who see one for the first time are likely to ask, "If you ride up past the top floor, do you come back upside-down?" The answer is no.

Coming to his floor, Paul confidently transitioned from being a body in motion to one at rest on a firm, horizontal surface. Then he took his bearings and turned toward the office to which he had been directed.

Grogan readily answered the first question Paul asked him over the telephone. Barney had guessed right about the medium of the missing funds. It was bearer bonds. To answer the question of how he knew what happened after the rendezvous and transfer, Grogan summoned them to his office. There he began by showing them a defector report so sensitive they had to read it in his presence and were allowed to make no notes. They were seated, as usual, in front of Grogan's desk.

The report, actually an electrical message, was short. It merely advised concerned parties that a Ministry of Interior troop had recently defected from the People's Republic and might be made available to authorized persons with an interest.

The subject, codenamed Patroon, had surrendered to authorities in the country to which he escaped. He was currently under

US protection in West Germany while his request for asylum in the United States was being processed. The message briefly listed topics of which Patroon might have knowledge. The rest of the report explained who to contact for an interview.

Paul noticed one item in the topic list because of its date. That was January twentieth, the same day Paul was buried in the snow, Barney went on to the rendezvous, the opposition group was attacked, and the bonds disappeared. The topic for that date was simply listed as an unusual event.

"This still doesn't tell us how you know what happened after the rendezvous," Paul reminded Grogan, handing the message on to Barney.

"Just accept it. Dollop is dead. That's all you need to know. Now aren't you at all interested in Patroon and the unusual event in January?" Grogan was smiling now.

"Okay. So let's talk about Patroon."

"I hope he can tell us something. Will you go and see what he has to say?"

"Sure," Paul said

"I knew I could count on you. I've already made the arrangements. You will debrief Patroon at the IG Farben Building. You've been there, I think. Here are the details." He slid a manila envelope across his desk toward Paul. "Do you want Barney to go with you?"

"I won't need backup for this."

Grogan nodded in agreement.

"Any questions?" he asked as usual.

"One thing, Grogan."

"Yes?"

"No identity cover this time. From now on, I'll use my own, authentic passport wherever I go."

"Do you think that's wise?"

"It is for me. I'm through doing things the organization's way. Take it or leave it."

"If that's what you want."

Grogan was not smiling any more.

# 15

The small debriefing room in the IG Farben building had no two-way mirror, so Paul knew there was a concealed security camera somewhere. That was okay. Paul was here to get information, not to give it away.

Patroon was a slender, narrow-faced, brown-haired, brown-eyed, unbearded man of medium height. He looked to be in his early twenties. He was wearing khaki trousers with a matching, long-sleeved shirt tucked in at the waist. Alone in the room when Paul was brought in, he stood to shake hands. The pile of cigarette butts in a ceramic ash tray at the center of a small conference table suggested he was a chain-smoker.

*Maybe,* Paul thought, *he is just overreacting to the luxury of American cigarettes his keepers are providing.*

Patroon knew his handler as Bill. At his own instruction, Paul was introduced by his true first name. Bill presented Patroon to Paul as Otto, which Paul knew was not his real name. Patroon was just a handling tag Otto would know nothing about, and Otto was what strangers were told to call him.

Bill offered to excuse himself, but Paul asked him to stay. Bill would be watching anyway. Besides, Paul had observed that people in Otto's situation tended to bond with their handlers. Otto might be more comfortable and cooperative with Bill in the room than facing a stranger by himself. Bill was also a linguist, which would help if Otto's English was less fluent than Paul had been told.

Paul seated himself near the center of the table across from Otto and the ashtray while Bill took a chair at the end to Paul's right. To open things up, Paul asked Otto how he felt about his new situation.

"I am very happy here," he responded, carefully selecting and arranging his words before letting them go. "I will be even happier when I get to America. Bill is helping me do that. Eh, Bill?"

Otto gave Bill a wide-open smile that revealed some damaged teeth. It looked to Paul as if he might have been beaten at some time.

Bill nodded and smiled.

Paul followed up with several questions to which he already knew the answers. A primary rule for such interviews was to give nothing away to the subject. Otto may have assumed that Paul already knew some of his background, but Paul would not confirm that for him.

When Paul asked where he came from, Otto gave what sounded like a town name.

"Is that your hometown? Is that where you grew up?"

"Yes."

"Where is that?" Paul asked.

Otto looked a little confused.

"In the People's Republic," he replied.

"Oh yes, of course. What did you do in the People's Republic?"

"My work?"

"Yes."

"I was a soldier."

"What kind of soldier?"

"I was what you call a private."

"That was your rank. What kind of work did you do?"

"I was assigned to a Ministry of Interior border patrol unit."

Paul was pleased to find that Otto's English was pretty good. As the interview progressed, his responses were becoming less hesitant.

"What were your duties?"

"We patrolled the border and protected other…areas." Otto seemed to be searching for a word.

"What kind of areas?"

"They were special places. Secure areas? No, no. I know—sensitive areas. That's it." Otto was smiling at his linguistic achievement.

"That's very good, Otto. Now where was your unit posted?"

"Posted?"

"Posted, stationed, quartered? Where did you live when you were not out on patrol?"

"A little camp. It was called Blaskovod."

*Bingo*, Paul thought.

His captors had never revealed to Paul the location of his hospital detainment, but he had looked it up when he came back to work for the organization. It was a small Ministry of Interior camp near a tiny village of the same name—Blaskovod.

*Now,* Paul thought, *let's change the subject a bit.*

"What made you leave the People's Republic?"

"I want to come to America." Otto had apparently felt the gears shifting, and his speech was halting once more.

"Was that all?"

Otto stopped to pull a Camel cigarette—regular, not filtered—out of the pack on the table. He lit it with what looked like a new Zippo lighter. Then he made a gesture with the pack toward Paul, who just shook his head. Now Otto sucked the first drag deep into his lungs and exhaled with a great smoke-embellished sigh.

"No. I was afraid." Now he was concentrating his gaze on the tip of his cigarette.

"What made you so afraid?" Paul asked.

Otto looked down the table at Bill, who smiled but said nothing.

"What frightened you so much, Otto?" Paul asked in a firm but gentle voice.

"An officer threatened me."

"Threatened you—with what?"

"He did not say, but he was a very bad man—one who would do anything to somebody who did not obey him."

"You disobeyed him? Well, I suppose he could have had you punished for that."

"No. It was not that way. He could not give me army punishment for what I would not do."

"What then?"

"He could make my life very bad. He might even have me killed." Just talking about this man was a very agitating business for Otto. The hand holding the cigarette was trembling now.

"Tell me about this officer. What was his rank?"

"He was a major."

"What kind of things was he doing to make you so afraid?"

"I told you. He was a very bad man. He always had his hand out." Otto moved his fingers back and forth beneath the thumb of his left hand to make the universal sign for money. "All of us knew he was getting bribes from smugglers and other people who wanted to avoid our patrols. No one could say anything, because he had a few pets in the unit who would tell him. They would beat up anyone he told them to, and sometimes they would just beat men up for no reason."

"Did they ever beat you, Otto?"

"One time, when I was new in the unit," Otto said, putting the fingers of his uncigaretted hand to his mouth.

"Was that how your front teeth were broken?"

"Yes," Otto replied, bringing his hand back down to the table.

"Tell me more about the major you made so angry," Paul said carefully. "What was it that you would not do for him? What made him threaten you?"

Otto crushed out his Camel in the ash tray, immediately lit another, and again pumped out a double lungful of smoke before responding.

"I would not kill someone he wanted me to."

Paul could see Otto's increasing anxiety. He did not like thinking about this man even now that he was safely in the west.

"Can you tell me what happened?" Paul asked.

"We had a prisoner, someone a patrol had dug out of the snow on the twentieth of January. I remember the date because something else was going on that day."

"Yes?" Paul encouraged him to go on.

"Almost a week later, the major called me in and said he had a special job for me. He said the prisoner, who was being held in our small hospital, was going to try to escape. The major started to tell me where and when the escape would happen because he wanted me to shoot the man. He said the prisoner had to be shot dead—not just wounded. He promised me a promotion for it."

"What did you do?" Paul prompted when Otto seemed to hesitate.

"Maybe I should have pretended to go along at first, but I did not. I told him no. He slapped me and cursed me and said he would fix me later."

"Fix you?"

"That is the closest English word I know. Anyway, after that I could not stay with the unit. He might have killed me or had someone else do it. I loaded up my field pack and deserted in the same hour. I took one of our snow cars—I am sorry, I do not know what you call them in English—and headed straight for the border. I was off duty at the time, so I knew the car would be missed even before I was. I knew the patrol routines well enough to get across the border without being caught. I was very lucky."

"Yes, Otto, I believe you were. Who was the major that threatened you?"

"He is called Major Anton Khrabovich."

"Will you write that out, please, to be sure of the spelling?" Paul asked, passing across a small pad and a ballpoint pen.

"Of course," Otto said, taking another long draw on his cigarette and crushing it out before writing the name down.

"By the way, Otto," Paul asked after recovering the pad, "how many officers were assigned to your unit?"

"There was only Major Khrabovich."

Paul resisted the urge to smile.

"Otto," Paul continued, "I think you said you remembered the twentieth of January because of something else that happened. What was that?"

"Yes, that is true. I was coming back from patrol just before daybreak. That was how I saw one of our other crews bringing in the prisoner. At the same time, I happened to see the major and two of his pets going out in a snow car. The major never went out on patrol, so I wondered what was going on."

"Did you ever find out?"

"No," Otto said, as if feeling guilty.

"Don't worry about that, Otto," Paul said, standing and reaching across the table to shake hands. "I've enjoyed talking to you very much. Good luck in your new life."

"Bill," Paul asked, "can I have a word with you before I go?"

"Sure," Bill replied, rising from the table and moving to follow Paul. "I'll be right back, Otto."

Otto just waved, took another cigarette out of the pack, and lit it.

"Do you think you will be able to get him into the states?" Paul asked Bill when they had left the room and closed the door. "He's not exactly a high profile defector with lots of information to spill."

"I know that, but I'm working hard on his case, and I have hopes. I don't think he'll be safe from retaliation in Europe."

Paul knelt on one knee and balanced his note pad on the other to write. Not for the first time, he regretted that people in his former line of work rarely carried business cards—at least not their own.

"Take my work phone number. I don't expect to be there very long, so here is my home address and telephone too. If Otto needs any sort of sponsorship or there is something else I can do for him, please let me know right away."

"I don't think I've ever seen an interviewer react quite this way to a subject," Bill said, looking quizzically at Paul.

"Me neither, pal," Paul replied. "He'll never find out why from me, but I owe that kid big time."

# 16

Paul had arrived in Frankfurt the evening before he was scheduled to talk to Patroon, which allowed him to be fully rested for that. He checked out of his hotel the next morning before going to the IG Farben Building, but left his bag with the concierge. He picked it up on his way back to the airport for a mid-afternoon flight into BWI. This gave him an opportunity before his boarding time to enjoy a Henninger Privat beer and a delicious open-faced ham sandwich with a fried egg on top.

It was now April, and the Frankfurt weather was perfect. This spared him the kind of delays he had suffered on his way back from imprisonment in late January. It also promised an on-time arrival at Baltimore-Washington International around five-thirty that evening. This time, he was riding coach, but the aircraft was not fully loaded, so he had the advantage of an aisle seat with an empty one next to him.

As soon as the plane reached cruising altitude and the seatbelt sign was off, Paul made a good writing surface of the pull-down tray from the seat in front of him. He opened his portfolio with its standard-sized tablet of lined yellow paper and began to draft a report on Patroon.

Paul never took notes at an interview like this. Watching someone write things down distracted a subject and might disrupt his memory. Making notes later let Paul review, organize, and assess his observations before permanently recording them. All that he wrote now would omit names, dates, times, locations, and other precise details. Later, with memory for a key, he could decode it and fill in the final report.

What approach should he take—chronological or topical? Patroon had given him several lines of information that came together in different ways.

*Maybe*, he thought, *I should clear away some of the mental underbrush first.*

*Where do we start?*

Otto says Major Khrabovich wanted him to kill me. Otto just doesn't realize I was the prisoner.

*Is this the same major that interrogated you?*

Otto says he was the only officer at Blaskovod.

*Could Otto have recognized you today and been trying to cozy up?*

He only saw me being brought in unconscious and half frozen to death.

*You were conked out in your cage for days. Anyone could have seen you then.*

If Otto knew I was the prisoner, he would have said so today.

*Okay. Then why would Khrabovich want you killed? You were no threat to him.*

Maybe, but just look at the coincidental events of January 20.

*Which are?*

I arrived at the hospital, and Otto saw the major taking out a snow-tracked Armored Personnel Carrier with a couple of cronies Otto called his pets.

*Okay.*

*What else happened on the morning of January twentieth?*

Barney made it to the rendezvous.

*And then?*

*Barney scrambled off to report your capture, the opposition group was ambushed, and the bonds disappeared.*

Didn't Grogan's mysterious source say the survivors were attacked by what looked like Ministry of Interior border troops?

*Aren't you stretching the bounds of coincidence?*

Remember how Otto described the sticky-fingered major? He ran his part of the border like a personal fiefdom.

*So what?*

Try this hypothesis. The major ran a protection racket. Pay him first, if you wanted to pull something in his territory.

*So Otto said.*

That kind of reputation gets out to people planning unlawful things.

*I suppose.*

Now think back to the late Andrei Plavin, alias Dollop. What if Plavin figured the major for a small-time crook it would be better to just pay off and keep out of the way?

*That's arguable.*

After taking Plavin's payoff, maybe Khrabovich smelled something bigger. We know about his greed. Nobody from the rendezvous was apt to complain about being double-crossed. Just being where they were that morning made them enemies of the state.

*That's plausible.*

So the major takes down Plavin and comes away with newfound wealth.

*It's a neat theory, but how do you support it?*

Think back. Why would Khrabovich want me killed?

*It begins to make sense. The major knows something is going down with Plavin, but he doesn't know what. He gets there too late to grab Barney, but after the killing he finds the bonds. He is now party to a national conspiracy. This stuff is really hot.*

So what does he discover back at his unit?

*You are cluttering up one of his hospital cells. He finds out when and where you were picked up and puts two and two together. The other man—the one who ran away when you were caught—made delivery to Plavin, but you were in on it.*

Don't you think this would make him uncomfortable?

*You bet. He still has to report your capture up the line. Too many people know about that to bury it. When you wake up, he tries to make you talk, but you don't.*

His time is running out.

*The big kids at headquarters are going to call you up there soon. They may succeed where he has failed. Then who knows what kind of questions will be asked about the events of January twentieth? He has too many dirty irons in the fire to let that happen. What can he do?*

He has to take me out of the picture in a hurry.

*Right, but he cannot kill you himself. That would be too obvious. He wants Otto to do it, but Otto won't play. Before he can set up something else, headquarters tells him to take you to the airport and turn you loose.*

Khrabovich's skin is spared.

*Right, that gets you out of the country and out of his hair. Now he can breathe and figure out what to do with the bonds. He will probably not be able to convert them to cash in the People's Republic. Besides, why would a wealthy guy like him stay in a crummy little country like that?*

You make the case. Only two questions left. What happened to the bonds, and where is Khrabovich?

*Find one, and you will find the other.*

# 17

Grogan's black eyes sparkled like polished onyx in bright sunlight as he read Paul's report on Otto's debriefing. It was typed on only three double-spaced pages, so Paul and Barney were delivering it in person. As usual, they sat facing him again across his desk.

As he read, Grogan would flip back to an earlier page, consult some passage, move ahead, and read on. Finished reading, he held the report in his left hand, thumping it emphatically with the middle finger of his right. Then he laid it face-up on the desk.

"We hit the jackpot with Patroon," Grogan proposed with a smile. "Nice piece of analysis, Paul. Where do you go from here?"

"Out the front gate I hope," Paul replied. "You wanted to know what happened to Plavin and where the bonds went. Here it is. Doesn't this fulfill my contract?"

"You've done great work. I knew you would, but we still don't have the bonds."

"Find Khrabovich and you will," Paul said, apprehension creeping into his voice. "I told you up front, Grogan. You need a cop for this game, not a has-been operator. I've never done law enforcement, and I'm not starting now."

Peripherally, Paul could see Barney concentrating his eyes on the wall about three feet above Grogan's head. He recalled once being caught in a test of wills between Grogan and Jason March in Okinawa. In the end Jason had died. That was not Grogan's fault, but the memory had a bitter flavor Paul did not like tasting again.

"Help me with this, Paul," Grogan said, leaning forward with his elbows and forearms touching the desktop. "I have always counted on you for flexibility. We will hire some outside help for this, but I don't have another asset like you. The way you handled Patroon proves it. We didn't have a clue to what happened or who did it. Now we know both. We cannot close this business until we find Khrabovich and the bonds. You said that yourself."

"For all I know," Paul said, "he is still sitting in Blaskovod stroking his money."

"But you don't think that."

"What makes it my job to find out? Tell me you're not just looking for a way to welsh on our deal. It wouldn't be the first time you've connived me into a corner."

At first Grogan looked pained by Paul's last comment, but he suppressed it, leaned back in his big chair, and went on.

"Believe me, Paul. I am not gaming you this time. The next stage of our operation demands oversight to keep from misreading the moment and blowing the action."

Grogan nodded absently toward Barney.

"I rely on you too, Barney, but I have to go where my nose leads me this time."

Barney showed no sign of resentment, but kept looking at the wall above Grogan. Paul was not sure he was even listening, and Grogan's eyes never rested on him.

Now Grogan swept his penetrating gaze back to Paul.

"Paul, you are the man I trust to bring this out right. If you insist, I will terminate your contract today, but I don't want to. Please stick with me until this job is done. I depend on you."

*Ouch*, Paul thought. Grogan waited for a reply while Paul imitated Barney's tactic, focusing his own eyes on the staff-mounted American colors behind Grogan's right shoulder.

*Now what do I do? I chose once between God and the organization. I chose God because I thought he wanted me to. Then I let Grogan shoehorn me back into the organization because he was holding all the cards.*

*Who dictated that? Was it God or the devil—or just Grogan and me all by ourselves?*

*Wait a minute. Remember what Grogan of the Vale—not the one across this desk—said about trying to stay focused on Jesus and failing every day as long as we live on earth?*

*In the Vale I was totally free from distraction, but on earth there is almost nothing else. Earth is what it is, whether I like it or not. Satan has power here, whether I want it or not. All I can do is trust God to guide and protect me.*

*Now all my cues are coming from Grogan. He is asking for my help. Isn't that part of the spiritual contract of love that is supposed to bind us all to God and each other—the love that grows within and seeks the souls of us all?*

In real time, Paul's tortuous reasoning took only seconds.

"All right, Grogan. I'm not giving you a blank check, but I'll stick around until mid-summer—let's say Independence Day. If we haven't turned up Khrabovich by then, I'm packing up and writing it off. If we have, I should already be gone. Fair enough?"

Grogan stood and came around the desk to take Paul's hand firmly in both of his. It was the first time they had touched since a similar handshake just before Paul's abrupt and unexplained resignation.

Paul had noticed the absence of any direct demonic attack since his mountain fog experience on the way to the Abbey of Saints and Angels. Was this because he had effectively been sidetracked from the pursuit of God's plan for him?

*Is the devil satisfied to have blocked me off, or is there more to it? Why am I diverting my attention from God's work to Grogan's, even when Grogan offered me a way out? Is Khrabovich more important to this than I thought?*

Wittingly or not, Khrabovich had become a hellish projectile launched at Paul's head the instant Paul was ejected from the Vale. By betraying Plavin, Khrabovich created doubt and suspicion about Paul's motives and loyalty to the organization. That had driven Grogan to interfere with every effort Paul made to find God's will for him in the world. Perversely, Khrabovich's exploits had turned

Grogan's fight into a mandate for Paul to clear his own name with the organization.

*With Satan as our mutual adversary,* Paul reasoned, *this must be God's fight too. I cannot read God's mind any better than I can Satan's. At least I know how Grogan operates.*

Paul found comfort in that familiarity, even when it was being used against him.

He had made no effort to contact Petra since their angry telephone confrontation just before he went on the run. At the time, he was trying to protect her. Once he was pulled back into the organization, contact with her became unthinkable. Her worst suspicions had come true. He avoided her now to protect himself.

# 18

For almost two months after his second surrender in Grogan's office, Paul dedicated himself to searching for clues to post-January events in the life of Major Anton Khrabovich of the People's Republic Ministry of Interior Border Security Command. At first his quest was fruitless. Neither intelligence sources nor public media reflected a trace of the man inside or outside his country.

Then Paul ran upon an obscure article in the People's Republic's state-propaganda newspaper. This quasi-news organ rarely published anything about the army except for boiler-plate coverage of the May Day parade and staged community assistance projects. That was why he noticed an item about recent events at a border-security station on the western side of the country. It said the Ministry of Interior had sent an inspection party to a unit near Blaskovod to rectify irregularities in political doctrine and military protocol. In communist-party parlance these terms were standard euphemisms for scandal and mutiny.

Discovery of some of Khrabovich's behavior might easily qualify as a scandal. Yet Paul could not imagine a mutinous outbreak under the major's closed-fisted control and ruthless use of the brutal informants Otto called pets.

If there was a mutiny at Blaskovod, Paul reasoned, Khrabovich was not there to prevent it. Considering the way the major ran his outfit, his absence alone could readily generate a breakdown in discipline.

The newspaper article gave no dates, but the edition was from the fourteenth of February. First, Paul factored in the typical bureaucratic lag between totalitarian governmental denial and even a hint of bad news getting into print. Then he computed a date somewhere between the closing days of January and the first few of February for the major's disappearance from his post.

Might he have run off but remained in the People's Republic? That was less than likely in view of his most recent activities and the high-value bonds he now possessed.

Would he have gone for the border alone the way Otto did? He had at least two accomplices he would not want to leave behind. They probably helped him escape.

This idea set Paul to a careful search of news from the country just west of the People's Republic, the same place Otto had gone for refuge. There he found something.

During the first week of March, the naked unidentified bodies of two adult men were found in the snow in a remote area about ten kilometers from the eastern border. Each had been shot once in the back of the head with what was only described as a small-caliber bullet. Paul could well remember the little semi-automatic pistol with which Khrabovich had threatened him in his hospital cell. It had looked like a 7.65-millimeter model. Proximity of the bodies to the border had initially suggested some kind of international incident, but the People's Republic had denied any knowledge of the men.

Continued search of the neighboring country's press produced no evidence of a People's Republic military vehicle being found. Surely, Paul thought, the deserters would have taken an APC, rather than try crossing the border on foot. When no APC turned up after spring thaw, he suspected the major had hidden it. Maybe some borderland farmer would be getting around next winter in an unregistered snow buggy.

Paul and Barney worked varied sources and regularly reported to Grogan. By the middle of May, they had solid estimates of when and how Khrabovich had left the People's Republic. Now they concentrated on following the money to find the man.

The bonds were of Swiss origin, and the fabled inflexibility of that country's banking and financial secrecy laws made it impossible to learn anything from the Swiss.

Would Khrabovich have fled to Switzerland? Paul thought not. The same laws that protected his redemptions could draw attention to his presence in a country where foreigners might be viewed with suspicion. A perfunctory search found nothing there.

Balancing the major's need for anonymity against practical limits on travel, Paul and Barney concluded he would settle somewhere in Central or Western Europe. Wherever he came to rest, he would be forced to minimize his visibility.

Gradually, they came to agree that Paris was the best place for a well-heeled foreigner to live in modest luxury without attracting too much attention. There were, after all, so many people of that sort already on the ground in the fabulous city of light.

If Paris was the place, there ought to be some trace of the money there or at least somewhere in the national range of France. A discreet survey by some unofficial French associates took over a month, but it turned up two sizeable redemptions drawn upon a single Paris branch of a prominent French bank.

The bank did not care about the identity of someone converting a bearer bond, but it did insist upon recording the name of any person to whom it was paying out so much money. As is customary throughout Europe, identification had to be shown by the payee, who in each case had presented a surely forged or stolen Austrian passport in the name of Wilhelm Brecht.

The first time, Herr Brecht listed his current address as the world-renowned Hotel Ritz in Place Vendome, where the French inquirers determined he had never stayed—at least not under the name of Brecht. At the second redemption, the man had provided an address in Rue Montmartre that proved to be equally bogus or at least not his residence.

The two known redemptions were made in February and April. By the time Paul and Barney were aware of them, it was nearly mid-June.

"What do you say about that?" Paul asked, when Barney and he had briefed Grogan in his office. "Isn't it about time for him to clip more coupons?"

"I suggest you refresh your knowledge of French," Grogan told them with a smile. "But don't think I'm going to let you two bunk at the Ritz. Enjoy your trip, and don't forget to visit the Louvre."

# 19

Seeing Petra March in the lobby of the Hotel Concorde in Paris brought Paul a twinge of *déjà vu*. It echoed their surprise reunion several years earlier at Washington's National Archives. That time they had not seen each other since the death of her husband seven years earlier. Since they both lived in the D.C. area, a chance encounter there was far more likely than bumping into each other in Paris, where neither spent much time.

The Hotel Concorde St. Lazare was a recent renovation of the revered Grand Hotel Terminus San Lazare. The original, built in the late nineteenth century, was modern for its day. All the rooms had toilets, and there was access to a bathroom down the hall. It was named, then as now, for the adjacent St. Lazare railroad station which continued to welcome transatlantic passengers off the boat train from Le Harve. Paul had stopped at the old hotel on his first trip to Europe in the early nineteen fifties.

This time, Paul and Barney shared a two-bedroom suite at the Concorde that cost just a little more than the organization was paying them to lodge. If it was not the Ritz, it suited their purpose equally well. An in-room bath was a plus, but Paul thought the lately sandblasted hotel facade on Rue St. Lazare had sacrificed something ineffably Parisian. A grand view from his bedroom window of the stark, white-domed spires of the Sacre Cours in Montmartre compensated him for that.

The Concorde's right-bank location offered tourists a wealth of attractions within walking distance. Paul and Barney chose it for geographic proximity to the area where they thought Khrabovich might be hiding.

The non-governmental French associates they worked with had narrowed his probable residence to this part of the city. Here the man called Brecht had cashed bearer-bond coupons two months apart at the same bank. Their French colleagues were watching to see if he came back. Apparently he had.

Just after noon, when the telephone rang in their hotel room, Barney was at the American Embassy maintaining their cover. Minutes later, Paul was headed out of the hotel to get a briefing. That was when he found Petra standing directly in his path. She was eyeing him as steadily as a falcon bearing down on some helpless rodent.

She was dressed comfortably for a temperate June afternoon in Paris. She wore a tapered, loosely fitting, wide-collared, white shirt outside calf-length, flared, light-khaki trousers. Her feet were well-shod in light, white-canvas athletic shoes, and she carried a small, tan-leather handbag with a no-nonsense shoulder strap that would stand up to the most determined purse snatcher in the street.

There was no one between them, so she strode right up to him and stopped about two feet away. She was wearing no makeup—not even a touch of lipstick—and Paul was reminded of what a naturally pretty woman she was. Her initial look of surprise gave way to a curious turn of her lips. She was standing almost at attention with her arms held straight to her sides.

Paul pre-empted an inquisition by putting on a smile and speaking first.

"Petra, I'm so glad to see you. What in the world are you doing here?"

She was caught off balance. Whatever she had meant to say was lost in her natural reaction to his question. She actually smiled at him, and her shoulders relaxed from their nearly military posture.

"I'm a chaperone and guide for some of my French-language students on a summer study tour." Now she caught herself and demanded information. "And what brings you here?"

"Business," he said, still smiling.

"What kind?"

"Which answer do you want—'Can't say,' or 'Same old'?"

"Didn't you tell me you were done with that?"

"It was the truth when I said it, and you didn't believe me. Now I'm saying something else, but I am being just as honest as I was before."

"Aren't you contradicting yourself?"

"No. What was true then is not true now. Something changed, but I couldn't help that. All I can promise is that it will soon be over. Then I will be free—of the job anyway. Can you accept that and move on?"

Their confrontation in the middle of the lobby had begun to attract attention. No one approached them, but Paul sensed the quick glances coming their way from hotel patrons and staff.

"I'll accept it now," she said crisply. "I'm not sure about the future. Haven't we been here before?"

"Indeed we have, and I am still not able to convince you of my sincerity."

"I'm not so sure of that," she said, tilting her face coyly up toward his and provocatively planting her hands on her hips. "Dinner might help."

Now Paul was the one off balance. She was offering him a chance he had only hoped for in a situation he could not control. On his way to an important meeting, he could not calculate what action he might have to take or how soon.

"I'm caught in the middle of something this minute," he said, talking fast. "Can I let you know later today?"

"I don't normally invite men to take me out, Paul, and I'm not much for giving rain checks. Take it or leave it." Her voice was firm, and her face and posture were daring him.

"I'm on my way to see someone who can tell me if I'll be free tonight. I'll call your room as soon as I get back. Is that okay?"

"As long as you're not on your way to see another woman," she said with a cute grin. At the same time, she took a small notepad from her bag, wrote what Paul presumed was her room number on a sheet, and handed it to him. "I'll expect to hear from you before three. If I'm out, leave a message with my roommate or at the desk."

"Depend on it," Paul said happily and turned back toward the door. He could not see her as he went into the street, but he hoped she was still smiling.

# 20

Entering the office of Jacqueline Nervier, Paul was uncomfortably reminded of Petra's proscription against going to see another woman. Madame Nervier and her husband Norman owned and operated a small security and investigations firm the organization had discretely engaged to look for signs of Anton Khrabovich, a man known to the Nerviers only as Wilhelm Brecht.

Paul's organization had no official standing or identity by which to enroll French intelligence or law enforcement elements in its efforts. That made it necessary to operate through private resources like the Nerviers. They charged high fees without asking for too many details.

The Nerviers shared a comfortable office with a window to the street on the first *etage*, what Americans would call the second floor, of their building not far from the Palais Royal. Anyone entering the office would see two, medium-sized, Scandinavian-style desks set at a right angle to each other. The window to the right of these provided plenty of natural light to the room. Four substantially padded, wooden chairs were scattered around the space facing the desks. In the corner behind the apex of the desks, a small dry-bar was set up with elegant crystal glasses and several decanters of what Paul could tell, even from a distance, were very impressive grades of brandy.

Paul had long ago learned that in Europe a dram of a strong drink often accompanies certain kinds of business—even in the morning. Once he and Barney graciously declined the first offer, no more were made. The corner directly opposite the bar held an oblong *faux*-teak table with six matching straight chairs deployed around it.

This time, Jackie, as Paul and Barney had been told to call her, stood and glided smoothly past her desk to meet him. With a mind-melting smile, she gestured gracefully for him to take a padded chair facing one corner of her desk. Her husband was apparently out of the office.

Jackie was a slim, very attractive woman with straight, radiant-blonde hair that hung to her shoulders and curled inward at the bottom. Today she wore an appealingly snug black business suit with a knee-length hem that rode up alarmingly for Paul when she bestrode the corner of her desk and leaned forward to speak to him.

"I think we have our man, Monsieur Paul," she barely whispered in a soft, breathy tone. Her English was excellent, but she delivered it with an urgently tempting accent.

"I hope so, Jackie. What have you found?"

Paul was deliberately aiming his gaze above her shoulders and away from the more alluring exposure of legs.

What, he wondered, made many mature French women seem so seductive in the most commonplace situations? Were they trained to it, or was it something in their choice of perfumes that was so distracting at close quarters? Right now, for example, Jackie's fragrance was rousing unbidden thoughts of playful mid-day love.

*It's probably just something left over from listening to World War I veterans talk about France when I was a boy.*

Paul took mixed comfort when she responded to his question by moving back behind the desk. There she remained standing while referring to some papers in front of her.

"Last Friday, just before eleven o' clock in the morning, Monsieur Brecht appeared at the same bank as before to redeem more of his holdings," she said in tones that still suggested intimacy to Paul's ear. "He has apparently become more confident in the security of his position. Instead of accepting a cash payment, he used the money to open a checking account with the bank."

"What address did he give?" Paul asked

"Alas, he no longer maintains false premises in Rue Montmartre, but has relocated to a fashionable establishment in Rue Lincoln."

"Is it real or imaginary?" Paul asked.

"Quite *bona fide*, I would say. At least that is the residence to which he resorted upon leaving the bank. It is in fact within walking distance. Who knows? He may have been there all along."

"I suspect so," Paul acknowledged. "What do you know about the layout of this *maison*?"

"Ah, Monsieur Paul, we have only begun to inquire into this matter. You must allow us a few days more, at least a week in all, to determine the details. Norman is at this moment pursuing every possible source. I think you do not want to flush this bird by running too soon upon the nest."

"As always, Jackie, you are correct. We will keep our distance until you have put together the information we need to prepare a more discreet approach. Please keep us informed."

"Of course," she said. "Our investigation is in progress, and we should be able to inform you reliably by the end of the week." As he stood up, she came back around the desk to escort him through the outer office. She walked, he thought, with delicate grace and charm on the eye-attracting, stilted footwear he remembered from his youth being called French heels.

When Paul called Petra's hotel room to confirm his availability for dinner, she insisted on selecting the restaurant but withheld its identity as a surprise.

"Won't your young charges need to be escorted this evening?" he asked.

"I have a co-director for the tour; she's my roommate. We sometimes trade off. Just meet me in the lobby at seven thirty," she said.

"What should I wear?"

"The evening ought to be moderately cool. We could go tourist semi-formal."

"I'm not sure I recognize that classification."

"I'll be wearing something white, something black, and flats. Does that help?"

"Skirt or slacks?"

"I might change my mind, but right now I'm thinking pedal-pushers."

"I'm comfortable with that."

"Are you?" she asked with a lilt in her voice. "I think you'll look pretty silly in pedal-pushers."

"You may have something there. Could you stand a loud Hawaiian shirt, Bermuda shorts, and sandals?"

"Ugh. I hate men who show up for dinner in sandals. Don't you?"

"Not really, but I'm easy to manipulate. Scrap the sandals and bring on some slacks."

"Barefoot?" She seemed to be subduing a giggle.

"Let's say loafers with black socks."

"I'll be there," she said and hung up the telephone.

When Barney came in, Paul was still standing by the phone and looking out the window toward Montmartre.

"Any luck?" Paul asked.

"Not really," Barney said, plopping disconsolately into an easy chair. "You know I hang around the embassy just to keep up our entrepreneurial image. I make contacts, and the embassy dining room still serves a great lunch."

"You're right about the food and the contacts. One of those investments might pay off. Meanwhile, I have encouraging news from Jackie."

"Oh, do you?" Barney was back on his feet and walking toward Paul with his hands spread and a smile on his face. "Just what did the enchanting Madame Nervier have to tell us?"

# 21

Paul was standing in the hotel lobby when Petra showed up promptly at seven thirty. She was wearing a crisp white shirt with wide lapels flared at the top. It was bloused smoothly into black, wash-and-wear pedal-pushers that came several inches below the knee above matching flat slippers. She had applied a mere touch of pink to her lips and was wearing small, gold-hoop earrings as her only jewelry. The absence of a handbag suggested a primp-free evening, which suited Paul fine.

Approaching him directly with a pixie-like smile, she put both hands on his shoulders and stood on tiptoe to brush his left cheek with her lips. She brought a fresh, clean smell of mildly aromatic bath soap that Paul found more enticing than the intoxicating perfume Jackie Nervier wore so effectively.

*Well a little more anyway.*

"Are you ready?" she asked, stepping back and placing her hand in his.

"Never more," he replied, forcing the words past an unexpected dryness in his throat. Then he grasped her hand to lead her out of the hotel and onto the sidewalk. "Where are we going?"

"Just follow me," she said, retaining his hand to guide him across the street and into Rue du Havre.

At first they walked briskly in silence, hand in hand. Daylight still lit their path, but twilight shadows began to announce the coming night. Passing small cafes, shops, and residences, they inhaled a range of cooking aromas unique to this great city. They said nothing until they had crossed Boulevard Haussmann and were headed down Rue Tronchet in the direction of the Place de la Concorde. By then they had slowed their pace a little and were no longer holding hands.

"How did you spend your day?" Paul asked after a while.

"It was very pleasant. When I saw you this morning, I had just come back from a bus tour to Versailles. In the early afternoon we made one of our tours through the Louvre. Then my partner took the girls to the Ile de la Cite for a look around Notre Dame while I went back to the hotel to catch up on paperwork and grab a nap. Showing young people the sites of Paris can be tiring for us older folks. Thank heaven for the prevalence of Metro stations."

Paul glanced over to see her smiling up at him.

"How about you? You were in a hurry when I saw you at the hotel."

"It was an important meeting, but it left tonight open. I'm grateful for that."

"Was it anything you can tell me about?"

"No," he said, seeing her face fill with disappointment.

"That makes me feel so left out."

"I know, and I hate it."

"The last time we talked on the phone you said you had to leave town and would call when you got back. You said it had nothing to do with your old job, and you would explain later."

She again took his hand as they walked on.

"I was angry and hung up on you, but I still thought I would hear from you later. Now I find you in Paris. You came home I guess, but you never called. Now you say you're back in the same business after all. What am I supposed to think?"

"I'm surprised you think of me at all, Petra—let alone walk the streets of Paris with me. It's a complicated situation. Let me try to sort some of it out."

"Go ahead," she said, gazing ahead as if there was nothing to see.

"Do you remember what I told you in the Pub about my afterlife journey?"

"Yes, but you left me wondering about most of it. You said you had died and gone to a place called the Vale on your way to heaven. Instead, you came back to earth. You said that would complicate your life from now on. Then the Ridleys came in, and you had to leave."

"That's right."

"That was the last I heard about the Vale. After you phoned and didn't call back, I remembered you saying you told Father Don about it. I went to ask him."

*Rats*, Paul thought. *The only contact I had with Don after I came back from the monastery was to say I would not be around St. A's for a while. He knew no more than Petra about what was going on.*

"He admitted you told him about the Vale, but said that was under a seal of confidentiality. I finally gave up thinking about you—until this morning in the hotel."

Paul could think of nothing to say.

"I want to know the truth, Paul—at least as much of it as you can tell me."

Now he let go of her hand and put his arm around her shoulder.

"I have more to say, and I will, but the street may not be such a good place."

"Look," she said, suddenly cheerful, "there's the Madeleine church. Isn't it lovely? Let's walk around to the front."

As if discovering it anew, Paul and Petra shared the excitement of circling the church of Ste. Marie Madeleine, which stood in stunning relief to face the fading summer sun.

"Where are we going for dinner?" he asked in front of the classical Greek structure.

"Actually, it's only a few blocks from the hotel. I just wanted to take a walk before dinner and keep you guessing for a while. We can go back through the Rue de l'Arcade and be there by dark."

Their passage had closed an emotional gap between them. Now they strolled, each with one arm around the other, pausing now and again for a quick embrace. Such affectionate demonstrations routinely go unnoticed in the early evening streets of Paris.

# 22

Paul had never noticed the restaurant Petra chose for dinner—a fairly small place called *Beau Ideal*. It was probably not recommended by a single food critic, travel guide, or concierge getting a kickback, but Paul liked that. Its iconic eateries aside, he knew no city so rich in great dining at bearable rates as Paris. Maybe Petra had found that there too.

She told him the specialty of the house was steak *Chateaubriand*, which is not so common on French menus because of the expensive center cuts of beef tenderloin used to make it properly. Ordering *Chateaubriand* most places in the world brings a portion of tenderloin roast that has been oven-cooked at high temperature. It is then sliced across the grain with the rarer slices coming from the center. In the United States and Germany, this great piece of meat is normally cooked to a tragic state of done-clear-through.

In France, where it originated and was named after the nineteenth-century author and statesman to whom it was first provided, preparation and presentation of *Chateaubriand* are quite different. Two very thick fillets are taken from the center of the tenderloin where it is widest and most tender. These are fried quickly to seal the surfaces and then broiled at very high temperature. Traditionally, this cut is served quite rare. An amiable French chef may be persuaded to produce one slightly more done, but that is as cooked as this luscious bit of beef is going to get in his kitchen.

Paul and Petra ordered *Chateaubriand* with a bottle of the current edition of Beaujolais and decided to share a dozen *escargot de Bourgogne* while waiting. Sipping chilled dry vermouth from small *aperitif* glasses, they settled into their chairs and gratified their palates with the garlic-and-butter tang of those warm, delicate creatures, sopping up leftover broth with crisp-crusted fresh bread.

With their snails gone, Paul resumed his account of the Vale for Petra.

"What I told you at the Pub was just the beginning of what happened to me in the Vale. Even now I worry about bringing you in on it because just being near me could put you in danger. That's one reason I left in January, but here we are again, back together and looking ahead."

"I think it's wonderful," she almost whispered, taking a sip of the robust red wine their *sommelier* had just uncorked and poured for them.

"I want to stop holding out on you, but this is important. Being close to me could also mean trouble for others you love."

She leaned forward to reject his warning, so he raised his hand, palm out.

"You may decide to accept the risk, but first listen to me. The danger I'm talking about is not of human origin. You're brave and savvy enough to handle that. This is different. You might be going up against the power of hell itself."

She smiled in simple disbelief.

"I am not exaggerating. I have seen this thing in action, and it is not a joke."

Her mouth opened a little. Had his warning begun to sink in?

"Does this have anything to do with your return to the organization?"

"Not exactly, but it is related. The events that forced me out of retirement were meant to divert me from something else. I had to come back and deal with them. That is why I'm in Paris now."

"I don't get it."

"I am bound by oath and law to tell you nothing about what I do for the organization. Its existence is a secret you share only because of what happened to Jason."

"Okay, but you haven't sworn any oath about the Vale, have you?"

"No, and I need to tell you about that. But first you have to know the chances you take by being involved with me at all."

"I'll accept those chances," she said with a warm and encouraging smile.

"We did not order any courses between the snails and the steak, so we probably have some time until the meat arrives," he said, turning his head and not finding their waiter in sight. "Maybe I can cover a little of the story before that."

She remained silent, but continued to smile.

"Before Hank and Ida interrupted us at the Pub, I told you I had died and gone to the Vale. That is where souls wake up on the way to heaven, unless they are bound for what is called the terminal ward. I was told that terminal souls actively resist awakening in the Vale."

"Why would they do that?"

"Because they want to maintain the distance and independence from God they built around themselves in life. They have purposely confounded God's original intent for them and transformed themselves into souls he did not make them to be. They do not wake up in the Vale, because that would be turning to God. They are no longer able to do that. Their wills have prevailed over God's. That is at once their victory and their eternal, self-administered damnation."

"Your terminal ward cases remind me of what you and I went through after Jason died. But you did wake up there—in the Vale I mean. Isn't that what's important?"

"Yes, and you are right to emphasize that. What I could see of the Vale was awesome, but my view of it then was very limited. I was told that the longer I stayed and the more I learned about the afterlife, the more of it I would be able to see. Where I sat was something like a barber's chair in the upright position. From there I had a view of limitless space in every direction. I saw no sun, moon, or stars, but everything near and far was brightly drenched in light from some other source.

"The infinite space around me was filled with constantly moving shapes and ever-changing colors. At first it all seemed random, but as I watched, things began to look more purposeful. I could see shadowy, colorful bodies moving at great speed as they abruptly vanished from one place and instantaneously popped up in another. I could detect a kind of speech coming from some of them, but I could make nothing of it. I learned that some of these were human souls, like me, making progress through the Vale on their way to heaven. What I saw was representative of the way things are in the dimension of simultaneous infinity where God always is."

"What is simultaneous infinity?" Petra asked with excitement.

"Good for you; you're paying attention. Simultaneous infinity is a way of describing time as God knows it. Defining that will help you understand what goes on around God and what happened to me in the Vale."

Now Paul paused, looking past Petra. He had miscalculated the speed of service for he could see their waiter rolling a cart toward them.

"Simultaneous infinity," he told her, "is not so simple. Let's put it off until after dinner."

The chef, they found, had liberally applied his own interpretation to their order for medium steak. This rewarded them with delightful bursts of flavor as each tender bite was transferred from its plate to their grateful mouths. Until the dinner plates were removed, most of their words were reserved for satisfied praise of the meal.

# 23

Once they were relaxing over *demitasses* of chicory-flavored coffee and some tasty selections of *gruyere* and *camembert* from the cheese cart, Paul decided to resume his description of the Vale.

"What do you mean, Petra, when you use the word *infinity*?"

"Something endless I suppose: endless space, endless time, or endless anything."

"What do you think about our universe? Is it infinite?"

"Maybe not, but it looks that way to us. We're inside it and can't see its limits."

"Do you believe there is anything beyond it?"

"Well, of course there is. Where else would God be? He is certainly not here."

"I like that. So God is not just off somewhere among the stars."

"Surely not. How could he create a universe he was already in? God is all-powerful, but that doesn't make sense. Wouldn't he have to be somewhere else before creating where we are now?"

"So if heaven, the place we believe God lives, is not up in the sky, where is it?"

"I've never thought much about that," she replied, bringing a finger to her lips, "but I guess he would have to operate from a different dimension. Didn't you say something about that before the steak came?"

"Yes, and we will get to that, but right now we are talking about another aspect of God's being. Are you suggesting that the space where God dwells is totally separate and different from the space we inhabit?"

"It would have to be, wouldn't it?"

"It would, if you mean that God's space might be infinite in ways ours is not."

"I think I said that."

"Okay then. Is that compatible with the idea that God can be everywhere all the time and all at once?"

"I don't know how, but I believe it is."

"Why?"

"Because I have experienced the presence of the Holy Spirit, and I knew that other people in widely different places were having a similar experience at the same time."

"You're talking about feeling God's presence. Do you mean physically or spiritually?" he asked.

"Both, I think, but mainly spiritually. After all, God is spirit, isn't he? Didn't Jesus say that?"

"He did, and you are on exactly the right track."

She smiled happily.

"But what about time?" he asked.

"Huh?" Now she looked puzzled.

"I told you we would talk about God in time, and we are getting there. We started off talking about infinity. I'd say you have pretty well described the infinite, spiritual quality of God in space—his and ours."

"You are talking about omnipresence, right?"

"Yes."

"Well, naturally. All Christians know that God is omnipresent."

"You mean in space?"

"Yes."

"Then what about time?"

"This may be a little harder," she said, pursing her lips for a second. "I told you I have thought about omnipresence, and I'm comfortable with that. Time is something else."

"I understand. The concept of simultaneous infinity gave me trouble too, even though I could see evidence of it right in front of me in the Vale."

"So how did you resolve it?"

"Think about this. I knew I was dead and in the afterlife. A lot of things there were obviously different. One was that I kept meeting people I knew were still alive when I died."

"How could that be?"

"Think again, Petra. If God is always everywhere, wouldn't he have to be everywhere all the time?"

"I'm not sure what you mean."

"Someone once told me that Edgar Allen Poe wrote this in one of his mystery stories: 'For God everything is now.'"

"So?"

"If Poe was right, then where God is there is no past or future."

Her brow wrinkled slightly as Paul went on.

"What we call *was* and *will be* have no meaning for God. The same thing is true for all the souls who leave our universe to be with God where he always *is*."

"This is hard for me."

"I understand," Paul told her. "Let's drop back a little. Why do you think God named himself to Moses in Exodus as 'I AM'?"

"Isn't that translated differently by some scholars?"

"Yes, but most of those translations literally equate to the description of a being that exists all at once and everywhere throughout all time. You said a while ago that God is spirit, and that is true. Everything around God, where he always is, must also be spirit, just as we will be when we go to meet him where he is."

Petra nodded in understanding.

"The Vale is a stop on the way to heaven, but it is close enough to be part of God's simultaneously infinite milieu."

"Can you amplify that?"

"I'll try. The same temporal rules apply to every soul that wakes up in the Vale whenever it does. That is why I could meet souls there who had departed the earth long after I died. Yet they could still speak to me with authority and experience about what goes on in the Vale and beyond."

"Whoa," she said, clasping both of her hands in front of her below the astonished expression her face now wore. "Speaking of 'the Vale and beyond,' you are getting way out in front of me."

"I understand, darling," he said, not even recognizing his unprecedented use of the endearment. "I need to back up a little and talk about what simultaneous infinity is not—the way time is here on earth."

Paul's use of such affectionate language probably did not escape Petra's notice, but she smiled without acknowledgement to go on pursuing what he had to say.

"Okay," she said, drawing out the word and bringing a hand up to cup her chin. "Tell me all about that."

"Time for us here on earth is always linear and relative. Does that make sense to you?"

"The linear part does. That just means we are always progressing along a line in time from the past to the present and into the future."

"That is truly the way it seems to us. We feel like we are always moving from *was* to *now* to *will be*, but is that really where we are?"

"What's your question, Paul?"

"Think about it. You may remember *was* and wonder about *will be*, but are you ever actually anywhere but *now*?"

"I think I see what you're getting at. *Was* is just a bunch of former *nows*, and *will be* is simply made up of all the *nows* yet to come."

"Very good. You're picking this up faster than I did."

"I'm trying, but what about relativity? You said our time here is linear and relative—relative to what?"

"Relative to everything about us and around us in time—it is our relationship to everyone and everything in the intricate tapestry of time that makes up our very finite universe from one end to the other."

"You'll have to simplify that."

"Try picturing our universe as a very long race track through time."

"That's the linear part."

"Yes, but now think about all the human souls who have lived and will ever live along that track. Nothing is still; everyone is moving. Linear time is constant, so they are all moving from the time they are born onto the track to the day they die and vanish from it. Everyone is running at precisely the same speed in exactly the same direction. None of them can ever overtake or pass another, and nobody ever changes position."

Petra cocked her head back a bit, but Paul plunged on.

"They are all moving from past to present to future, but nobody ever exists anywhere but *now*. Yet, even *now* is never constant, because every *now* is always changing to the next sequential *now* for each person everywhere on the track all the time. Everybody's temporal existence is always relative to that of everyone else. Of course, it is hard for us to see things that way on earth, because we ourselves are so caught up and trapped in the clockwork."

Petra was now facing Paul head-on with a bright look of dawning comprehension.

"You're starting to sound like one of Zeno of Elea's paradoxes of motion, like Achilles and the tortoise."

"That is a very astute observation. I was told in the Vale that Zeno thinks he was really onto something in the fifth-century B.C., but he finds he took it in the wrong direction. I'd say you're getting a pretty clear picture of the linear relativity that restrains our earthbound existence."

"I think so," she said, "but what about God? Where is he, and how does all this relate to simultaneous infinity?"

"Thank you for asking. That is my next point."

# 24

Paul paused to finish his last bite of cheese and sip some warm coffee from a cup the waiter had stealthily refilled without intruding or interrupting the conversation. Then he placed his forearms flat on the table and leaned forward with one hand resting across the other.

"Earlier," he said, "I asked you to consider the continuous succession of *nows* that represents a straight line of time from the beginning to the end of our created universe. You see how that works, right?"

"Well enough to go on," she responded agreeably.

Paul smiled back to encourage her.

"Okay," he said, carefully, "I want you to think about God outside our universe, where he occupies a parallel straight line that extends in either direction to true infinity—not the pseudo kind we know here."

"So far, so good."

"God's line is not composed of tiny dots of *now* the way our line here is. There is nothing linear or relative about God's time. He always occupies that whole infinite line all at once and whichever way we look forever and ever. That is what makes him simultaneously infinite. For God and all that surrounds him, there is just one great *now*. That ultimately includes those souls that go out of earth's universe to be with God for all time. They—we—all become a part of his simultaneous infinity."

"Are you telling me there is no past or future—only *now*—where God is, and we will know the same kind of temporal freedom once we leave this universe?"

"Yes, dear Petra, and much more than that. What happens on earth does not track at all with what goes on beyond our petty universe. That is how I could meet people in the Vale who were still alive here when I died. It also explains how I could be sent back here without really interrupting my experience in the Vale. I am still there along with the others I met, even though all or most of us are still here finishing our lives in the linear and relative constraints of time on earth."

"This is blowing me away," Petra said, pressing the fingertips of both hands to her forehead. As she slumped back into her chair, her face still held an expression of intense interest.

"I understand," Paul replied. "It is not an easy concept to get your head around. I had a very difficult time with it even in the Vale, where I could see examples of it."

"How does it affect us here and now?"

"Not so much, perhaps, except to help us understand how God operates in our earthly lives. It lets us appreciate how God is able to be omniscient, omnipresent, and omnipotent. To be any of those things he simply has to be infinitely simultaneous. It is the only way the *omni* stuff could work"

"That's great, but how does it operate in our lives right now? Give me an example."

"Try prayer."

"How do you mean?"

"In our linear, relative prison of earth, we are apt to think God endures the same cause-and-effect restraints that exist for us. He doesn't. He answers today's prayer anywhere in our time that suits him. There is no paradox, because God's intervention is not related to when we asked. His answer can be rendered before or after that. It's already done."

"Give me an example."

"Sure. I remember you telling me how often you pray for dead animals you pass on the road."

"Yes. I just pray for God's mercy upon them, but I know they are already dead. I don't expect them to come back to life."

"But don't you see? Since God is not hindered by linear time the way we are, he can answer your prayer the day before or whenever the animal was struck. Maybe he just grants it a quick, painless death. This is how an effect can precede its cause in our time, yet remain perfectly consistent with the way God sees things."

"So the answer to my prayer is just the way things already are because for God that's what always is. Cause and effect are all the same to him."

"And God sees everything infinitely, all at once, and all the time."

"Does that mean that when God spoke to his prophets, he was only conveying information—not predicting the future?"

"That's a very appropriate conclusion to draw. Another would be the understanding of predestination as a simple matter of God's foreknowledge, rather than his selection or decision-making about whose name is written in the Book of Life."

"What a wonderful thought. You are opening my mind to all kinds of things in the Bible that used to seem inconsistent. I've always had trouble with proclamations by Jesus and the apostles that the kingdom of God is at hand. That seemed to lose validity in light of all the passing centuries since they said it. Now you're telling me it was and is true, but we just can't see it yet from where we are."

Paul smiled, recalling his discussion of this very thought with Brother James in the abbey graveyard.

"That's a beautiful observation, Petra. It explains how understanding simultaneous infinity can influence our whole outlook on Scripture. What happens here on earth is just not relevant to what is going on where God is. His realm is the true reality. Looking back from there reveals our lives here as something like a dream from which we will soon awaken to glory and unending joy."

"Whew! You've given me a lot to think about," she said with a smile as radiant as any he could remember. "You know, I may have trouble getting to sleep tonight."

"Me too," he said, reaching across to take both her hands in his and gently kiss her fingertips.

# 25

Friday afternoon after Paul's night out with Petra, Barney and he were conferring with Norman Nervier around the table in the investigator's business office. Jackie had excused herself and gone out just as they were sitting down.

*Norman is almost too typical*, Paul thought.

Norman would not stand out in a crowd or anywhere else. He dressed neatly without being stylish or out of date. His suits were as nondescript as his bland physical features. His face would be hard to recall; it had little character. He looked somewhere between thirty and fifty years old. His hair was an unparted blur that bordered between blond and gray.

Even the blue pack of Gauloises cigarettes on the table in front of him was a prop, an iconic salute to French masculinity. There was no ashtray in the office, and Paul had never seen him light up. He was a theatrical walk-on that no one was expected to remember.

*Norman*, Paul decided, *is the perfectly self-made man who is never there.*

"Now, monsieurs," Norman said in his quiet, unremarkable voice, "let us examine the situation of Herr Brecht."

Paul and Barney nodded and leaned forward to look at the items Norman was taking, one by one, from a manila folder in front of him.

"Here," Norman went on, "we have *chez* Brecht." The first exhibit was an eight-by-ten color photo of a Parisian dwelling of the more elegant sort.

"Is the man on the steps Herr Brecht?" Paul asked, pointing to a figure in the photo.

"Indeed," Norman answered. "I regret the image is so poor, but it is the only one we have. We hope to obtain a better one, but I fear he rarely goes abroad."

Norman passed Paul a handheld magnifying glass of considerable power.

*The picture is grainy and the angle is poor,* Paul thought, *but it could be the major. If Brecht has the bonds, it has to be him.*

"Was this taken of the man coming back from the bank?" Paul asked.

*"Oui, Monsieur."*

When Paul said nothing more, Norman continued his presentation.

"The house is located here," he said, pointing to an enlarged print from a Paris street map. "Not two blocks from the Champs Elysees. It is an expensive home in an exclusive neighborhood."

"He has a lot of money," Barney commented, "but I doubt if he has converted enough to buy that place."

"You are correct, Monsieur Barney. He merely rents, but he has taken it for a year. I am sure the advance deposit comes to more cash than we can yet account for."

Barney, unlike Paul, had assumed the fictitious identity of one Barton Jacobs. That permitted the continued use of his real nickname, which made things easier for Paul.

"I would guess," Paul injected, "that his current bank is not the first institution to which he has applied for service."

"Manifestly so," Norman agreed, "but Herr Brecht seems to avoid any appearance of excessive opulence. He occupies three floors, but has only one servant living in the house with him. That is his cook and valet who maintains an apartment on the lower floor. I will speak more of him in a moment. The cleaning staff is composed of two women who come in twice a week. They arrive by nine and are gone by noon."

"How efficient," Paul observed.

"We have seen no one else coming or going. However, our observations have been for only a week. It is quite possible that Brecht may occasionally invite a woman in to provide him comfort. We have not been watching long enough to discern that."

"Did you say there is more to tell about the manservant?" Paul asked.

"Indeed there is. Herr Brecht has employed a most unusual fellow to serve him."

"How so?" Barney inquired as Norman laid out what looked like a black-and-white enlargement of a police mug shot. The man, Paul noticed, had a rough look about him, but such official photography generally emphasizes the hardest lines in a subject's face.

"He is in fact a very competent under-chef, who has worked in several well-regarded kitchens of this city," Norman answered. "I am quite certain that Herr Brecht dines well. We have learned that he sits down every night except Saturday to a full dinner and retires around nine to take coffee and brandy in his study. On Saturdays he lunches sumptuously at midday and apparently takes a cold supper to permit his cook a night out. That, except for shopping, is the only time his manservant leaves him alone in the house."

"And you say that Brecht himself keeps pretty much to the house?" Barney asked.

"As we have observed, his visits to the bank are irregular. Other than that, there are reports that some who provide him services, a tailor for example, have called on him at home. That is why we suspect there may be a woman. Otherwise, he does not seem to leave the house except with the servant."

"The cook?" Paul was surprised to find Khrabovich pursuing human fellowship, especially with a servant.

*Maybe even the devil craves company,* he thought.

"In late evening when the weather is fair, the two of them have sometimes been seen together, walking through the quiet streets and even venturing out to the Champs Elysees for exercise and a restful *digestif* at one of the outdoor cafes. At those times, it is reported, the man is treated not as a servant, but as an equal companion."

"How interesting," Paul commented.

"Of course, we have not been watching long enough to establish all the normal patterns of movement to which Herr Brecht may be given."

"I'd say you've gathered plenty of information, considering you've had only a week to watch the place," Barney said.

"*Oui, monsieur*, but our inquiry has not been confined to direct observation alone. We consult with varied sources."

"Of course," Paul acknowledged. "Is that all you know about the servant?"

"Indeed not, Monsieur Paul," Norman said. Now he laid out a clear color enlargement of the cook coming out of the house on Rue Lincoln. It was more flattering than the police photo, but Paul sensed something unpleasant that he could not define.

"This valet is a man of fairly dark history. Once, while he was working in a very well-known restaurant—the last one where he was employed—there was apparently some kind of dispute between Francois Declaire—that is his name—and another member of the kitchen staff. They were seen to argue over a woman who also worked in the establishment. Late one night, when most of the staff had departed, Declaire's rival became the tragic victim of a fatal gas explosion in the kitchen. There were no witnesses, and the body was badly burned."

Norman paused.

"Is that all?" Paul asked.

"Regrettably, no. The woman in question was heard to say she suspected Francois of foul play, but she disappeared before the police could question her. A search was conducted but the poor girl was never found. Of course Francois came under suspicion, but nobody else was able to give evidence. The police finally dropped the case, but Francois became *persona non grata* in the kitchens of Paris."

"And then?" Paul prodded, when Norman again appeared to hesitate.

"No one seems to know quite how he earned a living after that, but his methods were most likely criminal. It is known that certain members of the city's more sinister class came to fear him, and he never stopped living anything but well."

Again Norman paused, but went on when Paul and Barney remained silent.

"He was rumored for a while to have connections through drugs with some esoteric practitioners of the occult, so when he dropped out of sight four months ago, many thought he may have come to a bad end. Now we know he merely found a less risky way of living comfortably without working too hard. Evidently, he still derives pleasure, as well as good earnings, by employing his culinary art."

"Saturday is tomorrow, isn't it?" Paul said. "Tomorrow evening Monsieur Declaire will be out of the house."

"How fortunate," Barney injected. "I think we can be ready to move by then."

"I must warn you," Norman said gravely. "I cannot assist you with anything violent."

"You won't have to, Norman," Paul told him. "We only want to talk with Herr Brecht. After that, we hope he will cooperate with us. No violence unless he starts it."

"No violence—period," Norman emphasized.

"As you wish, *mon ami*," Barney said with a smile.

Paul said nothing, knowing they could not guarantee such a passive transaction.

# 26

Her tour obligations kept Petra from seeing much of Paul after their evening out. Their first chance for more than a few minutes together came the morning after he and Barney met with Norman Nervier. That Saturday her cosponsor took the group on a *bateau* cruise of the Seine, so Petra joined Paul for breakfast.

They left the hotel after eight with no plan for where to go. The sky was clear and the morning cool. Thinking ahead did not seem important. Across Rue St. Lazare down an uncrowded street they were wrapped in the scent of brewing coffee, redolent with chicory and coming from cafes with service on the sidewalk.

Picking a place favored by working-class men in blue smocks, they sat down to order coffee and croissants, which came with plenty of butter and a choice of thick orange marmalade or strawberry preserves. Paul always took his coffee black, but for breakfast Petra preferred *café au lait*, which she blended expertly in a large cup from separate pitchers of steaming coffee and warm milk.

"Nobody does breakfast like the French," Paul said, breaking and buttering half his croissant. "It's simple, satisfying, and fairly cheap."

"I know," she replied brightly, while dealing with her own flakey pastry. "It's really the smell. Nothing stirs my appetite like this kind of coffee on the open air."

"I don't know. Hunger might help," Paul speculated.

"Huh uh," she said, lifting her cup and holding half a croissant next to it. "Other breakfast is just nourishment. Real French coffee with croissants fresh from the bakery is divine."

"It is great stuff—in the right company of course."

"How true," she said, as they began to eliminate their bread and sweets.

Appetites quelled and all but the coffee cleared away, Petra returned to the topic of their previous meal.

"The other night you told me some of what you learned in the Vale—especially about simultaneous infinity. I am still intrigued by that."

"There is more to tell."

"I know that, but why?"

"Why?" Paul echoed.

"The purpose," she said. "Why were you taken away only to be sent back? I'm thrilled to have you here, but how did that happen? Why aren't you still dead?"

"How direct," Paul replied, smiling. "Actually, you have isolated the single thing that troubles me most. Nothing like this could happen unless God did it. That's why it's so important for me to find out what he wants from me."

"From you?"

"I told you before. I was not just a little dead—taken by mistake and accidentally brought back to life. I was totally dead, or I could not have awakened in the Vale. God isn't confused about when I die. He knows. Does God make mistakes?"

"How could he?"

"What I learned in the Vale convinces me he cannot. That would be a contradiction in terms. If he juggled our souls like we do, he would not be God."

Paul spoke fervently, but not demonstrably. No one around them could have assessed the force of his remarks. His face was calm and his voice level. This was a bit of tradecraft the organization had taught him. He and Barney had used it in January at the Frankfurt Flughafen to talk about Paul's accident, capture, and release without appearing to discuss anything of importance. Even with no training, Petra readily adapted to Paul's technique for suppressing signs of emotion.

"So what have you figured out?" she asked.

"God took me and sent me back for a reason. Dying is normal; returning is not."

"I'd call it impossible."

"Not really. The Bible tells a lot about God's prophets being taken away and told what to do back home. St. Paul wrote of doing that in the spirit."

"You're a prophet?" she gasped.

Paul's face remained serene, and his voice was level when he answered her.

"I'm no longer sure what prophets are. I only know I've had an experience like theirs. I share one thing with them—a roundtrip. I went out, and I came back. That means God did it on purpose."

"What purpose could there be?"

"I'm stumped about that. I learned a lot in the Vale. My old school teacher showed me how all true paths to God merge at last into one. There we meet God and each other in the same place at the same time and know the whole truth."

Petra nodded.

"Next an old colleague named Matt Harriford explained simultaneous infinity and the importance of happiness in knowing who and what we are. Then Grogan came to see me. You remember him, don't you? He was the heavy-set, gray-haired guy with the crew-cut who escorted you at Jason's memorial service on Okinawa. He is still alive by the way; so is Matt as far as I know. That's the way things are in the Vale and beyond. It doesn't matter what's happening on earth. God's reality just keeps on going where he is—all of the time for all of us. That is true reality. This world is not."

"Slow down. You're already stretching my limits for simultaneous infinity."

"Here it's hard to keep that straight. I slip up all the time."

Paul took a sip of his coffee.

"Anyway, I was talking about the transformed version of Grogan I met in the Vale. He emphasized the universality of God's love for us all and the way that love binds us to God and each other. It is the image of himself God planted in every one of us. It is the source and content of our souls—the true and unique identity God gave each of us at creation."

"That's a nice description, but there is more isn't there?"

"Yes, but putting all that together on earth is hard. Once we get out of here, the truth about our souls becomes obvious. In the Vale I knew it without identifying it. Now I remember it without having it. It is most easily defined as joy."

"Joy?"

"Yes. Here we have fleeting bursts of it like the one you had when God freed you from torment over Jason's death."

"I remember that!" she erupted, reaching across the table to clasp his right hand with both of hers. "But it was so wild and uncontrollable."

Paul dropped his pretense of equanimity and responded directly to her happy reaction.

"Earthly joy is rare and so quickly over. Beyond here it envelops you. It is the way you feel all the time."

"You make me shiver. I've thought so little about heaven. Maybe I was hung up on the Biblical imagery of pearly gates, purest gold streets, and crystal fountains. What you say sounds so perfect."

"Isn't that what you've always expected? Of course, we can't know it here. There is too much confusion and what I call static in our universe. When we enter God's dimension he transforms us into the truly free souls he made and ordained to live on with him forever."

"I am overwhelmed," Petra said, glancing at her wristwatch. "I want to hear more, but it's getting late. I have to catch up with the girls before noon. I wish I could see you tonight, but we're taking the group out for a sample of Parisian night life, or at least"—now she grinned as if sharing a secret—"as much of it as we have decided to let them see. What will you be up to?"

Paul recalled the plan to confront Khrabovich.

"Nothing you're apt to catch me at," he said with a worldly grin. It was a pointless inanity that would return to haunt him before the night was over.

# 27

Khrabovich knew what Paul looked like and would recognize him on sight. That meant Paul had to stay away from Rue Lincoln until the operation was launched.

On the other hand, Barney was a complete stranger to the major. He could reconnoiter the area with much less chance of provoking suspicion. That is what he did with Norman after a noontime meeting in the Nervier office to finalize intentions for Saturday night.

Norman's plan was simple. After Francois went out for the evening, Barney would quietly enter the house. Norman had obtained keys to get him through the gate and in the front door.

Norman would be waiting in the rear to discourage any escape that way. His mere presence in a lighted alley should stop their man from trying to get out that way.

Norman had already given Paul and Barney a rough floor plan of the house, showing the room where Brecht was most likely to be at the time of entry. That, he predicted, would be the study upstairs on the first *etage*.

Paul was supposed to watch the front of the place from the shadows across the street. Accordingly, Norman provided him with a key to a currently unoccupied apartment directly across from Brecht's study. Unless drapes were drawn, Paul should have a good view of what went on there.

Norman knew Barney would be negotiating for the return of some improperly obtained bearer bonds Brecht had been cashing in. He showed no surprise when Paul told him that the provenance of those bonds was something neither Brecht nor they would want publicized. This and their reassurance that no force would be used seemed to satisfy Norman with his role in arranging an *impromptu* meeting of the principals.

When Norman and Barney left for Rue Lincoln, Paul went back to the hotel. He spent the afternoon there thinking through the concerns and decisions he and Barney had worked out since their Friday meeting with Norman. Neither of them was happy with the situation on the ground.

This was not how Paul and Barney normally did their work. They were used to having backup from a headquarters planning staff. Those were experts who checked and rechecked every detail to find what did not fit or might not work in an operation.

At birth, an operation was given a cover name like *Bung Tick*. It seldom began as more than a brief objective with very few ideas on how to get there. Then staff members carefully organized an operation plan to gain the objective with minimal risk to the operators executing it. Operators were drawn from overseas sites or the headquarters staff. In the latter case, the operators could be directly involved in the planning process.

The planning staff began by listing a series of enabling objectives. Each of these had to be defined, tested, and approved before work on the next one could begin. When complete, the OpPlan formed a chronological list of major and minor actions required to achieve its goal.

The full plan, including special annexes for things like communication, transportation, and logistics had to be approved by a designated headquarters director for the operation. Except for the most mundane affairs, final approval rested with the Director of Operations, who was now Phil Grogan.

Comfortable as this process usually made him, Paul had seen how it might fail. No human plan, however carefully crafted, was immune to the influence of bad luck. God was the only source of help against that.

Even so, Paul knew that precise planning was a vital tool to the job he did. Its absence in the present case was making him edgy. Barney and he were about to be out on a limb all by themselves. They had heard that from Grogan himself.

After their talk with Norman the day before, Paul and Barney had put together a hand-coded message and invoked a special protocol to have it passed to Grogan through the American Embassy. The answer, when decoded, read, "Nice work. Bring it home. Forget K. You are not cops. G."

*So much for the organization's much-vaunted powerhouse of planning,* Paul thought.

Norman's scheme was only the beginning of what Paul and Barney planned to do. Their part was much riskier than either of them liked to think. Francois the cook was expected to leave the house around seven in the evening, but Paul and Barney would not move until after nine. It would be dark, and traffic in the street should be minimal. Khrabovich ought to be relaxed and settled in his lair by then.

The major might suddenly decide to go out for a walk alone, but that was not known to be one of his habits. If he did, Barney could enter the house and be waiting for him. He might even find the bonds and steal them back, but neither Paul nor Barney thought that likely.

However the stage might be set for Barney's arrival, he would at once need to introduce himself and calm Khrabovich's fears. The major might bluster, but he was not apt to react like an honest citizen by summoning the police. He was in no position to have his identity closely scrutinized by the authorities.

Paul and Barney expected him to have a gun in the house. Surely he would have kept the pistol he used to dispatch his fellow escapees from the People's Republic. It would probably be handy, but they hoped he would not be carrying it at the moment of confrontation.

Once the situation was stable, Barney would identify himself as an agent of the bonds' rightful owner. He would explain that his employers held the major's fate in their hands. If he turned over the still unnegotiated instruments, he could keep the cash he had in hand. Otherwise, he would be simultaneously exposed to the French and to authorities in the People's Republic.

This was intended to give the major a tight dilemma. The French were bound to give him trouble over his fabricated identity. Remaining in France meant prison. At the same time, his native country would be clamoring to have him extradited for past crimes. By law or extra-legal means his former compatriots would find a way to take him down.

Would the bonds even be in the house? Aside from his larcenous nature, Khrabovich seemed to be a careful and deliberate man. He might recognize the prudence of hiding the bonds elsewhere, but Paul reckoned he would behave differently. From the moment the major had them, they had governed everything he did. He would feel compelled to have them at his side, should he need to decamp in haste. Paul was convinced the loot would be there tonight.

Barney's primary job was to panic the man into turning over the paper right away. Of course, neither Paul nor Barney expected that to be the major's first reaction. He would panic all right, but he was at least as likely to lash out at Barney, grab the bonds, and run for it. Barney would have to talk him out of that, and he seemed to think he could. Paul retained grave reservations.

Paul expressed his misgivings on Saturday afternoon when Barney came back to the hotel.

"So what else can we do?" Barney asked.

"Why not just have Norman get somebody to blow the whistle to the French police. Let them arrest this suspicious character. Give them a clue to his true identity, and he'll be back in the People's Republic before you can shout 'firing squad.'"

"Have you forgotten the little matter of the bonds? Say the police find them. We can't very well come forward and claim them. Grogan wants the money back, and he's willing to let Khrabovich walk to have it that way."

"Count the cost, Barney. The major is liable to kill you. Have you forgotten the gun? He has one in there, and you will not be armed."

"Of course I won't. We brought no weapons, and I'd be foolish to go in like that. Remember Grogan's message. We're not cops."

"That doesn't mean you have to be a sitting duck," Paul observed caustically.

"How would you suggest we minimize that risk? We can't very well eliminate it."

"The only resort I can think of will be to your well-known, silver-tongued line of blarney, Barney."

Barney smiled and made a slight bow to acknowledge his alliterative duty.

# 28

The beginning went well. No one entered Rue Lincoln before Francois Declaire was seen leaving by the Champs Elysees. Even then they all held back, waiting for darkness to fully engulf the street and foot traffic to subside.

Then they moved into position one at a time—first Norman up the rear alley, next Paul to his apartment perch across the street. Finally Barney moved silently over the cobblestones to the gate of Khrabovich's dwelling. Norman had somehow arranged for a nearby streetlamp to fail, so Barney's form simply merged with all the other shadows.

Once in the apartment, Paul went immediately and quietly onto the balcony. From there he could look straight into the lighted study where he expected to see Khrabovich. As his eyes adapted to the scene, he saw somebody sitting at a desk that faced the open window between them. The room was lighted by a bright lamp to the figure's left, but Paul could see no face, because the head was bent forward to look at something on the desk.

*No matter*, Paul thought. *Khrabovich is the only one in the house; it has to be him.*

Shifting his gaze to the steps at the front door, Paul saw the door just being closed from inside. Hearing no sound, he at first gave thanks for the absence of an alarm, but his gratitude was brief. The figure at the desk had turned his head and was standing up to face around. Something unanticipated by Norman, maybe just a small bell attached inside the front door, had gone off. The quarry was alerted. Through the open window across the street, Paul could barely hear a male voice calling out to Francois.

Paul heard no reply, but seeing the form in front of him relax, he presumed Barney had responded with something simple like, *"Oui, monsieur. C'est moi."*

Paul could imagine Barney quietly hotfooting it up the spiral staircase to enter the study before Khrabovich had time to think. Then Paul saw Barney come into view in the back of the room. The still-standing figure of Khrabovich stiffened sharply for confrontation.

The ensuing conversation must have been conducted almost in a whisper, for Paul heard none of it. He could only watch as Barney gestured slowly with his arms and opened them wide to show he was not armed. For tonight's work Barney was clad in close-fitting, black garments that had made him nearly invisible entering the house.

The figure of Khrabovich seemed to grow taller, even though he was moving away from Paul towards Barney. He stopped near the middle of the room and appeared to give Barney his full attention.

So long as Barney was talking, Paul did not need to hear a voice. He knew what Barney was doing—telling the major his true identity was known and his position at risk, offering options of freedom or exposure, and urging a choice between cooperation and death. Barney had to keep the man fearful and off balance, and it looked to Paul as if that might be working.

After a moment, the initial crisis of discovery seemed to pass. Paul could see Khrabovich pointing for Barney to sit down. Consciously or not, Barney selected a light-colored chair that was in Paul's line of sight. Unfortunately, the major must have seated himself across from Barney in a part of the room Paul could not see. Now Paul could only guess at the distance between the two men.

Still nothing was audible, but Paul knew Barney was making a fast and eloquent pitch to Khrabovich. He was telling the man how to remain at large and save himself by just returning what he had taken. This would be a hard sell because the major had so totally and irrevocably turned his back on the past, reinvented his identity, and invested himself in his newfound fortune.

*Give it up, major*, Paul thought. Then he thought again. *How can he give it up? The money is all he has left.*

It might be a dire thing to risk being taken back to the People's Republic. It meant death for sure, but so what? Too late, Paul could see that he and Barney had fashioned a plan for failure. They were backing a vicious animal into a corner and expecting him to accept a civilized accommodation. It would not work; it could not work.

What was going on in the house across the street? Barney had risen from his chair. His stance showed no sign of alarm. Khrabovich was back in view, coming toward the desk near the window where Paul had initially seen him. For the first time Paul got a clear view of his face. He was definitely the officer who interrogated Paul in January. Now he bent over, possibly to open a desk drawer or go into some kind of container next to the desk.

After less than half a minute, Khrabovich stood up facing Paul with his back to Barney. The desk lamp showed him clasping a folio-sized, leather or plastic pouch against his chest with his right hand. It also flashed a blued-steel reflection from something held in the man's left hand. Now Paul recalled something from his mock execution in captivity. The major was a left-handed shooter.

# 29

The pistol was out and Barney was seconds away from his own afterlife. Paul had to change the script before the major could turn around.

Paul acted almost without thinking. Before Khrabovich could pivot away from him, he knelt, scooped up a heavy potted plant from the floor of his balcony, and hurled it onto the cobblestones below.

The pot landed with explosive echoes that ran through the street like the report of an artillery piece. At the same time, Paul squeezed up the air from his diaphragm to shout a piercing tenor order that bounced loud and sharp off every surface for a half-block around. Happily recalling the major's fluency in English, he had no need to translate.

"Murderer Anton Khrabovich, you are under arrest. Come out now with your hands up."

Hearing his true name being loudly published in the street drew the major's attention away from Barney. He must have seen Paul's shadowy movement in launching the pot, because he now aimed and fired his pistol twice into the darkness of Paul's balcony. One round ricocheted from the balcony railing into the street, and the other passed through the open door to bury itself in one of the apartment walls.

Meanwhile, an alerted Barney reacted to the racket outside and the gunfire inside by diving across the room and hurling himself into the major's back hard enough to dislodge the pistol from his hand. Whether it was lost somewhere on the floor or flew out the window, the firearm ceased to be a component in Barney's struggle. He was fully occupied just trying to keep Khrabovich from getting away. Failing that, he was fighting to get hold of the pouch that both he and Paul were sure contained the bonds.

All the action was now on the other side of the street, and Paul could do no more to affect it where he was. With a final glance at the wrestling match in the study, Paul abandoned his perch to run downstairs, across the street, through the still-open gate, and up the steps to the front door. Before he could reach for the handle, the door withdrew to disgorge a hurtling figure that knocked him down and trampled him into the steps on its way to the gate.

"Monsieur Barney, Monsieur Barney," Paul heard Norman calling from the back alley. He was apparently reacting to the sound of Paul's distraction in the street and the consecutive gunshots from the house.

From his prone position on the steps Paul could see lights coming on up and down the street. Norman would be trying to help Barney. That left Paul to try and catch Khrabovich, who was already a few houses away.

Was he carrying the bonds? Paul had to presume so, because he was headed for the Champs Elysees, Paris's busiest avenue. There he might blend into the dense evening crowd and become invisible once more.

Coming out of Rue Lincoln onto the brightly lighted Champs Elysees, Khrabovich paused and looked back over his shoulder to see Paul coming after him. Ignoring the people in his way, he risked the hazard of crossing the avenue and turned left, bumping and jostling the pedestrians in front of him.

True running is not possible among the crowds that fill the Champs Elysees on any fair spring or summer evening. Yet, desperate to escape, Khrabovich forcefully broke through the brightly lighted, passive masses along this grandest of all nighttime byways.

Unable to close with his man in the press of bodies, Paul could not tell if he still carried the pouch that might contain the bonds. Paul simply had to assume he did.

Forced to continue the chase in the wake of his quarry's growing crowd of hostile pedestrians, Paul became the object of their unleashed reaction to the long-gone offender. He rapidly became the target of hateful looks, curses, occasional thrown elbows, and a few deliberate efforts to trip him up. Trying to catch Khrabovich in so aroused a mob was a difficult proposition. Just keeping up the chase was a challenge.

*At least*, Paul thought, *I'm dressed for this.*

Khrabovich had begun a street race clad for an evening at home in leather-soled shoes, while Paul was wearing a short-sleeved tourist tee-shirt, Bermuda shorts, and running shoes. Paul reckoned this advantage allowed him to hold position, despite the obstacles placed in his way by people Khrabovich was inciting to bitter resistance.

After more than four blocks of being shoved, obstructed, and shouted at, Paul still had the major in view and thought he might see an end ahead. The fugitive was nearing the Etoile with Paul gaining on him.

The *Place de l'Etoile* was renamed Place Charles de Gaulle in 1970, but more than a decade later, almost nobody called it by the new name. The magnificent, historic site of the Arch of Triumph gracefully remained simply the Etoile. The world's most famous traffic circle, it gives convergence to twelve major avenues with ten full lanes of close-packed, fast-moving traffic that declines only in those few hours when most of the city sleeps. This great central pavement is reserved for automotive traffic and attempting to cross it or even walk out to the Arch at high-traffic periods is an act of suicidal intent.

Paul knew the pedestrian presence would begin to thin out around the Etoile. Khrabovich would be forced out of the Champs Elysees crowds and have to change his route. Then Paul might be able to overtake him and recover the bonds. He was already edging around to intercept the major at the next avenue to the right, when the crowd suddenly cleared and Paul found himself looking at the man's back only a few yards ahead. He had stopped at the brink of the Etoile's surging sea of automotive activity.

With a jerk, Khrabovich took a step backward and turned around to find Paul directly behind him. In the bright lights Paul could see he was not carrying the pouch.

*I'll bet he lost it when he ran over me on the steps.*

At first the major appeared stunned and momentarily paralyzed. Had he recognized Paul as his former prisoner? Possibly, but there was more going on than that. His face had filled with such revulsion and horror that even Paul was startled. Whatever the man might be, Paul did not imagine him a coward.

The effect of their confrontation was much different for Paul. The pitch of the chase went flat, and he stopped in his tracks. If Khrabovich no longer had the bonds, pursuit was pointless. Even Grogan did not care about punishment. Paul lost all interest.

"I believe our business is finished, Major," Paul called out to him and was about to turn away.

What followed was a surreal scene Paul would not soon be able to cleanse from his mind. Khrabovich was somehow looking beyond Paul and over his head. The terror in his expression greatly intensified, and he took a cowering step back.

Then the major twisted violently away and deliberately threw himself out into the oncoming flow of cars. He ran only a few feet before he was struck by a fast-moving taxi. His body executed a high arc to land less than a yard from where Paul stood. He was obviously dead; his head was twisted halfway around on his shoulders. His face, Paul saw, was still frozen in fear.

Paul felt almost numb. Lifting his eyes from the body, he looked into the manic traffic reactions being produced by the accident. Then he saw a reason for the man's aberrant action. The thing hung just above the body before swiftly descending upon it.

It looked like a thick black cloud of darkness so dense and repellant of all light that it fired Paul's memory. He had once been caught in a cloud like that, praying desperately for deliverance on a narrow, foggy road. Paul watched, but no one else seemed to see the cloud settle itself all around the major's body. Finally, Paul could see only an oily spot of impenetrable, throbbing ugliness that oozed above the ground.

*The demon is feeding*, Paul thought, recalling his own terrifying experience with one.

Then the blot was gone, but the corpse remained.

*Dear God. It has eaten his soul and taken it away. Khrabovich was already dead, but that did not save him. Did he go straight to the terminal ward?*

Turning to leave, Paul recognized something else he would rather not have seen that night. It was the shocked, unbelieving appearance of Petra March, before she coldly dropped her gaze from his face and turned to escort her small group of girls away from the bloody scene behind him.

# 30

Nobody in the gathering crowd seemed to relate Paul to the accident, so he simply turned away and melted into the group. If any of them had seen the recent footrace, none appeared to remember Paul as one of its obnoxious contenders.

Crossing the Champs Elysees and turning back the way he had come, Paul continued across Rue Lincoln. Glancing to his right, he saw the pulsating blue light from a police van parked in front of Khrabovich's place. He was confident, or at least hopeful, that Barney and Norman had cleared out before the police arrived. He hoped even more that they had picked up the major's pouch on their way. That was no longer in his hands, so he just kept walking until he came to the Place de la Concorde. There he turned left and continued by a series of quiet, narrow streets to his hotel.

Walking home, he somberly recalled Petra's obvious distress at the Etoile.

*How will I ever explain it? I can't possibly tell her the truth. She wouldn't believe me if I did.*

Paul had speculated that Barney and Norman might be waiting for him at the hotel, but the suite was dark when he got there. Closing the door before turning on a light, Paul was instantly aware of something out of order.

The entry alcove to the suite gave way directly to the bathroom and water closet with bedrooms located to the right and left. Paul and Barney habitually left their bedroom doors open, so Paul could see some outside light coming through the open-draped windows. He saw only unmoving shadows in each room, but he knew he was not alone.

After a quick analysis, Paul called out, "How did you get in here, Jackie?"

"Ah," she said softly from the right-hand bedroom, "Norman always says that I am very good to pick the lock—but how did you know it was me?"

"I could not mistake your scent," Paul said, turning on the light as he stepped into the room, which happened to be his own. "Your perfume is very distinctive."

*Actually*, he thought, drunkenly inhaling the smell of her, *it is barely short of disabling.*

Jackie was seated and facing him in an armchair by the window. This was the first time Paul had seen her in the evening, and she was dressed even more glamorously than by day. Tonight she wore a wine-colored, form-following, satiny, cocktail dress. Her legs were exquisitely crossed in a way that distracted him almost as much as when she had sat perched on the corner of her desk.

"Do you like it?" she asked with a lipstick-glossed smile.

"How could I not?" he replied, not sure if he was talking about the perfume or her provocative pose.

"Why have you come?" he finally forced himself to ask.

"To bring you a message from my dear husband, of course," she said, carefully uncrossing her legs and standing up. It was a single, sinuous motion that made Paul even more aware of her imposing sexual presence and power.

"Yes?" he croaked with a catch in his throat.

"Norman asked me to inform you that he and Monsieur Barney succeeded in recovering the bonds and getting away before the police arrived. We did not, of course, want to use the telephone to tell you that."

"Certainly not, and that is very good news."

"I knew you would be pleased," she replied in a luxurious tone.

*Is steam coming out of her mouth?*

"Since the police have become involved," she went on softly, "we thought it would be a good thing to complete all our transactions tonight. That will permit both of you to get an early flight out. I have arranged your reservations."

"What time?"

"Three o'clock."

"This morning?"

"Most certainly. Norman suggested you pack Monsieur Barney's bag for him and check out of the hotel. Then you can both proceed directly to the airport from our office."

"No moss grows under your shoes, does it, Jackie?"

"*Pardon?*" she asked wrinkling her brow in curiosity.

"Just an American figure of speech," he said with a smile. "I guess I turned it into a mixed metaphor."

Her quizzical silence persuaded him to abandon further effort at translation.

Paul had spent a lot of his adult life packing up and moving out in the middle of the night, so he was done in ten minutes. Changing clothes could wait. He and Jackie had the bags in the alcove ready to go, when there was a knock at the door.

"I planned to carry the bags down myself. Did you call for service?" Paul asked, as he reached for the door handle.

Then he and Jackie were looking straight into the upturned face of Petra March with the long hotel corridor behind her. She began speaking hurriedly in a contrite tone before she had taken in the scene in front of her.

"I am so sorry, Paul. I couldn't stand going to bed without letting you…"

Her speech slowly ground to a halt, and her face went blank. She kept looking at both of them, trying to understand. She took in everything from Jackie's arched high heels and well-curved calves to her provocative dress, perfect makeup, and lustrous blonde hair.

*She's probably getting a good whiff of the perfume too.* Paul felt like he had swallowed a giant snowball.

"Petra," he stammered, gesturing first toward Jackie and then to the bags. "Please meet my business associate, Jacqueline. Something came up suddenly, and I have to go home right away. We're on our way to the airport now."

Petra's expression quickly passed from blank to hurt to furious. Without another word she turned and stormed down the corridor with an arm-swinging gait that spoke equally of anger and pain. Disdaining the elevator, she made a sharp turn and dove out of sight into the stairwell.

# 31

Jackie drove Paul the short distance to her office in a Citroen sedan, and they left the bags in the trunk for later transport to the airfield. Climbing the stairs ahead of Paul, she tried to comfort him about the blowup with Petra. Following her, he found himself even more overpowered by her inescapable womanliness.

"I regret the misunderstanding with your friend," she said. "American women become so easily jealous. It is not at all French."

"It isn't your fault or hers, Jackie. She saw something tonight that shook her confidence in me, and she had come to me to talk about it. When she found us there together, she just went over the edge. She was not wrong, because I really have been keeping things from her."

"What did she see tonight—besides us in your suite I mean?"

*Jackie knows nothing about the Etoile. None of them do.*

"She saw a man—Herr Brecht—killed," Paul said. "I suppose she thought I might have had something to do with it. In a way I did."

They had reached the landing outside her outer-office door, and she was putting a key into the lock. Now she hesitated. Clearly, this was the first she had heard, or even considered the possibility, of Khrabovich's death.

"Did you truly?" she asked, turning the key slowly. Her normally perfect composure was quickly dissolving right in front of him.

"I did not kill him, but I was certainly a party to the events that led to his death. I guess we all were," he said, gesturing into the office where Barney and her husband were waiting.

"The woman you saw at the hotel trusted me once—several times actually. Now—again—she thinks I have failed her. Maybe she's right."

Jackie remained silent as they walked through to the inner office where Barney and Norman were seated at the conference table. Paul took a chair with them while she went to her own desk, sat down behind it, and began paging through a file folder that was lying on it. Now it was time for Paul and the other two men to compare notes.

"Are you at all aware of the way my pursuit of Brecht ended?" Paul asked.

"We thought he probably gave you the slip," Barney answered.

"No," Paul said, glancing at Jackie, who continued the stoic examination of her folder's contents. "I caught up with him at the Etoile." Then Paul explained exactly what happened, omitting only the demonic manifestation he had seen.

"We had no idea," Norman said with a grave expression. "Monsieur Barney recovered the bag of bonds our fugitive must have dropped in his flight. He brought them when he joined me in the courtyard behind the house."

"Brecht must have lost them bumping into me when he came out the front door," Paul told them.

"Having fired his pistol," Norman went on, "he must have been too fearful to come back for them. He knew the police would soon be there. You may even have been chasing him before he realized they were gone. A police car was in fact arriving as we escaped through the alley. We did not go through the Champs Elysees. Even if we had, we would not have seen what you describe, because we were headed the other way."

"What do you think, Norman?" Paul asked. "Will the police connect Brecht's death in the Etoile with the ruckus in Rue Lincoln?"

"Maybe not yet, but before long; our police are very good at piecing together violent events that take place only blocks and minutes apart."

"Then it is even better that Barney and I leave right away."

"Yes," Norman said, looking reproachfully at Barney. "Any loss of life is a great pity. I know Herr Brecht shot at you, but I deeply regret this outcome."

"I would not have chased him," Paul objected, "if I had known he lost the bonds."

"I know that, Monsieur Paul, but surely you understand the difficulty this creates for Jacqueline and myself. Now there must be what you call the cover-up. Even the most discreet investigation leaves footprints, and we will be at great expense and some risk to erase ours from the closing days of the deceased gentleman. Please understand if we are compelled to apply to your principal for added reimbursement."

"We will be sure to speak of that when we get home," Paul said.

"I am most grateful, monsieur. Now I think we should hurry you both to the airport. We must remain here," Norman said, speaking of Jackie and himself, "but you should not stay a second longer than you can help."

A man stood silent and hidden in the early-morning shadows of a narrow alley just across from the lighted window of the Nervier office. A gentle rain had begun to fall when he saw a beautiful blonde woman come out of the building and speed away with two men in a late-model Citroen. He did not know any of these people—not yet—but he would find out who they were. He would learn all about them very soon.

He had been told that trouble would strike tonight, but his warning came too late. By the time he got back to Rue Lincoln, it was all over. His base was invaded and already under police seal. He dared not approach, having to abandon all he had left there.

The pretentious pseudo-Austrian with so much money was gone too—dead nearby. Even the police had not connected that yet, but they would. That was one more reason he could not go home. The one he served, who Brecht barely knew, had shown him what happened and guided him here. Now he whispered what soon must be done.

The money he should have had was now out of reach. No matter; more would come by the master's will. When it did, he must be ready to act.

*Francois Declaire*, he told himself, *will happily repay this insult.*

The light in the office window had gone out, and now a male figure came out of the building in a light-colored raincoat and a dark beret. When the man had turned to proceed on foot, Declaire came out of the alley into the street. He spat once upon the already moist cobblestones. Then he blended himself into the darker shadows on his side of the street, silently following the man he would come to know as Norman Nervier. The rain was picking up, and he bitterly remembered the excellent waterproof garment he had left behind in Rue Lincoln.

# 32

Paul and Barney went straight from the airport to headquarters on Sunday morning to secure the bonds and write a debriefing report of the Paris operation for Grogan. They would have liked to end the job that way, but both knew better. They gave the report to Darlene Parker at eight o' clock Monday morning. By eight thirty Grogan had them in his office for their expected verbal beating.

Paul recalled his January exchange with Grogan at BWI after his repatriation from the People's Republic. There Grogan had similarly roasted Paul over a faulty decision that had left him buried in the snow, rescued, captured, and finally imprisoned.

Grogan's current disposition seemed the same, but this time he had both Paul and Barney to flog. For at least a quarter of an hour he had excoriated them with a mounting crescendo of abuse that appeared at last to be cresting.

"Didn't I tell you to leave the man alone? When will I ever learn? Putting you two together is like casting Lon Chaney in *Rebecca of Sunnybrook Farm*. If Paul weren't leaving anyway, I would have to fire one of you just to keep it from happening again."

*Grogan was right to chew me up last time*, Paul thought, *but not now*. Barney, he could see, was keeping still and taking his medicine like a good Spartan. His eyes were again fixed on that favorite bit of wall behind and above Grogan's head. Paul decided to speak for them both.

"Be reasonable, Grogan. Every move we made was meant to get your paper back. We were unarmed, and he pulled a gun. He was a lousy shot, but he fired two rounds at me when I distracted him from shooting Barney. Barney still had to wrestle the thing away from him or take the third bullet. That was the only time anyone laid a finger on him. I only touched him when he ran over me on the steps. For all I knew, he was headed out of town with the goods. Would you be happy if he had been, and I just let him go?"

Grogan was not used to being interrupted during one of his righteous rants. Maybe that was why he abruptly changed the tone and tempo of his blame-placing fit.

"All right, I know you had to think and act fast, but look at the mess you made. I wanted a simple, quiet transaction. You were supposed to scare the guy into giving back what he stole—no noise and no trouble."

*He's not giving any ground,* Paul thought, *but maybe he's through snarling.*

"Now you've stirred up a swarm of hornets that might expose a valued asset," Grogan continued. "The Nerviers are a useful resource. They do good work, and they don't ask many questions. I cannot afford to lose them, so I'll help them any way I can. Besides that, I'll be activating some extremely sensitive channels to make this thing go away. I hope it works."

"I'm glad you're doing something for Norman and Jackie," Paul said. "They helped us a lot, and I admit we blindsided Norman about the potential for violence."

Grogan gave a nod of acknowledgement as Paul continued.

"We should have known all along—maybe we did—how impossible it would be to separate Khrabovich from the money with mere reason and intimidation. Everything he cared about depended on keeping the loot. Maybe that is why he killed himself when he found the only thing he cared about was gone."

Paul knew he was fudging Khrabovich's motive for suicide. He had told no one of the major's terrified look, and he would remain silent about demonic apparitions.

Now Paul shifted the focus of the meeting by putting a question to Grogan.

"What would you have done differently?"

Grogan sat back in his famed executive chair, folded his hands in front of him, and rolled his eyes toward the ceiling.

"Beats me, guys," he said. "I just give the lectures and reprimands around here." Then he sat up and looked directly at Paul.

"What's your plan now, old friend? Your contract is almost wrapped up. Prior complaints aside, I'd like to see you stay on, but I'm pretty sure you won't."

Paul shook his head, tacitly dismissing Grogan's offer.

"The reporting phase will take a few days," Paul said gently. "We have to complete the paperwork on *Bung Tick*, as well as this one; I'll help Barney with that. We should finish up by Friday afternoon. That seems like a good time to terminate."

"Agreed," Grogan said with a tired look around his mouth. Paul could see he was disappointed but not surprised. "If I may ask, what will you be doing next?"

Paul looked down at the carpet for a few seconds, before lifting his eyes to reply.

"I wish I knew, but I don't. You learned enough from Ralph's polygraph session to guess what I'm waiting for—what I'm still trying to work out. I don't think I'm looking for a job so much as a purpose or a cause. I believe in time I'll be led to it. Coming back here for the last few months was almost relaxing—until we actually came to grips with Khrabovich, of course. That was no fun, but it reminded me that this is not supposed to be my life any more."

Paul paused, but Grogan did not speak.

"In the past few days, I have seriously botched my personal life," Paul added, thinking of Petra. "I'm not sure I'll be able to fix that, or even if I should try. It's just one more thing I need to patch up. I can't do that by staying here."

Paul stopped now. He had nothing left to say.

Grogan leaned forward over his desk, clasping his hands in front of him.

"I may not fully understand your situation, Paul, but we have seen a lot of the world together. I squeezed you hard to get this one last job done, but I will always care about what happens to you."

Now Grogan took a small bit of white pasteboard from his desktop and handed it to Paul. Business cards with valid information were not common in the organization. Paul was sure he had never seen Grogan with one. This card bore only the name 'Philip Grogan' and telephone numbers for office and home.

"Please inform me from time to time, and don't hesitate to call if you need help—with anything."

Paul was overcome by Grogan's untypical moment and could only nod his head.

"One more thing," Grogan said, producing a manila folder from one of his piles of paper. He handed it across the desk to Paul while looking away from him. "I asked a friend of mine at the Pentagon to get this for you."

Before Paul could open it, Grogan leaned back and began reading from one of his piles.

"Good day, gentlemen," he said dismissively.

Paul knew how rare it was for Grogan to end any discussion without a call for questions. This time he did.

"What's in the folder?" Barney asked after closing Grogan's door behind them.

"I think I know," Paul said, opening it to see.

Inside he found an honorable-discharge certificate and official forms releasing him from service in the US Navy Reserve.

## 33

*Where am I,* Paul asked himself? *How did I get here?*

A dense atmosphere hung still and fetid everywhere. Something here hated light, and there was none. Darkness ruled without contest, where no shred of form might emerge. His memory of a pig farm in summer compared quite favorably to the reeking stench that now enveloped him with a smell like human offal.

Was something trying to move beyond the shadows? He could not tell. Did he hear grating sounds from heavy masses scraping past each other, or was sound as alien as light to these inchoate reaches where he had come?

The place oozed a massive sense of suffocating closeness and impending dread. Its vacuous, invasive mood masked any evidence of Paul's human form. What did he look like here, or was he just another blob of clotted darkness?

*Everything is backwards.*

He was trapped in some gruesome reversal—a bitter parody of all that was true, holy, and good. He was surrounded by grotesquely opposite images of what he had seen when he opened his eyes in the Vale. The all-revealing source of light and life was replaced by emptiness—not just quenched, but never there. Stillness ruled, and nothing truly lived. No love survived here. Everything was dead and pitifully darkened forever.

*But that's impossible. How can I be in the terminal ward when I already woke up in the Vale?*

Paul felt a sudden rush of terror surge through whatever survived of him here.

*Don't panic. This cannot be what it looks like.*

Then he heard a strange laugh, triumphantly devoid of merriment, from the darkness around him. When the laughter stopped, Paul heard a cool, ingratiating voice coming to him from every point of the compass.

"Welcome to the end of your beginning. Look around. Tell me what you think."

"I don't think I'll stay," Paul said, trying to sound bolder than he felt. "I am not meant to be here."

"Do not be so sure." The voice was now urbane with a pedagogical flair. "Very few who come here thought they would. They do not foresee it. Many think nothing faces them at the end. We try to keep them thinking that. It is the most useful tool we have. Skeptics are so easy to catch. They are barely worth the effort."

"I already told you," Paul said. 'This is not my destiny. I have seen what lies ahead. I know the truth, and you cannot deceive me."

Paul heard something like a muffled explosion and felt a crushing pressure building around him. Unseen, grinding forces enclosed him from every direction at once. The voice, when it returned, was a scratchy, bowel-chilling trumpet of rage.

"Hear me, foolish mortal! Are you safe from me just because you were once caught up from earth? Did you stay that way?"

The shrill interrogator barely paused before shouting the answer himself.

"No! You went back to your puny universe, and I rule there. All on earth suffer my pleasure, and you will suffer more still. I can kill everything you love. Do you doubt me?"

There was a punctuating pause, because Paul gave no response. Why did this persecutor threaten only what Paul valued? How great was his power over Paul?

"It does not have to be like that."

The physical pressure relaxed. The voice was again soft and persuasive.

"Abandon your service to him whose name I will not speak. My rewards are real and my pleasures immediate. You have taken them before. If you want happiness and safety, just choose me and renounce my enemy."

*How absurd*, Paul thought, and his contempt welled up in ridicule.

"Rewards like this place? I watched you reward your servant, Khrabovich. You took the money he coveted and drove him to a violent death. He is yours forever, and this is his reward."

When there was no immediate response, Paul escalated the level of scorn.

"You could speak the name of your enemy if you would. You know it well enough, but you are afraid to say it. To pronounce the true name of God the Father, Son, and Holy Spirit would gag and silence you forever. You cannot bear to hear it. Someday—right now in God's holy time—you are being dealt with, and you know it. You know the outcome of this charade. Why continue it?"

Now Paul heard what sounded like a roaring, angry protest of agony. When the abusive voice spoke again, it was measured and deliberate.

"Look around you, mortal fool. Make sport of me while you can, but I will drag you here when the time is full. You will fail in your attempt and lose the prize. I promise it. You will gladly fall back into my arms. Know you not that your world is mine? I can take you from it when I choose."

"Maybe you can, but you cannot bring me here." Not wanting to test his adversary's threat in the present moment, Paul began shouting every powerful prayer that came to mind.

"Oh God, make speed to save me. Oh Lord, make haste to help me. Glory to the Father and to the Son and to the Holy Spirit, as it was in the beginning, is now and ever shall be."

There was no response, so Paul kept going.

"Holy God, Holy and Mighty, Holy Immortal One, have mercy upon me."

The tormentor's voice was stilled, but the foul surroundings remained.

"Lord Jesus Christ, Son of God, have mercy on me, a sinner."

Abruptly, the gloomy, threatening scene dissolved, and Paul awoke, desperately clutching the arms of the easy chair in his apartment. His tormentor was gone, but Paul's pulse kept racing.

The last thing Paul remembered before his horrific vision was sitting down in the evening to look over the *Washington Post*. He had skipped reading the paper that morning to treat himself to a leisurely day at the National Gallery of Art and strolling along the Mall. That was how he celebrated the Saturday after he finished the Khrabovich reports with Barney and once more processed himself out of the organization.

He must have barely begun to read when he fell asleep and found himself facing the Prince of Darkness.

Since his sojourn in the Vale, Paul had experienced three demonic encounters: first in the mountain fog, next at the Etoile watching Khrabovich die, and now in a dreadful place that whispered to him of what he knew about the terminal ward and souls that do not wake up in the Vale. The first two involved greater or lesser demons. This time, while his body slept in the chair, his soul had gone to meet the chief executive officer of the lot.

Could Satan have killed him outright? He said he could, but he is a notorious liar. Paul had nearly died on the mountain road, but he called on God to save him and was delivered. The same tactic had worked for him tonight.

Tactic? The word felt wrong but seemed no less true. Whatever the devil and his servants might do to Paul's mind and body, his soul was bound for the Vale and beyond. Experience confirmed it. The devil might destroy his mortal form, but Paul was still going to see God. His eternal life was already in progress where God is, and nothing could change that. It was already done.

# 34

Paul got up early Sunday morning and drove out to St. Athanasius's for high Mass. It was the first time he had attended there since passing through the Vale. He had of course visited Father Don in his office right after that experience and telephoned him several times since. Even the telephone calls had stopped after he became once more engaged in the work of the organization.

Today Don nodded to Paul as he passed on his way up the center aisle to proclaim the gospel. At the end of the Mass he was standing at an inner door off the apse, speaking to people who were on their way to either the coffee-hour social downstairs or the parking lot outside. As Paul passed him, Don gripped his hand and spoke with a serious look on his face.

"We need to talk. Go through the sacristy and wait in my office."

Paul wanted to speak with Don anyway, so he made a left turn into the vesting area behind the altar, passed through an anteroom, and sat down in Don's office.

Don came in a few minutes later and immediately took his place behind the desk. He had removed his vestments and was wearing a black, short-sleeved shirt with a white clerical collar.

"Where have you been?" Don asked impatiently. "I tried calling you all week-before-last, but had no luck."

"I was in Paris. I got back last Sunday."

"Ouch!" Don barked, slapping himself lightly on the left cheek. "Looks like I gave up at just the wrong time. How was your trip?"

"It was a mixed bag. I ran into Petra there."

"What a wonderful coincidence. I think she's due back this week. Did you two settle your differences?"

"Briefly, but not still. We had a few great days, but it all fell apart. Not her fault—mine I suppose."

"Sorry," Don said, dropping his eyes.

"Wait." Don reacted, abruptly looking up. "I still have something to tell you."

"Good time to change the subject. What's up, Don?"

"Brother Arnold has been trying to find you. Do you still have his number?"

"I don't believe I ever had the number. You've got it, don't you?"

"Right here." Don opened his card file and scribbled a note for Paul.

"What does he want?" Paul asked.

"I asked, but he dodged the question. He sounded pretty agitated though."

"May I use your phone?"

"Sure. I need to circulate in the coffee hour, so you'll have the room to yourself." Don paused. "What were you doing in Paris anyway?"

"Same old stuff; just moving furniture around."

"Is there anything you'd like to talk with me about?"

"There is. Will you have a minute after coffee?"

"Certainly. Here or in the rectory?"

"Here would probably be better. It's not exactly family-hour material."

"I'll bring you back a cup. Black isn't it?"

Paul nodded, and Don left him alone in the office.

From Don's chair behind the desk, Paul dialed the number Don had given him. He waited through six rings before a familiar, slightly accented voice came on the line.

"Frank's House; Brother Arnold speaking. How may I help you?"

When Paul identified himself, Brother Arnold replied cheerfully.

"It is so very good to talk with you, my friend. I have heard nothing from you since late January. Remembering the danger you faced, I was worried for your safety."

"Thank you for your concern, Brother, but I'm doing quite well at the moment."

"So you have had no threatening encounters. I am most happy to know that."

"To the contrary, Brother, I have had several encounters. At least two of them were pretty threatening."

"You must come tell me what happened. Maybe I can be of help."

"I would like that. When would it be convenient?"

"My business usually falls off on Sunday afternoon. That would make today a good prospect, and in daylight your vehicle ought to be safe here. May I expect you?"

"I will come as soon as I finish with Father Don."

"Wonderful, and please give him my best regards."

"Certainly," Paul said before hanging up the telephone.

# 35

Paul had returned to his original chair when Don came in with two steaming, ceramic mugs of coffee. One of these he placed on the desk in front of Paul before taking his seat on the other side. After a sip of his own coffee, he extended his left hand, palm up, and nodded for Paul to proceed.

Paul tested his own cup carefully. Then he set it aside to cool.

"I just spoke with Brother Arnold and arranged to see him this afternoon. He told me to give you his best regards."

Don simply nodded. He made no other response, so Paul continued.

"I never brought you up to date on my January discussion with Brother Arnold. After I told him about my time in the Vale and what I thought it could mean, he warned me I might be targeted for trouble by the devil himself."

"That's interesting. Brother Arnold is a man of unusually broad experience. Was he right about your peril?"

"I was given immediate cause to suspect so. While I was talking with him, my car was stolen. That was after dark the same day I last visited you here. I thought the theft might be a shot across my bow, but it could have been coincidence."

"Maybe, considering the neighborhood where the good brother does his work."

"That's what the police said, but I could not so easily dismiss some later events."

"Such as?"

Paul went on to describe his demonic encounter in the fog and how that concluded. Telling about what he saw at the Etoile, he withheld the location and details, except to say the victim had run in front of a car just seconds before.

"The demon attacked him after his death, but I think he saw it first. That's what he was running from at the end—not me."

"You've never been prone to hysteria or hallucinations, Paul."

"I've told you what I saw and felt in the first two cases. They happened in different places more than four months apart, and I was very wide awake each time. The next encounter was different. It took place while I was asleep, but I am convinced it was not a dream. It was a visitation."

Don did not respond, so Paul described the previous night's eerie interlude in the terminal ward.

"Are you sure this wasn't anything more than a vivid nightmare?" Don asked in clear surprise.

"Believe me. I know the difference between a dream and a vision," Paul said, remembering his nocturnal visit with Jason March in the Vale.

"What's the difference?"

"My dreams are rarely coherent. They ramble all over the place. Some I even recognize as dreams in progress. My worst nightmares fade as soon as I wake up."

Paul paused, but Don made no comment.

"Last night was not like that, Don. Everything I smelled, saw, heard, or felt is indelibly etched in my mind. I will never be rid of it in this life."

"So you were actually transported into a spiritual vision of hell to be threatened and tempted by Satan?"

"I could put it no better, Father."

"You are seriously convinced of this?"

"I couldn't be more certain. God took me to the Vale for real, so I'll believe the devil can bring me an illusion of hell. Was I really there? No. You have to die to be there. Besides, I know I wake up in the Vale; I'm already there. Still, this was no mere dream."

"Your argument is all too compelling," Don said. Then he thoughtfully stroked his clean-shaven chin, as if considering a reply. Paul waited and sipped his now cooler coffee.

"In the church these days," Don at last began, "we do not talk much about the devil. He is still in Scripture of course, but we priests keep him out of our homilies. When we have to mention him, he becomes an allegory for what evil men do in the world. He is no longer the immortal antagonist of God, seeking to spoil everything good and to lure God's children away from him. We do not describe him any more as our eternal enemy. We don't warn our flocks about him. We leave that to groups we think of as evangelical extremists.

"Our parishioners don't want to hear about damnation and the devil, so we are silent. We forget the truth about the father of lies, even while the scriptural facts are read out in the morning lesson. The truth about Satan is just too ugly, and neither end of the nave wants to look at it very closely.

"We emphasize love—and we ought to—but we sweep the devil's dirty little secrets under the altar cloth. We don't want to scare people—and we shouldn't—but we leave out the hard parts and hope everything will still turn out okay. When someone like you brings us evidence of the enemy's filthy work, we find ways to go on ignoring it. We suggest you might be hallucinating."

Don abruptly stopped, looking at Paul with a blank expression. Paul took another sip of coffee before responding.

"Brother Arnold," Paul began, "describes the threat of the devil in our world with words like yours."

"I have heard him use those words. That's one reason I sent you to him."

"Aren't you being too hard on yourself, Don? Your job is to lead souls to God and encourage them on the way. You do it all the time, and I think you do it right. You don't deny the devil exists—you shouldn't—but that isn't the focus of your ministry. You are totally dedicated to feeding Christ's sheep, and that is what you do every day. You did it for me ten years ago in that hospital in the Philippines."

"I really didn't have much to do with that," Don objected.

"You just don't know. I was hitting bottom when I met you there. I was a self-absorbed, pitiful drunk. I am grateful that the ward nurse would not give me a pass during the week I waited for surgery. If she had, I would have just gone to the Officer's Club and gotten rotten-socks drunk every day.

"Instead, I had to stay on the ward, getting to know you, and watching your simple ministry to wounded men who needed it. My wound was different, but you helped me too. God needed some way to get my attention and draw me back to him. He sent you for that, and it worked."

"That's kind of you, Paul, but right now I feel like a fool."

"Let me share a few more things I brought back from the Vale."

"Go ahead."

"For one thing, I learned how different each soul is from every other."

"Okay, but what about it?"

"How we see ourselves acts upon every choice we make, especially in our religious elections. Look how different, yet similar, some of those seem to be. As we search for the truth about God, why do so many routes claim to be the one true path? How can that work?"

"How indeed?" Don asked.

"It can't, unless our focus remains on God. God never changes; we do. As long as we are here, we change every second. Everything that happens from birth to death affects us. It becomes one more part of our completely personal history. It may be trivial or life-and-death stuff. It adds up to the person we think we are at any given moment. It limits our options and guides our choices."

"So?"

"All who practice or care about religion are trying to find God. We are all looking for the exact same place where God, who never changes, always is."

"Of course we are."

"Yes, but even while we seek the same place—the same God—not one of us follows the same map. Each soul is unique. That is how we wind up taking so many different roads on our way to the same destination."

"Wouldn't a cynic just call that part of life's futility?"

"Aren't the cynics always wrong, Father? Let me share one of the most important things I learned in the Vale."

"I'm listening."

"When it comes to saying which of us is worthy to see God, he alone decides. No God-created being is competent to judge the value of another soul. That is why Jesus told us not to. We may be even less competent to judge ourselves."

"Of course that's true, but how does it relate to the way some of us cover up for the devil?"

"First, I would not call it covering up. Did I ever tell you about Dr. George Fatheringill Trumbull?"

"I don't remember it."

"He was my childhood pastor. He converted me, but I spent my life despising him until he turned up as one of my therapists in the Vale."

"I recall you saying you were terrorized into joining the church as a boy."

"That's right. Dr. Trumbull was a master painter of the eternal torments waiting for anyone who died without Jesus. He had a valid point, but he made it sound like God wanted things that way because God hates sinners so much. I was afraid God was about to throw me under a streetcar for not making up my mind to follow him fast enough.

"I was only ten years old when I ran down the aisle to be saved, but later I started to worry. Had I faked my conversion just to escape eternal punishment? Had I been insincere? I wasn't sure, but I knew God was. That scared me most of all. I was a teenager before I figured out what was wrong with the preacher's technique. Anyway, I saw him again in the Vale."

"What happened then?"

"He was different, but that is true of everyone in the Vale. Nobody there or in heaven holds a grudge or ridicules another soul for foolish behavior on earth. We are all fools here, but that is past tense there. Nobody says they are sorry or begs forgiveness. There is nothing to forgive, because God's grace wipes all that away. No soul in God's reality ever feels guilt again."

"So Dr. Trumbull just went on preaching hell and damnation?"

"No. He told me about his later ministry. There the Holy Spirit led him to understand that his emphasis—not his message—was wrong. He learned to stress God's saving love as much as the consequences that overtake us when we fail God and others.

"I had already learned from another of my Vale teachers that God is not into punishment. He does salvation. He does redemption. In this universe of ours, that confines the discussion of good and evil to a matter of balance. I doubt if any preacher of the gospel can get that balance exactly right all the time—not in this world. A former colleague explained that to me when he was no longer in this world."

"Huh?"

"That's a different story for another time," Paul said with a smile.

"Okay. Maybe you're right," Don replied, smiling back, "but I can't help thinking that some of us on the liberal side might balance our message better than we do."

"After last night I can agree with that. I understand that I was not actually in the terminal ward—not in the sense that I died and really went to the Vale. Still, knowing what I saw and felt in both places gives me a very sobering sense of what is at stake for every human soul at life's end. The younger Dr. Trumbull was not wrong about that. He was just placing the em-*pha*-sis on the wrong syl-*la*-ble."

Don laughed at the way Paul intentionally misplaced the stress on those words.

"Bless you for seeing that, Paul. I think it may be time to take a good look at some of my own pronunciation."

# 36

"Friend Paul," Brother Arnold said after hearing a full description of his demonic encounters, "I find myself reconsidering some of the advice I gave you before."

He and Paul sat at the table normally used by the brother's guests to eat. The windows of the row house were all open to the summer weather, but a light breeze kept the room only a little warmer than the street outside. Seasonally, the coffee urn had given way to iced-tea dispensers and the soup pot was gone. Instead, the refrigerator door bore a menu of the sandwich and snack items within. Consistent with the old Franciscan's telephone prediction, they had the room to themselves. A thin halo of perspiration over each man's face was the only sign of discomfort.

"What changed your mind?" Paul asked. "Haven't your fears come true?"

"Not the way I expected."

"I don't get it," Paul said, opening his hands with a shrug.

"First, I did not anticipate visible demonic exposures. Satan usually operates unseen. You have become sensitive to the presence of evil in a way few people do. That ability comes from one of two sources."

"Which are?"

"This gift proceeds only from God or the devil. Yours, I think, comes from God."

"What about the terminal ward visit I just made?"

"You are right. Satan set that up to bully you. I am curious about that."

"Why?"

"It does not fit my first assumption about your gift. Unlike the devil, God does not send visions to deceive or frighten us. What you saw last night was meant to scare you away."

"From what?"

"The path that leads to God's will. Maybe you are getting closer to it. I wonder what it could be."

"I don't know."

"What have you been doing lately?" the brother asked.

"Not much I can talk about. I was forced to return to a job I thought I had left."

"You quit this job?"

"Just before I came to see you the first time."

"Can you tell me why you decided to quit?"

"It was not consistent with what I felt God calling me to do."

"Have you determined what that is?"

"No," Paul replied. "I still don't know a thing about that."

"Why did you return to work you no longer wanted to do?"

"My arm was twisted, but I also had some unfinished business."

"Is that now finished?" the older man asked.

"I hope so. I wrapped it up on Friday."

"Tell me more about your first demonic event on the mountain. Where were you going and what for?"

"I was running away. I was being chased, and I didn't know why. Besides that, you had just told me people I loved might not be safe around me. I wanted to avoid that danger, and I was still looking for guidance from God."

"Where were you going for guidance?"

"I was on my way to the monastery Abbey of Saints and Angels in Virginia."

"That's a wonderful place to rest. I have taken retreat there myself. Did you find something there?"

"I became confident that God will show me the way in time. I also decided to stop running."

"Since then, you have been tying up leftover loose ends from your former work?"

"More or less."

"Was your second demonic sighting part of that?"

"Yes, but that time I don't think I was a target for the malevolence. The other man I told you about seemed to see the manifestation and was driven to his death by it. I just happened to be there. We were in a crowd, but nobody else seemed to see the demon."

"That is a perceptive observation. Maybe it will lead us to another. You say you left your job for good on Friday."

"That's right."

"And when did you have your visit with the devil?"

"The next night; that was Saturday."

"Do you see where this goes?"

"I think so, Brother."

Brother Arnold did not react, so Paul tested an explanation.

"Before last night, the only demonic activity actually directed at me was in the mountains while I was on my way to try engaging God. I could see the demon because God gave me that ability. The attack was meant to kill me or at least divert me from God's purpose. God gave me special sight to protect me from that. I also believe the devil created the complications with my former employer. Those disrupted my life and distracted my attention for more than five months. I don't suppose I was any threat to satanic concerns during that time."

The Franciscan nodded but did not speak.

"The next time I saw a demon—when the other man died—it was mainly by chance."

"Are you sure that is all?" Brother Arnold finally asked.

"Not entirely. The situation was intricate. I had crossed paths with the victim of that attack immediately after returning from the Vale. He was doing things that were opposed to purposes of mine in ways I only learned of later. Even now I cannot tell how the schemes of hell and a web of human concerns might have overlapped that way.

"I only know that the devil seemed to leave me alone so long as I was back at work. When I finished and walked away from my job on Friday, I went back on his list of things to do. Then he summoned me in person."

"I agree," Brother Arnold said gravely, propping his elbows on the table, "but surely you see the difference between the first two demonic manifestations."

"What difference?"

"In the mountains, they wanted to kill you."

"Yes."

"The next time, when the man died before your eyes, you saw what they can do—the kind of fear they could inspire. Do you remember what I told you about humans who are able to see these beings?"

"I needed no lessons in fear after the first time, but I remember what you said about the gift of seeing demons. It comes from God or the devil."

"Do you believe God endowed the victim of your second observation with that kind of sight?"

"Hardly," Paul answered.

"Now suppose this victim had more than a casual acquaintance with the demonic side of things—something you don't know about?"

*Could Khrabovich have been in service to Satan?* Paul asked himself. *He was a criminal, but would he sell his soul, or whatever one does, to sign on with the devil?*

"I'm not sure, Brother. The man was a thief and a murderer. I suppose he might have become a devil worshiper."

"I have said enough about that possibility. Let's move on to the third event—last night. You said earlier that demonic manipulation might have been used to draw you back into your former work. Now you conclude the devil renewed his interest in you only after you eliminated that distraction?"

"Yes."

Brother Arnold sat silent and unmoving.

After about fifteen seconds, Paul spoke up.

"I get it. Satan was not trying to kill me this time—last night I mean."

"That does not mean he will not," Brother Arnold added.

"I know, but it makes me wonder why. Last night brought only temptation and a threat. Maybe Satan knows I have awakened in the Vale. He cannot threaten my soul—only my mortal body."

"What an interesting prospect, Brother Paul. Let's think about this a little."

They both sat silent for a moment. Then Brother Arnold spoke.

"He can be very frightening."

"Tell me about it. Last night he threatened me with death and hell."

"But he declined to follow through."

"I taunted him for not being able to bring me to hell, but I'm sure he can kill me."

"Why didn't he then?"

"Just as I did on the mountain side, I began praying for God to save me. In both cases the threat subsided."

"That is a wonderful lesson with lots of encouragement for our side. Satan has great power here on earth, but he is no match for God when we call for help. I am glad to learn how readily you do that."

Now both men sat silent for a bit.

"Before I leave," Paul finally asked, "what do you think of me trying to resume normal relations with people I care about?"

"Thank you for reminding me. I had almost forgotten to speak of that, even though I was thinking about it at the beginning of our talk. I remember cautioning you very strongly, but with all that has happened, I am now of a different mind."

"How so?"

"The devil, as you have learned, is a great mischief maker. That is what he does here on earth. I expect he will continue to interfere with you at every turn. He will want to distract you from God's purpose any way he can. He will not become kind, no matter what you do. He will hurt you if he can, and he will not spare those you love just because you avoid them. I suggest you simply live your life as best you can, praying always for God's help and trusting him to provide it."

Now Brother Arnold slapped his right hand firmly against the tabletop and looked squarely into Paul's eyes.

"Meanwhile, listen for the Lord. He reaches out to us when we are still."

"I pray for that, Brother. Right now I have nothing else to do."

"Do not be impatient. Remember what you have learned about God's time."

"Thank you. I've been back from the Vale less than six months, but I keep falling back into earthly habits of thought."

"I am sure you need no lectures from me, but oh my friend, be extremely careful and always prayerfully seek to do the will of our Father in heaven."

Paul bowed his head, and both men stood.

Transiting the steps in front of Frank's House, Paul gave a silent prayer of thanks that his car was still parked where he left it.

# 37

Paul carefully considered Brother Arnold's advice for two days, revisiting his long, sometimes tempestuous history with Petra. Now truly free of the organization, he needed to salvage what had been reemerging between them before that last, terrible night in Paris.

Early Tuesday evening, he called Petra's home telephone. The coarse-but-friendly voice that answered was Katya's. When he identified himself, she became much less friendly.

"How loathsome to call here after what you've done. You want to talk to Petra? Forget it. She's over the Atlantic on the way home."

Her voice was barely less bitter than her words.

*She must know about my last night in Paris*, Paul thought.

"You have the advantage, Katya. I can only guess at what you're talking about."

"Oh sure, but I'll bet you could come pretty close."

"Maybe, but why don't you tell me? Then we'll both know."

"I'll tell you all right."

Paul kept his mouth shut.

"Maybe you don't know how much you hurt her in January. She came home on a cloud after you met her at the Pub to say you had quit your job. Before that, I used to kid her for not making you more than a family friend. She never told me why. She only said it was something about your work. I thought it was all the time you spent out of town."

"Okay, Katya. Can we go back to January?"

"All right, you bastard!" she exploded, and her tone matched the epithet. "When she got back that night, she could not wait to tell me your new status. She was as happy as the day she married Jason, but it didn't last twenty-four hours."

"I called the next day. I tried to explain."

"Explain what—how you lied to her? I was in the next room when she answered your call. She sounded like a bird for a minute, but the chirping ran out fast."

"I recall her reaction."

"She told me what you said. You said you were pulling out and would call when you got back. When did you call? The children asked about you at first, but they stopped when they saw how it got to Petra. She didn't talk about you any more. She'd just gaze into space sometimes—you louse."

"I explained all that when we met again in Paris. I think she understood."

"I know about that too, at least what she wrote after having dinner with you."

"I didn't know she told you about that."

"Oh, did she ever—three full pages on both sides of the stationary about you. She was in love again, and she had to tell me all about it."

"I see."

"No you don't, Paul. Loving you must have more ups and downs than a manic-depressive on a pogo stick. In January you didn't last a day. This time it was less than a week."

"What did she tell you about that?"

"Just that you were the same, crummy liar you've always been. She phoned early Sunday morning in Paris, but it was still Saturday evening here—weekend before last."

"Was that all she said?"

"That was all I could understand. She ran on about the Arch of Triumph, a dead man, and some woman she didn't like much. She just wanted me to know what a bum you are and how stupid she'd been to think she still loved you. Any excuses?"

"Not for now, but I am grateful for what you've told me. Do you have her flight number and ETA? Is she coming into BWI or Dulles?"

"Why would I tell you, snotball?"

"So I can meet Petra at the airport and tell her about the dead man, the woman, and how I feel."

"Why would she take a ride from you?"

"She might if you're not there."

The telephone line fell silent.

"Katya, are you still on the line?"

"Yeah, I'm just stunned by your nerve."

"Get over it, girl."

She did.

Petra had told Katya not to meet her at BWI unless she called. She would catch a ride with someone in her group.

At ten o' clock Paul was waiting with others outside the customs inspection area for disembarking passengers. Traffic through the double-doored exits moved only one way, so greeters watched patiently for their expected arrivals. Paul had already seen several high-school girls from Petra's group emerge with luggage to meet parents, siblings, and friends.

The earliest tour members were accompanied by Petra's co-leader, who made sure each one was met.

*Petra,* Paul thought, *must be hanging back to guide everyone through the inspection.*

Finally, Paul saw her come through the doors behind the last member of her group. She was dressed for the humid Maryland summer in a light, short-sleeved print blouse worn outside knee-length white slacks with the walking shoes she had worn in Paris. Making long strides, he managed to intercept her as she came up to her partner, whose name he remembered was Doris.

"Welcome home, Petra," he said, gently taking her right hand in both of his and looking into her eyes. "Did you have a good flight?"

"I suppose so. What are you doing here?"

*Good*, he thought. *She does not want a scene.*

"Katya told me when you were coming in, and I thought you might need a lift. What about you, Doris? Do you have a way home?"

"Thanks, but I'm fine," Doris replied, pointing to an approaching man. "See you at school in August, Petra."

"Who do you think you are?" Petra rumbled ominously.

"I'm here to take you home. Are you ready?" Paul asked, holding her at arm's length and looking into eyes already agleam with moisture.

Uncertain if these were tears of rage, he picked up her bag, put his arm around her waist, and guided her out to the car. Nothing was said while he loaded her bag, settled her on the passenger side, and slid behind the wheel.

"How was the food on the plane?" Paul asked after exiting the parking lot.

"Airline standard I guess, but I ate it anyway. I'm not hungry." Her voice was giving way to fatigue. No anger or complaint remained.

"Why did you come to get me, Paul?"

"Didn't I tell you on the arrival deck?—to drive you home."

Petra was silent.

"Listen, Petra. There are a lot of things we need to talk about, but they can wait a few minutes. If I don't come straight to the point, I'll lose it."

"Go ahead, Paul."

"We have known each other more than ten years. In the beginning a lot of what happened was difficult-to-downright ugly. The rest—except for the last six months—was the greatest blessing in my life. Just those few days with you in Paris were the happiest I have ever known, because we were together, and you trusted me. Now, unless you're too tired, I have some explanations to make."

"I'm waiting."

Paul had to keep his eyes on the road, but he could feel the fleeting, gentle touch of her hand against his upper arm. Instead of plunging directly into an explanation, he asked her a question.

"How did it look to you that night at the Etoile?"

She sat for a moment considering her answer.

"We had just come up the Champs to the see the Arch lit up. I was planning to cross the avenue there and stroll back to a Metro station. I was in front, and Doris was bringing up the rear, so she saw nothing except that there was some kind of accident. We hustled the students away, so none of them had a chance to see much either. I don't think anyone but me got close enough to recognize you. No one mentioned it if they did."

"That's good, but what did you see?"

"I was looking ahead, so I saw nothing until two men ran past us. One a few feet behind was obviously chasing the other. The first one pulled up at the curb and turned back to face his pursuer, who stopped running too.

"I could see the face of the man at the curb. I don't think I've ever seen anyone look so frightened. Then he turned back around and lunged into traffic. Some car hit him right there and threw his body at the feet of the second man, who turned around and looked into my eyes before I could start herding the girls away. That was you, Paul."

Paul had stopped for a red light, so he was able to face Petra, who was looking patiently at him. Then he turned his eyes back to the road and spoke.

"Your account is correct as far as it goes. I was chasing that man because he had stolen something, and I was trying to get it back. When he turned to face me, I could see he did not have it with him. That ended the race for me. I was about to leave him standing there when I saw the same horrified expression you did. At first I thought he must be afraid of me. After all, he had tried to kill me that night and had wanted me dead five months before. He had reason to fear me, but that was not why he leaped into the Etoile."

"Why then?"

"He saw something else; something not of this world that he thought had come for him. I don't know how or exactly why, but he was right about that."

"How could you know?"

"Because I saw it too."

"What?"

"A demon."

"A demon?"

"Yes ma'am—a genuine, soul-eating demon straight out of hell."

"You're joking."

"Not at all; it's a talent I've picked up since coming back from the Vale."

"You're going to have to tell me more about this."

"Maybe later; for now just take my word."

"Okay."

"Can you accept that I ran after the man and cornered him, but did nothing to cause his death?"

"I believe you, but of course I knew none of this that Saturday, and I was very disturbed by what I saw. I was also worried about you."

"Thank you, Petra. That makes me happy."

"I came to your room that night, because I wanted to hear your side of things. I wanted to understand. I suppose I wanted you to console me."

"Then you ran straight into something else you did not understand, something that only aggravated your initial concern."

"Darn right I did," she said, but her tone was lighter than before.

"I told you at the time. The woman you saw me with was an associate. She was helping me with the business I had come to Paris to do. Fact is she is the one I was on my way to meet when I ran into you in the lobby of the Concorde."

"Just as I suspected," she said, mockingly triumphant. "You really were going out to meet another woman."

"Yes, but as I told you, it was strictly business."

"You'll have to do better than that, Paul. She looked like a headliner from the Follies Bergere. She was dressed for the job too, and her perfume was the kind that turns men's minds to molasses."

"You are correct to identify Jackie—that is what I called her—as a stunning example of French womanhood. I may have found her attractive, but that is as far as it could possibly have gone."

"Oh, sure."

"For one thing, my other French associate was her husband. As much as Jackie likes to throw her femininity around, I don't think she would be unfaithful to him."

"Do I just take your word for that?"

"There is one more reason I would never go after her."

"Like what?"

Paul took a deep breath and spoke with deliberate precision.

"I am spellbindingly in love with you, Petra March. I think I always have been. I hope you've suspected that, but I needed to tell you right away. That is truly why I picked you up tonight."

Petra hesitated a few seconds before responding in a low and fervent voice.

"Just don't you ever forget you said that, Paul, because I'm not going to."

Paul was unable to look across at her, but he thought she was smiling.

"About Jackie's fidelity to her husband?" he ventured playfully.

"Don't be cute."

"Let's clear the record. I did not invite her to my room. She came with a message from her husband and let herself in before I got back. She is good with locks. Had you not been so distracted by her glamour, you might have noticed we had baggage in tow. I think I told you at the time that I was headed for the airport."

"Of course you did. Thank you for reminding me."

He did not need to see her this time. Her voice was definitely smiling.

"Are we all right now, Petra?"

"Oh, yes. I'm very glad you came to get me."

"Me too."

Now she nestled her head warmly against his right arm. He liked the way that felt. She stayed quietly there until he brought her home.

# 38

On the night Paul drove Petra back from BWI, he stayed only long enough to make peace with Katya and accept an invitation to come back the following evening for an outdoor barbeque.

After breakfast in the morning, he gave serious thought to his next move.

For the second time in six months he faced a life-changing moment. The first had gone nowhere because of Grogan and the organization.

*This time has got to be better. I need a clean break with the past, and Petra ought to be part of it.*

He decided quickly and began working the telephone to create a surprise.

Late that afternoon the children were doing something in the house, while Paul simmered bratwursts in a pan of beer on the outdoor grill. That was when he told Petra and Katya what he had in mind.

"School is out, and I'm no longer employed," he told Petra. "Why don't we take off for a week in the Smoky Mountains? It's one of my favorite places to relax."

"Didn't we just get back from Paris?"

"Yeah, but that was mostly work—not a vacation. I haven't had one of those for years. What do you say?"

"When do you want to go?"

"How about tomorrow?"

"You bold, impetuous man, I'd love to. I've caught up with the bills and paperwork that piled up while I was away, but…"

"But what?"

"Katya needs me to help with the kids when they're not in school. She's away from home showing houses, and they're not old enough to be left alone all day."

"Oh no, you don't," her sister objected. "I'm not blocking the road to romance. You two go ahead; I'll get someone to take care of Spike and Patty."

Bobby, the older child, was now passing through puberty. His voice had changed, and he preferred to be called by his gym-class nickname, Spike. His mother, his aunt, and now Paul had elected to honor that wish.

"No need for that," Paul said. "They can come with us. I've already planned for it. The reservations are made."

"What a great idea," Petra said with enthusiasm.

Katya shook her head.

"I don't know about that Paul. Won't they kind of—be in the way?"

"Not at all. In fact, they will be our chaperones. We ought to pay them to come."

Petra laughed with her hands over her mouth, and Katya cackled raucously.

"If that's what you want," Katya agreed. "But won't four of you be cramped in your little Daytona?"

"No problem. We'll have lots of room in Petra's Buick."

"Absolutely. It's time we started sharing things, isn't it, Paul?"

Paul smiled and slightly bowed his head.

"I'll tell them now," their mother said. "They're going to love it."

"Good timing, Katya. I'm just getting ready to grill the sausages. Bring out the hard rolls and some hot mustard too."

The prospective travelers were delighted when Paul revealed he had brought a bag with him and was ready to begin the trip right away.

"Don't worry much about clothes," he advised. "Light, comfortable, outdoor stuff with swim suits and good walking shoes will do fine. We won't be going anywhere to dress up for. If you have summer reading, bring the books along. The hotel we're staying at is guaranteed to have no TV, and the only telephone is at the front desk."

"I'd like to get an early start in the morning, Petra. Is it all right for me to bunk on the rollout sofa in your family room?"

"Of course. I'll make it up for you. We'll pack after supper, get everyone to bed early, and be up before dawn. Will breakfast be here or on the road?"

"On the road," the children shouted in unison.

"So let it be written; so let it be done," Paul announced in the gravelly tones of Yul Brenner's Pharaoh from *The Ten Commandments*.

"I've always known you were a man of action," Petra murmured to Paul, "but this time you caught even me off guard."

"You may find me good at that," he said, clasping her hand with the one of his that was not encumbered by cooking tongs. Raising his voice for the benefit of all, he called out, "All right, everybody, come get the bratwurst."

Remembering his mountain-crossing experience in January, Paul took I-70 west, merging onto I-81 south through Virginia into Tennessee. It was an uneventful passage with light, midweek traffic and mostly clear skies. Petra and Paul alternated driving until they were well into Tennessee.

Near Knoxville, Paul brought them onto US Route 441 which cut straight through the Great Smoky Mountains National Park. The children grew excited, watching the massive, gray-mountain eminence steadily growing ahead.

Paul left the main road at Pigeon Forge to take rural, Wears Valley lanes into the park at Metcalf Bottom. The effect was striking as they drove abruptly from bright sunlight into cool, green shadows under a thick, forest canopy. A picnic ground in the bottom gave access to the narrow, winding Little River Road that linked sites east and west on the Tennessee side of the park.

"Do you remember what I told you at breakfast about the Wonderland Hotel?" Paul asked as he turned left onto Little River Road.

"Yes," Petra and the children responded in ragged unison.

"You might think hotels don't belong in the park, and you would be right. Gatlinburg, where lots of visitors stay, is on the edge of the park, but not actually in it. The Wonderland is still around only because it was here before this place became a park. It will not always be here though. I've been told the lease runs out sometime in the 90s. Then it will be abandoned and left for the forest to take back. Right now, I think it's one of the most beautiful and relaxing places in the world."

"I can see it," Spike called out.

"You have a good eye," Paul said.

Ahead of them, a road entered from the south, and the standard park sign said it led to Elkmont. Just yards away, a very plain, white sign with black lettering read Wonderland Hotel.

Paul turned at the sign and proceeded slowly along a narrow, winding, valley road that paralleled a fast-moving, stone-filled stream on their right.

"Elkmont," Paul told them, "is a camp site at the end of this road, but we're not going that far. In a little while, we should see the hotel above us on the left. It's a white clapboard building more than fifty yards up the mountain from the road."

"There it is," Paul said about ten minutes later. Before anyone could look, he threw the Buick into a tight, 180-degree turn to the left and careened up a steep gravel ramp around the mountain. The hotel came into view only when he turned into the gravel parking lot behind it.

"Okay," he said turning off the engine. "Here it really is."

They all laughed.

"Katya was right about one thing," Paul told Petra while they unloaded the car. "That last turn would have been a lot easier in my Daytona."

A stay at the Wonderland Hotel meant trading modernity for a remote part of the early twentieth century. The only evident additions were electricity and indoor plumbing. Communication was limited to a lone telephone at the hotel desk. No newspapers were delivered. Radios never seemed to be heard. The old-fashioned, polished-wood console in the hotel lounge might have worked, but nobody ever seemed to turn it on. The surrounding mountains blocked any television signals. Nothing was air conditioned, but that went unnoticed in the temperately cool mountain air.

The hotel was steeply perched above the road below, and the rushing stream beyond it fed eventually into the Little River for which Little River Road was named. Wooden steps from the steep-sloped front yard, along with the hotel's main door, gave access to a wide, embracing front porch full of rocking chairs that faced mountains to the west. The sun went down early, and the night showed no lights except from the hotel and occasional vehicles on the road below. The porch was well used day and night, but it never seemed crowded or lacking available rockers.

Inside the front door were an antiquated reception desk and a large lounge, richly fitted with comfortable wooden furniture and electric lamps for reading after dark.

All the single and double rooms were upstairs. They were small, sparsely decorated, and cleanly kept. The bathroom fixtures were adequate, but looked like they might have come from World War II army-surplus outlets. The room rate was higher than that of more comfortable quarters in Gatlinburg, but no one complained. These rooms were not meant to entertain or be lived in. They were places for guests to sleep, wash up, and store clothes while they did what they came for—wandering the park, relishing its beauty, and luxuriating in the peaceful serenity of it all. Petra, Paul, Spike, and Patty each had their own room.

Despite the Spartan tone of the quarters, Wonderland guests enjoyed one of the park's authentic indulgences. That was the home-style mountain cooking from its simple dining room at the back of the main building. Breakfast and an evening meal were served there on red-and-white-checked tablecloths. Choice was minimal, but the price was the same. Whatever the entrée, the sides all came in heaping-full, family-sized bowls.

Fortunately, the active daily routine of Paul, Petra, and the children minimized any likelihood of gaining weight from such indelicate gluttony twice a day. They swam at least once a day in the ice-cold stream that collected in a deep, rocky pool called the Sinks just west of the hotel.

They gradually explored as many features of the park as they could. There was a full day of driving and walking among relics of nineteenth-century mountain life in the meadows of Cades Cove. They designed one daytrip around a steep trek to the park's highest point at Clingman's Dome and spent another visiting the Cherokee Indian Reservation on the North Carolina side. Other days brought leisurely treks into sites of gorgeous waterfalls and primal scenes of remote mountain beauty.

Many hours went into simple hikes around the hotel or just relaxing with a book and the view from its vast front porch. Such local expeditions commonly made contact with deer and other wildlife in the area.

Only once did they venture into Gatlinburg to procure some obligatory souvenirs for friends and family in Maryland.

# 39

On their last afternoon in the park, after a farewell swim at the Sinks, Petra and Patty had gone for a final inspection of the variant wonders surrounding the hotel. Spike and Paul were simply enjoying some unfinished books and light conversation on the porch. Abruptly, Spike steered the talk to something less light.

"When are you and Aunt Petra getting married?" he asked bluntly.

"I don't believe she and I have directly talked about that yet."

"Well you're going to, aren't you?"

Paul leaned forward to place his open book face down on the porch railing. Then he leaned back in his rocker and turned to the boy, who was carefully looking straight ahead at the misty juncture of two distant peaks.

"I'd say we're proceeding on that assumption, but we're taking our time."

"Is that why you aren't sleeping together?" Spike asked, now facing Paul.

"There are several reasons for not moving on to that at the moment." Paul suppressed a smile and spoke casually. He did not want to appear condescending.

"Don't you love each other?"

"We do, but that is only part of the contract people make when they start exploring the prospect of marriage."

"Doesn't that mean sleeping together? Why don't you do it?"

Spike's matter-of-fact tone betrayed no guile so Paul proceeded with caution.

"You surprise me, Spike. Where did you get your information on the timing, order, and circumstances for love, marriage, and sexual relations?"

"Mom told me all about sex last year."

"I am grateful for that. Did she say anything about the part love and marriage play in the process?"

"She seemed kind of embarrassed about that part. She told me all about intercourse, but she said it was a very serious commitment that could even be dangerous—you know, pregnancy and diseases."

"Was this all news to you?"

"Not really. I hear a lot from the guys at school. Some of it was even in my Health Science class last year."

"This also comforts me, except for the stuff you hear from the other guys. Trust me. That is a case of the blind leading the blind—possibly over a cliff."

"I think I kind of knew that."

"Good for you. What did Katya tell you about how love, marriage, and temptation fit into the mix?"

"She said I was growing up fast, and I would start having feelings and physical reactions that might be very distracting."

"'Distracting' is an understatement. Just the recent change in your voice tells me that some of this has already happened. What do you say about that?"

"Sure it has," the boy said, lowering his gaze and now fiddling with the leg of his denim shorts. "It's kind of embarrassing sometimes, because I can't seem to control it. What I feel inside and show outside gets away from me. I can't hide what's on my mind. It's right out there for people to see."

"Don't bother trying to hide it; you won't be able to anyway. The important part is not your body, but what you do with it. Your mother is absolutely right about that. The intensity you feel will gradually become more controllable. That's what your mind and conscience are for. Just avoid doing things impulsively."

"I should not sleep with anybody, right?"

"It's not the sleeping you have to worry about. That's just a euphemism for sexual intercourse, which can easily crop up when gland-driven, adolescent bodies get too close together. Why do you think there are always faculty and parents at school parties?"

"I think I already knew that too."

"Beyond that, Spike, I have to admit that plenty of adults are not much better at handling sex than you might be right now. They just have less excuse for it than kids do. They know what's at stake, but choose to ignore it. That keeps a lot of divorce lawyers in business and helps them send their kids to Harvard."

"I think that's what my dad did to Mom," Spike said, suddenly looking straight into Paul's eyes.

"I'm sorry. It was thoughtless of me to use that example. I know nothing about your parents' breakup. A lot of divorces are not at all about adultery."

Paul paused, but the boy simply dropped his eyes and looked at his lap.

"Anyway, Spike, maybe this will help you understand why your Aunt Petra and I have left sex alone while we work out what is best for us both—now and for the rest of our lives."

"Don't you want each other?"

"We're in love. I think that has been true for years now—possibly since around the time I first met you—maybe even before that. Do you remember when we went to the Renaissance Festival together?"

Spike nodded.

"At that time, something stood between Petra and me. It kept us from being more than good friends. It was my job, but I recently gave that up. Can you imagine what might have become of our love if we had ignored that barrier and just gone to bed?"

The boy was looking at Paul again but did not answer.

"It could have ruined the real love between us. It would surely have magnified our differences and eroded our respect for each other. That's what happens when sex is just a sport. It's why Petra and I do not yet share a room or a bed—even if she would allow it—which I do not believe she would. Do you?"

The boy just shrugged, so Paul went on.

"Love, marriage, and sex go together, but only in that order. Other sequences are too risky. They can wreck everything and steal the joy and beauty God wants us to find."

Spike gave his chair several slow and deliberate rocks before looking over at Paul.

"I think I get it now—about myself anyway—but it won't be easy, will it?"

"You're right, Spike. Managing our sexuality is one of the trickiest things we grownups have to do. Ready or not, you are turning into one of us. Avoid every mistake you can, but admit to the ones you make. Don't hurt anyone else if you can help it."

"No," Spike said with an expression that was starkly grave for a fourteen-year-old. "That would be mean."

"Congratulations, young man," Paul said, reaching over to pat his shoulder. "You just made a very mature observation."

Spike nodded his head and resumed his reading.

Paul's analysis of the difference between love and libido had been as much an attempt to inform himself as to console the hormone-rampant youngster next to him. He left his book on the railing and looked off into the haze that was beginning to rise out of distant valleys.

# 40

It was after ten, and the children had recently gone to bed. Paul and Petra sat next to each other on the mostly darkened south end of the hotel porch. Only the sounds of the forest night were in the air. The two of them had barely spoken since seeing Spike and Patty off to bed. The silence felt comfortable and natural until Paul broke it.

"You'll never guess what Spike asked me about this afternoon."

"Let me think," she said, turning her head slowly to look at him. "Did it have anything to do with you and me not sharing a bedroom yet?"

Paul chuckled while Petra giggled immodestly.

"Do those two keep anything from each other?"

"Not that I've observed. Unlike many siblings, they are also best friends."

"How wonderful for them."

"I think so too."

"I would hope for us to be the same."

"Siblings?"

"Hardly. Am I safe in declaring that we are committed, if unconsummated, lovers?"

This was the first time Paul had spoken to her of love since bringing her home from the airport. After that, they had shared so much free-wheeling joy and affection that talking about it seemed unnecessary.

"Oh yes, Paul," she said standing up and turning to him as he rose to face her. Neither of them looked to see who else might be on the porch. It was late anyway, and the porch lights were off. They were totally absorbed with each other in that moment as they came together in a long, ardent kiss that knew little reserve.

Paul was reminded of his recent advice to Spike about keeping one's fleshly appetites under control. The adage that "talk is cheap" came sharply back to him. A moment later they were still closely embraced, but the right side of Petra's face rested comfortably against his chest.

*How wonderfully soft and warm she is,* he thought, *so pliantly loving and sweet. How could I ever let her go?*

"Would you like to visit Father Don with me when we get back to Maryland?" he whispered to her in the dark. "I think he might be able to help us do something we both want very much."

"Do you?" she asked coyly. "What would that be?"

"Maybe he would be willing to marry us around Labor Day—before we get even more impatient. I don't think we will need much instruction, and there is plenty of time for posting the banns."

"Oh yes, Paul," she said, eagerly pressing her palms against his back to draw him closer. "Right now if we could; maybe earlier than you said, to give us more time together before school starts."

"What did I just say about impatience?" he murmured into her hair, inhaling her honest scent and feeling the growing heat between them. "I wish I had a ring handy."

"Forget the ring. We'll get to that."

The warmth of their mutual passion kindled within him. Even now, he knew the emptiness he would feel every moment until they were one.

Unexpectedly, Paul became aware of a hand grasping his shoulder from behind. Reluctantly releasing his hold on Petra, he felt as if he had been thrown from the warm, safe deck of a ship into the relentless icy cold of an arctic sea.

Paul turned around to discover that the intrusive hand belonged to the old man who normally tended the desk in the evening.

"Yes?" Paul asked with a less than welcoming edge to his voice. He felt suddenly weak and confused.

"Excuse me, sir," the man said with obvious embarrassment. He appeared to be struggling with some great puzzle. "I think you have a telephone call."

# 41

"How did you find me, Barney?"

"Don't ask. I'm sure you will figure it out if you think a little."

"Okay, but why?"

"Is this phone clean?"

"Quit joking. Telephones are scarce around here. Outgoing calls go through a switchboard. I'll bet they come in that way too."

"It will have to do."

"Fine, Barney. Talk to me."

"It's about Norman and Jackie."

"What about them?" Paul's voice dropped to a lower register. He forgot about the hotel man a few steps away. Petra had come up behind him and was gently stroking his back, but he barely knew it.

"They nearly had a wreck last week," Barney enunciated very carefully to prevent any need for repetition.

Around the organization, saying someone had a wreck was a subtle reference to them being killed. Adding the word *nearly* suggested an attempt had failed.

"Was anyone else involved?"

"I cannot say for sure, but I suspect you are on the cusp of a pretty fair guess."

"Not so fast, Barney. I don't jump to long-distance conclusions without information. Is there any more?"

"Not now. When can you get here?"

"Who says I'm coming?"

"Aren't you?"

"I'm driving up tomorrow; I'll be there by late afternoon. Headquarters?"

"Good idea. I'll be looking for you—sometime after three?"

"More or less. It's not a special trip. I was coming back tomorrow anyway."

"That works for me."

"No promises, Barney. I just want to know how our friends are."

"We'll be here to tell you," Barney said just before the line went dead.

*Great,* Paul thought, hanging up the telephone. *Now what do I tell Petra?*

The two of them went back onto the porch to reoccupy their previous rockers and resume monitoring the dark forest before them. Turning in his chair to face her, Paul told Petra very briefly that he was being called back for a consultation about something left over from Paris. He did not anticipate going back to work over it, but for now he could not be sure. There were loyalties he might not be able to overlook.

Petra's reaction surprised him.

"I believe I understand," she said softly, looking straight into his eyes. "I've been thinking a lot this week. I remember what happened when I lost Jason. That time I shut myself away from everything that reminded me of him. I went to a dark place and locked myself in. Nothing got better until God opened my lightless cell to free me. Now that you and I are together, I will never go back there. Just tell me nothing will stop us from keeping the promises we made each other tonight."

"Nothing this side of death will ever change that," he said, briefly touching her hair with one hand. "Still, there is one more thing you ought to think about."

"What's that?"

"At the moment, you may have noticed, I am not working."

"That could not escape me, Paul, even if your former colleagues have not forgotten your phone number."

He laughed with her easily.

"I don't mean that I'm penniless."

"Oh, I'm glad of that."

"Seriously, I can take care of us for quite a while without drawing a paycheck. On the other hand, I cannot tell you what I'll be doing tomorrow, next month, or next year."

"Do you plan to stay unemployed?"

"Not a bit, but you should remember what I have said about my prospects. At the moment I am in a holding pattern. I expect to be working for God, but he still has not told me how that will happen or what I'll be doing."

"Do you think you might be called to the clergy?"

"Maybe, but I doubt it. Aren't there already plenty of them around? Why would God route my soul through the Vale just to get one more minister for his Church? That is only one of the questions I keep asking myself.

"I know the Lord will point the way when he is ready. Until then, I have to caution you about signing a long-term contract with a man who cannot tell you what tomorrow will be like."

Petra maintained a faintly tolerant look while he spoke. Then she took one of his hands in both of hers, brought the back of it briefly to her lips, and caressed it against her cheek.

"I hope it does not embarrass you to know that these questions have crossed my mind. I have considered them, prayed over them, and balanced them against the faith I have in God and in you. I believe God has a place for me in whatever lies in store for you. Why else would he have made you such an important part of my life?"

"God bless you, dear Petra. You make my concerns seem so trivial."

"All that aside, don't forget I'll be working too."

"You shouldn't have to."

"Maybe not, but you couldn't force me out of teaching with a charge of dynamite."

"I'm okay with that."

Rising from his chair, Paul gently took her upper arms, lifted her to her feet, and planted a quick kiss on her forehead. Then they told the deskman goodnight and went quietly up to bed in their separate rooms.

Paul's happiness was too overpowering for him to get to sleep quickly. He almost forgot about Norman and Jackie until the next day.

# 42

Paul and Barney occupied their familiar chairs, facing Grogan across his desk.

"Your security oath still holds you to protect any information you receive here," Grogan reminded Paul, while passing him a conspicuously classified electrical message.

"Okay, but I'll be glad when you stop showing me this stuff."

From habit, Paul first scanned the whole text. Then he went back to read for detail. It was a report from the organization's resident operator in France. Paul and Barney had not contacted him during their operation, but he was Grogan's official link to the Nerviers. Mainly, he was their paymaster.

Grogan and Barney remained silent until Paul finished and dropped the message in the center of the desk. Paul waited, but no one spoke. Finally, he broached the question.

"A mishap in the kitchen last Friday evening? A sudden, unexplained, gas explosion? Thank God Norman and Jackie were detained by their concierge only seconds before their apartment went up."

"What do you think? An accident or an attempt?" Barney probed.

"Be serious. The only accident was when they didn't die. The investigation ruled out chance. Besides, the Nerviers are professionally careful people. They avoid risky things."

"Was it to kill or just to warn?" Grogan asked.

"You don't warn people this way. Warnings are supposed to change behavior, not kill people or take out real estate. What else have Jackie and Norman got on their plate?"

Grogan propped his elbows on the desk and clasped his hands in front of him before responding.

"They had a few minor things running—mostly divorce and industrial stuff—nothing of substance except the Brecht case."

"Brecht?" Barney began before settling back in his chair. "I almost forgot. He may have been Khrabovich to us, but he was only Wilhelm Brecht to them."

"Right," Paul said, "but who do we know with a reputation for producing gas-driven accidents in the kitchen?"

"We too were reminded of Francois Declaire," Barney answered.

"But how would he learn about them, and why would he care?" Paul objected. "With his history and all the uniforms around Rue Lincoln that night, he couldn't have gone back inside. What would he have wanted there anyway?"

"He had personal effects in the house—maybe a little money," Barney responded.

"Yes, but he would have to go to the police to claim them," Paul answered. "Do you think he would have?"

Barney frowned and shook his head.

"I'd like to know," Paul went on, "how he connected the Nerviers to the affair at all. Even if he did, why go after them?"

"I've no idea," Grogan put in. "But what about the bearer bonds? Could they be a connection?"

"That or something close," Paul replied. "Declaire had to be in on his boss's stash of wealth. He may not have known where it came from or exactly where it was kept, but there was obviously a cash kitty around to pay him and keep the place up."

Paul now leaned forward in his chair.

"Who knows, Grogan? Brecht might even have given him a small housekeeping account. Maybe day-to-day expenses were too irksome for a man of leisure like the major. Norman said he treated Francois more like a companion than a servant on their evening excursions around the neighborhood."

Grogan nodded at that, and Paul continued.

"Such egalitarian treatment may have encouraged Declaire to be patient, but I'll bet he had plans for Brecht's resources that did not include Herr Brecht. Then the man was dead, and the prize went with him. Declaire's record with the law kept him out of the house while the police were there. Once they were gone, he had nothing left to look for."

"The bonds were out of play," Barney put in. "Either somebody had taken them, or the police would confiscate them. Still, wouldn't he want to know what happened?"

"Of course," Paul said. "He had nothing else to do, so he probably canvassed the neighborhood for gossip. Like the police, he may have tied the uproar in Rue Lincoln to Brecht's death at the Etoile."

"I'd bet on that," Grogan opined.

"It still doesn't tell us how he found Norman and Jackie," Barney said. "Maybe it was his connections with the Paris underworld."

"Just think about that, Grogan," Paul suggested. "He seems to have unearthed their involvement, even when the police did not."

"Keep talking," Grogan said, now grimly motionless.

"Even knowing who they were, why would he go after them?" Barney asked.

Now Paul remembered the conclusion Brother Arnold had drawn from knowing that Khrabovich was able to see the demon at the Etoile. God did not make that possible. Only the devil would give him that talent.

*What was Khrabovich's satanic connection, and how did Declaire fit in?*

"That's hard to say," Paul responded to Barney's question. "Maybe it was just meanness or revenge, but I suspect more. Could some evil business have been cooked up between Francois and the major? I saw something very strange at the Etoile when Khrabovich died. I don't think anyone else did—except Khrabovich."

"Is this more guesswork?" Grogan asked, unclasping his hands and lowering them to the desktop. "Or is it something you brought back from the afterlife? What kind of evil are you talking about? What did you see at the Etoile anyway?"

Paul was surprised to hear Grogan credit his Vale experience with any value. His earlier comments had been mostly dismissive.

"Never mind what I saw. I didn't dream it up, but I doubt if it would help us now. What we need is a way to deal with Monsieur Declaire before he gets lucky and blows up something besides empty kitchens."

"We're working on that," Grogan replied.

"Do you have anything yet?"

"Not much, but we suspect he's no longer in France."

"What about Norman and Jackie?"

"They're out of the country too. We are making them as safe as we can."

"I suppose that's the best you can do. Is there anything more before I go back to the real world?"

"As a matter of fact, there is," Barney announced.

"What is it this time?"

"I took a phone call for you here yesterday that I failed to mention last night. It just didn't come up."

"Who would call me here?"

"He said his name was Bill Farben. He was kind of cagey, but he said you will remember him. He left a phone number." Barney passed Paul a small piece of notepaper he had taken from his shirt pocket.

"Bill Farben?" Paul asked, wrinkling his forehead as he looked at the page. "Did he say what he wanted?"

"Yeah, he said he wanted to talk to you about someone named Otto."

"I get it."

"You do?"

"Yep, Bill was the cover name of the guy who was handling Patroon. Otto was the name given to Patroon when I interviewed him at the IG Farben building in Frankfurt. Remember?"

"Oh, right. Do you know what he wants with you?"

"I think so. Remember my report? I found out this kid Otto, whatever his name really is, saved my life by refusing to shoot me for Major Khrabovich. That's quite a debt, so I asked Bill to let me know if there was ever anything I could do for Otto."

"I hope this is good news, Paul," Grogan said. "Let me know if I can help."

Another anomaly in Grogan's behavior caught Paul's attention. Willingness to become involved in the personal affairs of others seemed entirely out of character.

"Thanks, Grogan. I will."

# 43

Back from the mountains, Paul had stopped at Petra's place just long enough to shower and change clothes. From there he took his own car out to see Grogan and Barney. After that, Petra was to meet him for a bite at J. K.'s Pub before he went home to D.C.

Driving back into Columbia, Paul thought about the two people who were just reappearing on his horizon: Francois Declaire and Otto. He would have to talk with the man named Bill about Otto, so now he focused on the shady Frenchman.

Paul had seen Declaire only once. Paul and Norman were sitting at a sidewalk café in the Champs Elysees just before the assault on Khrabovich. The tall, slender man strode smartly out of Rue Lincoln, turning toward the Place de la Concorde. Paul guessed him to be between thirty-five and forty years old. He was wearing a light-blue sport jacket and a brimmed, dark-blue hat. His features were regular enough, but his complexion was pale and his face had a brooding quality.

*He doesn't see much daylight,* Paul had thought. *But he is pretty trim for a professional cook. What is it I don't like about this guy?*

Despite the bizarre death of his employer, Declaire had seemed to escape the attention of the Paris police. Had they even connected him to the residence in Rue Lincoln? Whatever his motive, he was loose and seriously out to get the Nerviers.

Was this only about his former employer's wealth? He must have coveted that but failed to get much. How had he associated the Nerviers with what happened at the house or the Etoile?

Paul was the only remaining player present at the Etoile incident. He was certainly the sole surviving observer of that demonic apparition goading Khrabovich to his fatal leap. What was that thing there for anyway? Was its post-mortem attack just opportunistic soul-grabbing, or was it taking a trophy?

Suppose Declaire and the demon were driven by the same essence of evil Paul later faced in his vision of the terminal ward. Did that give Declaire power to track down anyone he went after? Would the Nerviers be his only target? Was Paul on his list too?

What about Khrabovich himself? He lived a vile enough life, but Paul could not directly connect him to the devil—at least not until Declaire came along. Paul remembered Norman's reference to Declaire's occult-narcotics connection. Might Declaire have introduced the major to something darker than drugs? Had Declaire become his satanic intercessor in return for some of the major's money? Who was really in charge at the house in Rue Lincoln?

*Aren't you getting a little close to the edge, Paul?*

What edge?

*You're bordering on paranoia, and you may be drifting south of the border.*

Paul was just pulling into the small parking lot next to J. K.'s. The car windows were already down, so he took a parking place close in, turned off the engine, and prepared for a quick self examination.

*Good idea. No more driving until we've checked your brain for pinholes.*

Okay, but I am not going out of my mind—not even close.

*Oh, no? Then what's all this stuff about dark arts and satanic priests?*

Does that bother you? Weren't you with me when I toured the terminal ward? Haven't I been attacked or threatened by demons often enough to get your attention?

*I don't deny demonic influence in the world, but aren't you going a little overboard by pulling out witchcraft and wizardry as if they really work here?*

Don't they? Don't Satan and his spiritual servants walk the earth? What are they here for? Most of the humans they influence don't even know it. The devil wants it that way so that anyone who tries to expose him looks like a superstitious crackpot.

*Just because Declaire is a bad guy doesn't make him an accomplice of the devil.*

What would?

*I don't know: forming a coven or running satanic rituals I suppose. Do you have that on the Frenchman?*

I saw a demon performing at the Etoile when a man who might have summoned him died. Khrabovich saw it too. You're not saying God gave him that talent, are you?

*Brother Arnold was clear on that point, but the old Franciscan isn't infallible.*

He has been a reliable source so far. Why would Khrabovich get personal demonic attention if he hadn't been one of the devil's own?

*Maybe for the same reason one of Satan's servants came after you on that mountain road. That might even have been the devil himself. How would you know?*

You're way off track. I'm the devil's target because God has a job for me, and the devil doesn't like it. That is behind everything bad that has happened to me lately. Remember when the organization thought me a traitor? Look how long it took to clean that up. Now Francois Declaire is menacing friends of mine. Have I seen the last of him?

*Maybe not, but aren't you jumping to conclusions with all this Satanist malarkey.*

Give me a better idea.

*I can't.*

The prosecution rests.

# 44

The day bartender was going off duty, and J. K. was busy clearing the cash register when Paul came in. A few daytime regulars were still at the bar, but the supper crowd was only beginning to trickle in.

"Evening, J. K."

"So it is, my good man," the arch proprietor said, looking up. "Are you waiting for the lovely Petra to appear?"

"It's a barely concealed anticipation."

"Not hidden at all that I can tell. It's been quite a while since you've graced my modest establishment—late January wasn't it?"

"You have a good memory."

"I've hardly seen more of Petra, except for a few nights in May, when she came by with some of the ladies' softball crowd. You're early enough to grab a standing bar if you like. A draft Bass, isn't it?"

The publican had a good memory for the favorite drinks of his clientele, even when they had been absent for a while.

"Just what I wanted," Paul said, taking a seat at one of the standing bars. There he sipped gratefully from the pint glass of well-chilled, dark-amber liquid J. K. brought him before resuming his tally of the day's take.

The Pub had begun to fill for the cocktail hour and early dining by the time Petra arrived. J. K. greeted her near the door. With a clap of his hands and a voice like cracking pottery, he jovially invited her to sample his current supply of Merlot *ordinaire* and gestured at the same time toward Paul at the standing bar.

She was dressed in an open-necked, sleeveless, blue top, tucked into white shorts over well-tanned legs and the same street shoes he first saw her wearing in Paris. Her outfit paralleled the style to which she had kept during their past week in the mountains.

As she approached, Paul felt his heart surge and he rose to kiss her cheek. She smiled up at him and boldly returned his gesture by planting a quick kiss upon his lips. Then they sat down.

"You ought to be more cautious about such public displays of affection," J. K. said caustically, as he approached them with menus in one hand and her wine in the other. "You might give my bar a good name and drive me, perforce, into the street."

"Don't worry, J. K. He has promised to make me an honest woman before the leaves fall."

"I never thought for a moment you could be anything less, my child. Still, you wouldn't pull my leg about getting married, would you?"

"Not unless he's pulling mine," she said.

"That, dear lady, would call for pistols at dawn, and I rarely rise from my couch so early any more." Then he drew Petra's hand to his lips and reached across to shake Paul's.

"Congratulations," he added with a low-register laugh, "and please consider tonight's elegant repast to be priced at a celebratory, ten-percent discount."

Now J. K. moved away from their standing bar to speak with other customers and, no doubt, to share the news he had just acquired.

Tonight Paul and Petra both decided to make a meal of the Pub's bread-and-cheesy French onion soup, which was delivered to them hot from the oven in individual baking crocks. Richly seasoned and crusted over with thick layers of cheese, the soup went beyond its advertised role as an appetizer to become a fairly generous entrée.

At first, they talked very little while dealing with this gooey, tricky-to-eat, hot stuff. Most of their dinner discussion revolved around the recent change in their relationship from close friends to promised lovers. Other than today's travel in the car with the children, this was their first opportunity to explore their new roles.

"I was on such a short leash when we got back," Paul said, "I didn't have time to get Katya's reaction to our marriage plans. What does she think?"

"She's delighted of course," Petra replied, attempting to terminate a long string of cheese that awkwardly extended itself between her mouth-level spoon and the crock. It stubbornly refused to break loose even when she bit into it.

"Need any help?" Paul offered with a smile.

"No thank you," she mumbled, still talking around some of the cheese. "I can handle this. I've done it before."

"I know." Paul was struggling with his own cheese, which threatened to burn the roof of his mouth. "I've seen you do it."

Now they both burst into laughter that was muffled by their need to keep their mouths mostly closed.

"I give up," Petra said after a few seconds.

"Not me," Paul replied. "No stringy cheese is going to get the best of me."

"Oh no?" she asked between giggles. "Take a look at your shirt. The cheese has already won."

"Well, if it's going to stick to me anyway, so be it," he said, bringing a small spoonful of soup to his mouth and licking his lips, despite the residual strings of cheese that still linked it to the bowl.

"I suspect," said J. K., who had arrived to help Paul with what still adhered to his clothing, "we should conduct qualifying events before allowing amateurs to order our onion soup."

With that, all three of them lapsed into uncontrolled mirth. The remaining soup was consumed primarily in silence, punctuated by occasional fits of giggling from Petra.

Later, over coffee, they talked more about their future family arrangements. Petra told him that Katya had suggested moving out when they were married.

"What do you think about that?" she asked.

"Is it really necessary? I understand why you could not move into my place. Even if there was enough room, it would put you too far from your work. You already have your own room and bath at the house. Why not just upgrade to a king-size bed, and add me to the population?"

"That might work for a while, but wouldn't Katya start feeling like a fifth wheel?"

"Maybe, but it would give us time to look around and see what we want to do. Katya and the kids could be doing the same thing. She is a real estate agent after all. Hey, she could pick up two commissions in the process—one on whatever we buy and another for selling your place. She might even decide to buy it herself, so the children would not have to move."

"I like that idea," Petra replied. "She may just leave anyway, but she would have plenty of time to think things over and look at her options."

"Consider it a deal. When we get closer to moving time, I can get rid of my apartment and sell or put most of my stuff in storage."

"Incidentally," Petra added, "I did not get around to telling you what a good week Katya had while we were gone."

"That means you can tell me now," he said, reaching across the standing bar to take her hand.

"She has a new client she's excited about in more ways than one."

"Oh?"

"Yes. She calls him a walk-in—that's somebody who just came into her agency looking for a house when she was on floor duty."

"That means she gets the commission, right?"

"On whatever she manages to sell him, and from what she told me, he is looking for something near the high end of the market."

"Very interesting, but didn't you describe her excitement as being of more than one kind?"

"Yeah. She finds him very attractive."

"Is her attraction reciprocated?"

"She seems to think so."

"Why wouldn't it be? Except for being tall and wearing her hair blonde, she is the living image of her beautiful, younger sister."

"Thank you, kind sir," Petra said, nodding to the compliment. "She thinks he is very cosmopolitan."

"How is that?"

"She said he is European, apparently loaded, and a smooth operator. He's already taken her to lunch, and they are going out tonight after she shows him a prospect."

"What about the kids?"

"They're spending the night with friends to brag about their mountain adventure."

"How convenient," Paul drawled, gently squeezing her hand. "What's his name?"

"She just calls him Frank."

*Maybe I am paranoid*, Paul thought. *There's nothing here to justify suspicion.*

"What's his nationality?" he asked.

"She told me he's French."

*That doesn't help.*

"Really, how long has he been here?"

"I'm not sure, but I got the impression he just arrived from the continent. She says he speaks wonderful English."

"I cannot explain," Paul said in a very serious tone. "There is probably nothing to worry about, but I have to talk to Katya right away."

"What do you mean?" she asked, concerned by Paul's sudden change in behavior.

"I just need you to get her on the phone now. Okay?"

"I'll try, but she was almost ready to go out when I left the house. She wanted to take her client by a sale property while it was still light. I have no idea where they are going to dinner."

"Please try, Petra."

"I will," she said, rising to go to the pay phone. "Got a quarter?"

Paul handed her some coins from his pocket and waved to the waiter for the bill. By the time he settled up, Petra was back.

"No answer," she said. "I knew there wouldn't be."

"Do you know what property she was going to show him?"

"Oddly enough, I do. It is sort of a landmark. Is that where you want to go?"

"Yes. Maybe we can catch them there."

"I'll guide you. Just follow my car."

"I'm not sure I want you along for this, Petra."

"It's the only way you're going to get there."

"In that case, let's just take my car. We can come back for yours later."

"I'm good with that."

They waved at J. K. on their way to the door.

# 45

Petra guided Paul out of Columbia into some hill country northwest of Ellicott City and onto a narrow, paved road that wound gradually upward. Except for acknowledging her directions, he remained silent. He had nothing to say that would make sense to her. How could he explain his guesswork assumptions about someone he only imagined might be Francois Declaire?

Of all the Frenchmen on earth, why would the only murderer Paul knew turn up near people Paul cared about? How could he know anything about Paul or where to find him? If Frank was Francois, why was he after Paul?

Paul had asked the same questions about the attempt against Norman and Jackie Nervier with no better result. Declaire's motives went beyond criminality and greed. If Paul was right, Declaire was a dedicated agent of the devil, one of those conscious servants Brother Arnold talked about. If that was so, the man knew whatever he needed, and private revenge was only a spur to the larger design of his master's intent.

Paul was skeptical of his own suspicion, but he could not to take chances with Katya's safety. Petra might be placing herself in danger by tagging along, but she had insisted on it.

Paul's options were limited and growing fewer by the minute. He could not call the Howard County Police about a nefarious Frenchman who might do something bad because the devil told him to. Grogan might have helped, but time for that had run out.

"There it is," Petra called out, pointing ahead toward the right side of the road.

The house was an old, three-story, limestone-block mansion on rising ground. It sat among large, converging oaks, which had begun to bury it in shadows from the sun's continuing descent in the west. Paul stopped the car and killed the engine at the apex of a curved driveway in front of the main entrance. There was no other vehicle in sight.

"I want you to lock yourself in the car while I look around. The keys are in the ignition if you need to get away."

"Don't kid me. If my husband-to-be thinks my sister is in some kind of trouble, I'm not going to cringe in the car while he goes off to find her. Put the keys in your pocket."

"Forgive me," he said with an unrestrained smile as he came around the car. He helped her out of the low-built Daytona and put his right arm around her shoulders to guide her toward the house.

"I had forgotten I'm engaged to Wonder Woman."

"The place looks empty. I don't know if it's been lived in lately. Katya said it has only now come on the market."

"It won't do any harm to check things out," he replied, not quite sure he believed it.

Circling the house slowly, they saw no light coming from inside and no evidence of a car or other human activity around it. Paul held Petra's hand to coordinate their progress and keep them steadily moving. The place looked deserted, but he was taking no chances. Something might be waiting in the darkness that now reigned over the backyard. They had almost reached the southeast corner of the house, shrouded in oncoming twilight, when they heard sounds coming from the wooded area beyond.

Paul pulled Petra to him and gently placed a finger on her lips to command stillness and silence. They remained motionless as the noise of bodies passing through brush grew louder. Eventually, they heard quiet voices and saw intermittent signs that suggested a flashlight in the hand of a moving arm. Then a man and woman in light clothing came out of the woods. The man was carrying the flashlight. They continued moving forward, as if to pass the house on the south side. Paul took Petra's hand and walked out of the shadows into the path of the approaching hikers.

"Good evening," the man called out. "Did you come to look at the house? We've heard it's for sale."

"Yes," Paul responded, "but it looks like we're too late. We were supposed to meet an agent here, but we got delayed in traffic."

"That must have been who we saw on our way into the woods. There was this pretty blonde woman coming out the front door with a man. She was a smart dresser—high heels and all—like most real estate people on the job. She locked up, and they were headed for their car as we passed. They were talking to each other, so we didn't bother them."

"Just like a man," his female companion added, mockingly. "He can probably tell you how high her skirt was above the knee, but not a word about the man. He was tall, dark-haired, and sort of pale in the face. He was wearing a gray suit with a thin, black tie."

They all laughed at her keen observation, but Paul was not happy to learn that Frank bore even a general resemblance to Francois.

"Well," Paul said, turning to Petra, "It sounds like we missed her. We'll just call her tomorrow."

"Thanks folks," he added with a wave, as he and Petra walked back to the car.

*What next?* he thought. *Am I out of choices?*

Neither of them spoke until Paul had driven off the lot and they were back on the pavement headed down the hill they had come up to get there. Then Petra found her voice.

"All right, Paul. Are you going to tell me something now?"

"About what?"

"What are we doing and why?" Her tone was no longer patient. She would not abide his evasions much longer.

"I told you. I wanted to talk to Katya."

"Not until I started talking about her new client. Suddenly, you became concerned about where she was, what she was doing, and who she was with. I am a patient woman, Paul. I also love you to pieces, but there are limits, and you are nearing them."

*How can I help her understand?*

"Spit it out, Paul! What is going on with my sister?"

"I don't know. I only suspect, and there is nothing certain about my suspicion."

"What is it?" Now her voice had an edge on it like the squeal of a rusty hinge.

Paul remembered the last time Petra had spoken to him this way. That was on Okinawa many years before. Grogan had sent him to tell her Jason was dead. Paul was also supposed to talk her into suppressing the actual circumstances of his death.

*I couldn't even tell her what she was being asked to hold back.*

That meeting had brought them both the kind of anguish only God could heal. Now Petra was asking him again to tell the truth about a family member. No security oath held him back this time.

Still he feared for both Katya and Petra. Whatever hellish emissary might be sent to block his work for God, was he any less bound to protect those he cared for?

*Just a minute, you jerk. What makes you think you can do that anyway? Can you beat the devil at his own game? That is God's business, not yours.*

Paul gently slowed the car, pulled off the lightless country road, stopped, and turned off the engine.

"You're right Petra. The last time I kept something from you, we were both ruined for a long time. It nearly destroyed us. I can't let that happen again. God saved us then, and we have to believe he will do that now—but up front this time, before we mess things up by ourselves."

Petra turned in her seat to face him and took his right hand in both of hers.

*She is so wise and comforting. All the anger is gone.*

"What is it?" No tinge of challenge or accusation remained in her voice.

"There is a man, a Frenchman. I suspect him of great evil. He is certainly a criminal—a murderer. He recently tried to kill some friends of mine. Only today did I realize he is in direct service to the devil. Even then, I did not think he was in this country—not until you started to tell me about Katya's new client."

Petra squeezed his hand to encourage him.

"I have told you about my life in the Vale and my conviction that God has some very special work for me to do here. That makes me a natural enemy of Satan, not just because he hates all humanity—he does, you know—almost as much as he hates God. Still, any success God gives me in serving him spites what the devil wants done to oppose God. That makes me a target for whatever he can throw at me."

"I understand," she said, lifting his hand and softly kissing the back of it, "and I am afraid for you."

"So far, God has vigorously protected me from demons, but I want you to remember what I told you in Paris."

"You told me a lot of things there. Which do you mean?"

"I suggested that people near me—those I care about most—might become targets too."

"And I remember telling you I was up to that challenge. I also…" She stopped abruptly. Then she went on with fear in her voice. "Oh, dear God, do you think Katya could be in that kind of danger too?"

"She is, if the man she's with is the one I just told you about. Moreover, the description we heard from the woman at the house matches what I know of his looks."

"What can we do?" she asked in a shrill voice that now projected Paul's fear for her sister.

"I was warned about this by a very holy man, a Franciscan brother, and I know the wisdom of his counsel. I am ashamed of myself. Instead of following his advice, I have wasted time running all over the place like some kind of lab rat."

"Never mind that; what can we do now?"

"You already have one of my hands in yours," Paul said. "Now take them both, and do what I know has saved me before. Pray with me for Katya's safety. Remember what I told you about God and time? What we pray for now can be granted by God whenever it suits him—the plea we make now may have been granted hours ago. We have no way of knowing how or when God answers our prayers. We only know for certain that he does and he will."

"I believe that."

"Good. Pray with me for Katya's safety and soul. Pray with all your heart, as I will pray with mine."

"Dear God," he called out, "save your servant Katya from all harm this night, and protect her from the powers of your ancient enemy who wants only and always to confound your righteous will and love for us all. O God, make speed to save her, O Lord make haste to help her. Glory to the Father, and to the Son, and to the Holy Spirit. As it was in the beginning, is now and will be forever. Amen."

Now Paul released her hands and turned to the steering wheel.

"Pray, Petra, pray. Don't stop yet. Don't stop until we get home. Pray to God Almighty for the relief and protection of Katya."

Still praying in his heart, Paul started the car and drove straight to Petra's house.

# 46

Pulling into Petra's driveway, Paul was very encouraged when he saw Katya's car ahead of them and the house completely lighted from within. He doubted Declaire's worst behavior would be compatible with so much light. He also knew that Petra and Katya did not normally leave the place so fully illuminated when they went out at night.

"Don't stop praying yet," he told Petra, "but I think we are about to see another of God's great and wondrous works."

"Please, Lord!" she shouted, as they scrambled from the car to rush across the grass.

The front door was locked, which in itself was not unusual after dark. While Petra fumbled for a key in her small handbag, they heard Katya call out from inside.

"Who's there?"

"It's Paul and Petra. Look through the peephole," Paul responded.

The bolt was audibly drawn, and the door opened. Katya pulled Petra into the entry hall. Paul followed closely, pushing the door shut and locking it behind them. Maybe the danger had passed, but he was taking no chances.

"I thought you were going out this evening," Petra said as they moved up a few steps to the right and into the family room.

"I was, and I did," Katya told her. "But then my date went creepy on me."

She had apparently been home long enough to change from her day-and-dinner clothes into a green shorts-and-halter combination with simple, brown, leather sandals. Her face and figure were out of the same mold as Petra, but there was nothing petite about her tall and slender frame.

"What happened?" Petra asked.

"Wait a minute," Paul interrupted. "What is your client's name, Katya?"

"He told me to just call him Frank, but his name is Francois Declaire," she said, collapsing onto the corner of a sofa with Paul and Petra standing nearby. "He's French; I've seen his passport."

*He's in plain sight,* Paul thought. *He bailed out under his own identity right after the attempt on Norman and Jackie. Grogan said Declaire had probably left France. Now here he is.*

"He appeared to have resources," Katya continued, "and he told me he was looking for a large, fashionable place in the country to entertain and conduct business. He said he would be developing interests in both Baltimore and Washington. He was charming and seemed inclined to mix his real estate search with some fun. I thought that might be a kick, so I did nothing to discourage him. Besides that, my commission for the grade of place he claimed to want would have paid the bills for at least a year."

"Did he ask personal questions?" Paul inquired.

"From the start he wanted to know about my home and family. I even brought him here for lunch between two of our showings. That may have been a mistake, but he behaved perfectly—maybe too perfect. He didn't make anything remotely like a pass. I was almost offended, but that made him even more attractive to me."

"Did you tell him anything about me?" Paul continued.

"That's kind of funny. I didn't much notice it at the time, but he encouraged me to talk about Petra, and that led to telling him things about you."

"And since he is French, I'm sure you mentioned that she and I had recently visited his homeland."

"Now that you ask, yes; he was very interested in that."

"But you thought that was just a matter of patriotic pride."

"I suppose so. Was I wrong?"

"Not at all, but tell us what happened tonight. What set your teeth on edge this time?"

Katya settled back into the sofa, while Petra sat down facing her at the opposite end. Paul remained standing near the center of the room.

"I took him out early to show the house while there was still plenty of light," Katya began. "You know which one, Petra. I mentioned it this afternoon after you got back."

"Yes. We went there looking for you tonight, but you were long gone. A couple of neighbors told us about seeing you earlier."

Katya cocked an eyebrow but continued with her story.

"He made me feel kind of strange this time. He had seemed very attentive when visiting other prospects, but once we were inside this one, he showed almost no interest. He suddenly seemed to be just too tired of it all. The only thing he talked about was our evening out. It was as if that had become our sole purpose for being together. By the time we left the place, he was getting pretty free with his speech and even his hands. I've been around some weird guys, but this was a total reversal from the witty, considerate personality he had shown me before.

"When we got back in my car, I put him on notice about the hands. He appeared to back off, so I thought that was settled. He's staying at the Cross Keys Inn near the lake and had heard about the Rusty Scupper, so that's where we went for drinks and dinner. You know what the atmosphere is like there—pretty formal in the dining room, but kind of crazy upstairs in the bar."

Paul and Petra nodded.

"Happy hour ran until seven. I just had a gin-and-tonic, but Frank ordered double martinis back-to-back. He was getting well sloshed by the time we were called to dinner, but he still grabbed a third double to take in with him. You know what the dining room down stairs is like—all plush, comfortable, and dimly lit with a nice view of the lake. It can be very romantic."

"But not this time, huh?" Paul queried.

"No way; we decided on a London-broil-for-two, but I was the only one to eat much of it. He ordered a bottle of good cabernet sauvignon with the meal, but I only got a half-glass. He gulped down the rest while ignoring his steak.

"Conversation became very one-sided while we ate. I hoped if I kept quiet he might pipe down, but that didn't work. He just got louder and more obnoxious. I could tell that other people in the room were beginning to notice. I thought we would be able to leave after the dessert cart came by, but he suddenly decided we ought to try a very old and incredibly expensive XO cognac he found on the after-dinner menu. A slug of that stuff would have been fifty bucks at least—too much for me in more ways than one. That was the end of my evening."

Katya's face now reflected a revulsion she must have felt at the moment she was talking about.

"'Look here, Frank.' I told him, 'I've had as much to drink as I want, and you are way beyond the limit. Just pay the bill and let me drop you at the hotel.'"

"Was that the end of it?" Petra asked.

"Don't I wish?" Katya replied with another look of disgust. "Suddenly, he got a very strange look on his face. He was drunk of course, but I swear this was no part of that. In fact, his speech suddenly cleared, as if the alcohol no longer affected his tongue. It developed an eerie, echoing quality that was appealing and scary at the same time. Can you imagine that?"

"It's not simple," Petra said, "but we know some things about this man you don't. I'll believe anything you say, except that he gave you a good time."

Katya's expression turned wide-eyed as she continued.

"What happened next is still hard for me to figure out, but I saw it and heard it. His voice dropped to a volume only I could hear, and his manner went from boisterous to oily. Now he was like a carnival pitchman playing persuasive *gigolo*. First he talked about the pricey cognac, but the proposition escalated in a hurry. It was so arrogant and insulting I can repeat it almost word-for-word.

"'You don't understand, my dear,' he told me. 'This *liqueur* is a marvelous anodyne that will move you to take me with you. Let me give you peace through what I can make you become. I can help you know what I know and serve whom I serve. I can bring you pleasures you've never dreamed of. Wouldn't you like that, my lovely child?'"

Katya paused, indicating that her quotation was complete.

"What did you say to that?" Petra asked impatiently.

"Not a damn thing, but I kicked him under the table as hard as I could and as close as I could to the place I wanted to kick him the most."

"What happened then?" Paul inquired. He had an uncontrollable smirk on his face.

"The drunkenness regained control, and he almost fell out of his chair," she said with obvious delight. "By then, I was grateful. He had made my getaway easy."

"I can imagine," Petra put in with a note of amusement in her voice.

"On the way out, I told the head waiter that the gentleman was having some kind of fit. I also suggested he might need some help getting back to his hotel. The Cross Keys is nearly next door, but I'll bet Frank needed a cab to get there tonight."

"See, Petra," Paul said. "Never question the power of prayer."

Petra smiled and nodded.

"What's that about?" Katya asked.

"Nothing much," he said. "Petra can tell you about it later. By the way, you don't happen to know the number of Frank's hotel room, do you?"

The scathing look he received from Katya convinced him not to pursue that question.

"Skip it," he said. "Do you have any idea when he arrived here from France?"

"No, I didn't examine his passport that closely, but he came into the office on Monday this week, when you two were long gone to the mountains."

"Did you mention to him tonight that we had just come back?"

"Now that you ask, I did, and guess what?"

"You tell me."

"It was while we were on our way to the showing. He started acting crazy right after that."

"That's a very interesting observation," Paul noted.

"I didn't make the connection at the time, but that's exactly when he went nuts."

"After the way he bungled things tonight," Paul advised, "I don't think he will try reconnecting with you. If he does, keep your distance, and let me know right away."

"I'll have no trouble remembering that. Thanks for caring."

"Okay if I use your phone?" he asked.

In the kitchen, Paul picked up a wall-mounted handset and punched in the home number that Grogan had given him the last time he quit. Calling Grogan at home was something he had never done before. Grogan, he found, answered his home phone just as he always did at work.

"Grogan," the telephone receiver spat gruffly.

"Hi, boss."

"I'm not your boss. That is the only reason you have this number."

"I hadn't expected to use it so soon. I just happened to run into some information about Monsieur Francois."

"Is that so?"

"He has been in this country since at least Monday. He is a registered guest of the Cross Keys Inn in Columbia, Maryland."

"Is he still there?"

"He did a lot of drinking tonight. You might grab him there if you hurry, but don't bet on it. His scheme for tonight did not work out. He'll bail out as soon as he wakes up enough to recognize his risk."

"Is he registered under his own name?"

"I suspect he is. He has been very open about his identity and nationality. Judging from where he lodges and dines, he came into substantial money before leaving home."

"What's he doing in Columbia?"

"He spent this week shopping for real estate in Howard County. That was just a cover while he tried to dig up data on me. He ran a game on a friend of mine—probably looking for leverage—but came up short. He won't be sticking around."

"Will he come straight at you? Can he find you?"

"He knows my name and that I live in D.C. It wouldn't take Miss Marple to follow that up. He might come at me eventually, but not too soon. I'd love you to take him off the street, but I doubt if he's wanted for anything."

"Nothing I know of, Paul, but I'll follow up your tip. Call me if you learn more."

"Will do, boss."

"Don't call me boss."


Francois Declaire awoke fully dressed and stretched face down across a bed. There was no light in the room and his memory of the evening was ragged, but he was sure he was in his own room at the Cross Keys Inn in Columbia.

His mouth was dry and his tongue felt like dirty burlap. He knew it would be painful, but he sat up on the edge of the bed and turned on a lamp. The soft lighting pierced his eyes and brought throbbing pain to his head. Turning the light off would not help. He was already wounded. Besides that, he sensed himself a target.

How foolish he had been. Why did he expose himself to Katya so soon? She was so malleable and willing to believe whatever he said. She was infatuated and would easily have been his. Then she said her sister and the man from Paris were back.

It was too soon. He was unready for anything but making a fool of himself.

Why had he done it? Why was he always that way with a woman? Blinded by egotism, he always forgot the work and went for the reward. Now he was exposed and had to flee.

He would pay for his blunder, but he must not be caught. Then he would be abandoned and lose everything. He had to escape.

Still wearing the business suit he had slept in, he quickly picked up the telephone and called the front desk.


Barney Rice and a representative from Immigration and Naturalization walked into the Cross Keys Inn lobby at a quarter after two in the morning. The night desk clerk seemed surprised when Barney asked about Francoise Declaire.

"I don't know how you missed him," the clerk said. "He just now went out to a cab."

# 47

Paul rose early on Friday morning. He showered, shaved, ate breakfast, and browsed through the morning paper until shortly after nine. At a quarter past he dialed the telephone number Barney had given him for the pseudonymous Bill Farben.

"Warren," a male voice answered when the phone had rung twice.

"My name is Paul, Mr. Warren. Is there anyone at this number who answers to the name Bill Farben?"

"Only one and you have him," the voice came back cheerfully. "I'm Ted Warren, and I wanted to talk to you about our last meeting in Munich."

*A spook to the end*, Paul thought. *He has to be sure I am who I say.* "Wasn't it Frankfurt?"

"You're right of course. We were at the chemical building."

Paul could tell Ted Warren would not be saying much more over the phone.

"I just got back in town, and I'd like to see you. Can we make an appointment?"

"Certainly," the man said, dictating an address in Arlington, Virginia. "Can you make it at ten thirty this morning?"

"I'll be right out," Paul said.

"Try not to come early. I'll meet you at the desk downstairs. You can park in the underground lot across the street."

Paul imagined the place to be some kind of safe house. He would look awkward just strolling in without a resident out front to escort him.

"I'll see you then," Paul said.

Looking into his wardrobe, Paul decided to wear a jacket and tie, despite the midsummer heat.

The address Warren gave Paul was an unimposing three-story office building that shared the block with similar structures. Pushing his way through a single revolving door, he faced a wide reception desk manned at each end by a uniformed security officer. Two side-by-side elevator doors were located on his left several yards beyond, and a solid, metal door on the right probably gave access to a stairwell. The man he remembered as Bill came around the end of the desk to shake hands, greet him, and escort him past the silent, motionless guards into one of the elevators. Inside the lift, Bill operated the controls without speaking, so Paul kept quiet too.

Paul noted that Bill was dressed as unceremoniously as he had been in Frankfurt.

*Scrap the coat and tie next time.*

Leaving the elevator on the third floor, Bill led Paul to the end of a short corridor.

A door on the left opened into an office holding four work cubicles and an open conference area with a table and chairs at one end. For the moment, they seemed to be alone in the room. Paul reckoned the spaces had been hurriedly cleared on his account.

"Have a seat," Warren said, taking a chair at one end of the table.

"Should I just go on calling you Bill," Paul asked, sitting down one chair away on Warren's left.

"Go ahead. Otto still knows me as Uncle Bill."

"How is he doing?"

"I'd say quite well. I'm rather proud of him."

"Is he still a slave to those cigarettes?"

"No, and that is only one of the improvements you will notice. He made himself so sick in the beginning that he quit the habit entirely. Now he hates to be in the same room with a smoker. He is quite a different man from the one you met in Frankfurt."

"I can hardly wait."

"He is really a very bright kid."

"Which he demonstrated by getting out of the country before his commanding officer could arrange a fatal accident for him."

"He is still quite sure about that part of it."

"He is right."

"You know that for certain?"

"Yep, but don't ask how."

They smiled together in recognition of their mutual instinct to keep secrets.

"What's he doing these days?" Paul asked.

"He's looking for ways to restart his life."

"How do you mean?"

"I wasn't exaggerating about his intelligence. He has had plenty of time to himself, and he's used it wisely. Wait until you hear his English. Give him access to a library, and his first choices are philosophy, physics, and religion.

"After he polished his language skills, we administered IQ tests, first in his native tongue and then in English. His scores on both left most Mensa members in the dust. Then we gave him some college equivalency tests in mathematics and English composition. He blew the top off those too."

"Did that help get him into the country?"

"I would say so. His citizenship program is greased and nearly done. He only has to fulfill the residency requirement for naturalization."

"Wonderful."

"He's a good actor too. We gave him a West German background he picked up and turned into a perfect fit. He already had some German language. After intensive tutoring, he can pass for a native Frankfurter at the conversational level."

"That's very impressive."

"Like I said, he is very bright and a quick learner."

"That's great news, Bill. I'm happy you were able to put it all together for him."

"Actually, Paul, we still have a few hitches in the program to relocate him here. That is why I called to see if you would help."

"He saved my life at the risk of his own. How could I not?"

"I remember you hinting less specifically at something like that."

"So now you know," Paul responded, surprised by his own candor. "Incidentally, Bill, since I'm going to be involved, what is his name? I can't keep calling him Otto."

"We don't expect his native country to be out looking for him very hard, so we just gave him a German name and got him immigration status here. Today he calls himself Victor Guttmann."

"That has a prosaic touch. So what is the problem?"

"Even you mentioned it after debriefing him; he is not a high-value asset."

"He was for me, but I think I understand. Is it funding?"

"You said it, Paul. We usually set up the top-dollar guys with a complete change of identity. Then we protect and support them while they settle into a new and safer life. We can't do that for Victor. There's no payoff."

"I get it. He has no future value like the others."

"That's the point exactly. He's told us all he knows, and it isn't much. Since he's so smart, we were able to get him a full-tuition scholarship in D.C. We couldn't go to his true country for a transcript, so we fabricated his academic background in Germany."

"How did you get away with that?"

"Don't worry. His record actually exists in the archives of two West German universities. The university here has already received and accepted the transcripts. With those and his equivalency test scores, they're starting him in September as a junior."

"Wow. That's a giant leap. You already said he's set to gain citizenship."

Warren hesitated a few seconds before answering.

"That's where you come in, Paul. We still need a U.S. citizen to sponsor him, someone to guarantee he does not become a burden to the state. The applicant needs a place to live and food to eat until he becomes a citizen and gets a job. Are you still as anxious to help him as you were in Frankfurt?"

"No doubt about it. There's only one snag."

"Which is?"

"I am about to be married."

"Congratulations."

"Thank you, but maybe I should broach this topic with my fiancée first."

"I'd say so. You're not telling her who he really is, are you?"

"No way would I do that. She will know him only as the man you have described. Make sure he understands that too."

"Great. Do you expect any problem with your intended?"

"Not really, and I'm still giving you an affirmative. One way or another, we're going to take care of Otto—Victor that is."

"Can you give me a commitment by next week?"

"I've already given you a commitment," Paul said slowly and deliberately. "I will confirm that on Monday and sign whatever sponsorship documents may be necessary. You do have a notary around the office, don't you?"

"I'm sure we can find one," Warren said, breaking into a huge grin.

"When can I see Victor?"

"I'll have him here Monday. He'll go home with you and never come back here again. Will the same time do?"

"Ten thirty it is, but I need to ask a favor."

"What's that?"

"I will tell my fiancée this weekend that our marriage is bringing her the equivalent of a young adult stepson. She might want to see him at least once in advance. Can she come up with me to meet him?"

"Be serious, Paul. We're not social service administrators. Just getting you through the door required a two-page justification now that you've given up your clearances—yes, I know all about that."

"How very thorough you've been."

"I lined everything up before giving you a call."

"Okay, I had to try, but don't be surprised if she's waiting for us in the car across the street."

"Suit yourself, but she may be sort of sweaty by the time you get back to her. It's summer, you know."

"I don't think she'll melt after a few minutes in the underground garage. Just make sure that's all it takes."

"I'll do my best."

# 48

"What would you say about having a child?" Paul asked Petra on Saturday afternoon. They were in his car on the way to see Father Don about getting married, although they had yet to inform the priest of their purpose.

Petra turned slowly to look at Paul as he drove. With his eyes on the road, he could not see the enigmatic smile that moved across her lips before she composed them into a more serious image.

"We haven't talked about children, have we?"

"That's one reason I'm bringing it up."

"I'm surprised we haven't. I love children, and I'm young enough to bear one. Still, I can't help observing that you will be on Social Security by the time any baby of ours might be ready for college."

"That's an important consideration we ought to discuss very soon. Actually, I have something a little more immediate in mind."

"Are you talking about adoption?" she asked. The furtive smile was back, and he could almost detect it in her speech.

"Not precisely, but something close to that. He would be more like a stepson to you."

"You mean you already have a child?"

"Not that. Maybe I introduced this too abruptly, but I wanted to tell you about it before we set the wedding date."

"Good idea. Please continue."

"There is a young man in his early twenties. He is new to this country and has a scholarship to start his junior year of college here this September." Here Paul paused.

"Go ahead," she urged him.

"His name is Victor Guttmann, and I have no blood or legal ties to him—at least not yet." Again, he hesitated.

"Come on, Paul. What is it?" She reached across and lightly patted his knee.

"Like a lot of things in my life, this is something I can't give you much detail on. I still want you to understand my motive."

"I know I will."

"Very recently, just before I came back in January, this boy placed himself at great risk to effectively save my life."

"Thank God."

"I do, but I also thank Victor Guttmann. Please understand—this is very important—he does not know me that way. We have met only once, and he has no idea of the service he rendered me—nor must he ever. He's a very intelligent guy, and can be given no clue to what I owe him. He must know me only as a sympathetic benefactor."

"All right," she said, softly concurring with his explicit demand for future silence.

"At the moment, he needs my help and financial assistance to become a U. S. citizen and complete his undergraduate education. Since you and I are to be married, I will need your help and approval to provide that."

"Thank you for saying 'since,' rather than 'if,'" she responded warmly. "Now we are almost at the rectory. Maybe we ought to postpone discussing the details until later."

"Thank you, darling."

"I expect to revisit our talk about babies as well."

They both laughed as Paul guided the car into the parking lot.

---

The rectory of St. Athanasius's was a small, two-story, brick home that stood about twenty yards behind the sanctuary and its related structures. It was connected by an unobtrusive, asphalt driveway to the parking lot in front of the church. This was where Father Don lived with his wife and three children. It was a cozy residence under the proprietary vigilance of the family's large, fluffy, orange-and-white tomcat most respectfully addressed as Boniface.

Father Don wore a bright, expectant smile when he opened the door to greet them.

"I'm happy to see you both. Please come in," he said, leading them through the living room into a family-sized dining space.

"Everyone is out right now, so we have the place to ourselves."

"Not quite everybody," Paul said, taking a chair beside Petra on one side of the linen-covered table while Don sat down opposite them.

"Excuse me?" Don asked.

"Unless my lower legs deceive me, our friend Boniface remains on watch beneath us."

"You're right, of course. He is very territorial."

"And well he should be," Petra said, reaching her hand beneath the table to gently stroke the cat, who was rubbing the top of his head vigorously against her legs. "He's a very conscientious watchman."

"When I spoke with Paul two Sundays ago," Don said, shifting his gaze between them, "he was concerned about the state of things between you. May I assume that has been resolved?"

"You certainly may," Petra responded.

"I am very happy to know that. Now what can I do for you?"

"I think you know quite well, you crafty, old priest," Petra answered.

"Let me guess," he said, holding a serious expression. "There are only a few things I am empowered to do for people. Has anyone died or had a baby?"

"As a matter of fact," Paul put in, "we were just talking about babies."

"Nobody's pregnant I hope."

"Father Don, how could you?" Petra gasped.

"That's actually part of my job too, you know," he answered with a grin.

"I am not pregnant," Petra protested.

"I know that, but you still want to get married don't you?"

"Oh yes."

"Wonderful. Do you want the fast track or the slow track?"

"How long is the fast track?"

The priest pursed his lips and cocked his eyebrows, as if deeply in thought.

"About six months—as long as nobody is pregnant."

"Six months!" she exploded.

Neither man could continue with a straight face.

"Now I get it. Did you two cook this up together?"

"Not really. Don started kidding, and I just kept quiet."

"Well cut it out."

"Gladly," Don replied. "I am delighted to see how much you both want this. How soon would you like it to happen?"

"Posting the banns will take three Sundays. Is there any reason to wait longer?" Paul asked.

"In your case, I don't think so. May I suggest combining your marriage with the Mass on the Sunday following the third reading? Merging marriage and the regular Mass was an ancient practice, but it is not much done these days."

"If that's all right with Paul," she said, reaching to take his hand on the table top, "I like the idea."

"That's it then," Paul said.

"Consider the date set," Father Don replied, bringing the table back to order and writing a few notes in his pocket diary. "I will make the first reading tomorrow morning, and the wedding Mass will be scheduled for three weeks later at ten o' clock. You are both long-time parishioners, well known to me, so I believe we can complete all necessary instruction during the course of today's visit. There are just a few things we need to talk about. Do you agree?"

They both nodded.

"The peace of the Lord be always with you," the priest began.

"And also with you," they answered happily.

"Let us pray."

Petra thought she heard Boniface, who had moved into the next room, meow a loud, "Amen." Later on, Paul told her he heard it too. That is how a family legend was born.

# 49

Even after Ted Warren's description of the new Otto on Friday, Paul was impressed with the Victor Guttmann he met on Monday morning in Warren's office. His formerly thin face had filled out, but not with fat; the plain white tee-shirt he wore over tan slacks and clean running shoes revealed well-toned muscles Paul did not recall from their Frankfurt meeting. Of course the younger man had not been dressed to show much of his physique that time.

Victor had definitely gained weight but wore it well, like a man who ran or worked out regularly. His skin bore a moderate tan, and when he smiled, Paul saw evidence of expert dental attention to his formerly cracked front teeth. His brown hair was long enough to be parted on the left, but was now neatly trimmed away from his ears and neck.

Paul decided that Warren's organization, whatever its funding problems, had treated this temporary ward well. He was pleased with the result. When Victor confidently moved forward to shake hands, Paul's satisfaction rose to a new level.

"I'm very glad to see you again, Paul. You were the first person, besides Uncle Bill, to show much interest in me when I came to Germany. I was grateful for that; I still am."

Victor's handclasp was firm, and his unaccented English seemed to echo the measured speech of some mid-west radio commentator. Paul automatically related this clear, strong voice to the reported termination of his former tobacco habit.

*He sounds and looks like a preppie jockstrap,* Paul thought. *He'll fit right in at school.*

"I'm happy to see you too, Victor. You're looking very well. Has Bill told you why I'm here?"

Paul could see Warren hanging back with another man a few yards away. Compared with Friday, the office was densely populated with workers who appeared to belong there. Paul supposed Warren had cleared the place for his first visit to minimize the number of people he might see. That professional restraint seemed now to be relaxed.

*Warren is holding himself in reserve,* Paul thought. *He wants us to reconnect.*

"He told me," Victor answered, "you will be my new angel until things work out. Thank you for that. It is a great kindness to me, and I deeply appreciate it."

"You're more than welcome," Paul said, moving in Warren's direction. "Let's see if Uncle Bill can speed up the paperwork. I hope you will like what we have planned."

Across the street, after the notary business and other details were done, Paul could tell that Petra was as impressed with her new sort-of-a-son as Paul already had been. Of course, she had the advantage of not knowing about his formerly shabby state.

Paul drove them, along with Victor's sole traveling bag, to his apartment. This was Petra's introduction to the place Paul lived. She had never visited him at home.

Sitting with them at the small kitchen table, Paul explained that the apartment would be Victor's home while he completed his citizenship requirements and finished college. He might eventually want a car, but for now, public transportation was easily available, cheap, and adequate.

Until his marriage to Petra in three weeks, Paul would be sharing the place and showing Victor how to get around town. As soon as Paul moved out, Victor could move his sleeping quarters from the living-room sofa-bed into the bedroom. He and Paul would maintain close contact, and Paul would provide a maintenance allowance until Victor was able to take care of himself. Finally, Victor was delighted to accept Paul's invitation to be best man at the upcoming wedding.

Everyone seemed happy with the arrangements, and Paul left Victor to settle in while he drove Petra home to Columbia.

"I think we are going to be very proud of him," Petra said, as Paul pulled away from the curb.

"Me too."

Paul had to keep his eyes on traffic, but he could tell Petra was looking at him when she spoke again.

"Let's stop on the way home to shop for that king-size bed."

"Good idea."

*What an overstatement that turned out to be.*

# 50

*Holy God, have mercy on us,* Paul prayed silently as he struggled to throw open every window in the apartment. It was quicker than breaking the glass. He had no tool for that anyway and dared produce no spark of electricity.

The air conditioner had been off and the windows open when he left Victor alone. Shopping for a bed took time and delayed his return until after one thirty. Then he found the air conditioner still off but the place tightly closed up.

*Now where is the igniter? Never mind Victor. He doesn't matter until I find the igniter.*

Paul knew there would be an igniter as soon as he stumbled over the prone form of Francois Declaire. He had to force the front door open, because Declaire's body was in the way. Ignition was part of the assassin's method. It was the only way he could light off the gas after making his getaway. This time he just failed to get away.

*Jerk,* Paul thought when he saw the Frenchman stretched out on the floor. *He didn't expect so small a breathing envelope in here with all the windows closed.*

With the door and windows now open, Paul went straight to the kitchen stove to turn off the gas jets Declaire had left on but unlit.

*Never mind the pilot light. It won't put out much gas by itself. Find the igniter.*

Paul kept moving, while trying to minimize the amount of toxic vapor he could not help drawing into his own lungs. He tore off his already sweat-sodden shirt and held it against his mouth and nose to screen his intake of air while desperately looking for the igniter.

It had to be somewhere all set to blow the place up any second now. There were plenty of fumes left to do that unless Paul found and disarmed it—whatever and wherever it was.

*There it is; it's not a bit concealed. Why didn't I look in the kitchen sink first? Surprise, surprise; I haven't seen anything like this since my ROTC manual. How in the world did he get one?*

It was a concussion grenade—World War II stuff, designed to stun and disable rather than kill. Except for the pin-and-release apparatus, there was no metal on the casing around the tightly packed, explosive charge—no shrapnel-generating metal jacket like that of an ordinary fragmentation grenade.

The smooth, cylindrical body looked like cardboard and was hardly more dangerous, unless it went off in a roomful of gas. Here and now its flash ignition would blow the apartment to bits and remove any sign of what actually caused the blast.

Declaire had passed a wire loop through the grenade's activating ring and around the sink's water faucet. Now the grenade hung from that ring only by its arming pin, which would start an internal explosive process when fully extracted. Ten seconds later its non-lethal charge would instantly ignite a fatal one as the gas around it went up.

Paul figured the killer had loosened the pin enough to get it started, so that gravity and the weapon's own weight would finish the job. The wire loop was there only because the activating ring was too small to fit over the faucet.

Only one thing had kept the pin from coming out already. Without it the little bomb would have fallen into the sink of its own weight, fully armed and ready to blow. That single restraint was a five-pound plastic bag of ice the bomber probably brought with him in a small ice chest Paul had seen near his body.

Paul was sure the bottom of the bag had been slit to accelerate water release down the drain. As melting ice was displaced, the grenade descended slowly toward inevitable detonation. Tepid water, steadily trickling from the tap, had advanced the process until the ice was nearly gone. Hot water would have worked faster, but might not have given Declaire time to clear out. Even when he failed to escape, the process continued until grenade activation was now mere seconds away.

*Spare us, Lord. The pin is already more than halfway pulled. When it comes all the way out, the handle flies off, and a chemical reaction begins within. Once that starts, the sequence cannot be reversed. I couldn't get away now if I tried.*

*Don't waste time turning off the water, Paul. The pin is about to pop.*

"Shut up, stupid, and stop it!" he shouted aloud to himself.

His shirt was in the way so he dropped it to the floor. Carefully but quickly, he took the body of the grenade in one hand and pushed it upward, while bracing the arming ring with his other hand.

*All right, the pin is fully reinserted. It's back where it belongs.*

Now he cautiously withdrew the wire loop from the faucet and placed the weapon gingerly to one side on the sink draining board. He thought briefly about immersing the thing in water, but decided he did not know enough about its triggering mechanism.

*Don't meddle with it.*

The air was clearing more rapidly through the open door and windows. It was being assisted by an uncommon, summer afternoon breeze.

*Thank you for that, Lord,* Paul prayed, kicking the bomber's body as he went by. He observed no resulting sound or movement and was grateful for that too. A small, cloth bag in the man's hand, Paul assumed, held tools for the work he had come to do.

*Dead or alive, I can't help him now.*

Nobody around the building seemed aware of what had almost been a catastrophic urban event.

*Good. I have more to do now than waste time with the neighbors.*

Paul had seen no sign of Victor since entering the apartment, but he knew his young roommate must be there. Why else would

Declaire have rigged the explosion? He could not have known when Paul would come back. Might Victor have been his target?

*What kind of sense does that make? Victor had no connection to the Khrabovich affair—at least not in Paris. Why would Francois want to blow him up when I was not even here? Might he have mistaken Victor for me?*

With time to look, Paul found Victor's body face down on the floor of the bedroom between the bed and the inner wall.

*Praise the Lord. Down there he may not have taken as much gas as Declaire did, up and running around.*

*Is that blood-matted hair on the back of Victor's head? I'll bet that's what kept him out of Declaire's way.*

*Never mind the analysis, Paul. Just get him out of here.*

Lifting Victor's dead weight in a fireman's carry, Paul took him through the front door onto the stairwell landing and carelessly dumped him face up on the floor.

Out there the air seemed fully cleared. Checking Victor's vital signs, Paul found no evidence of breathing, heartbeat, or a pulse. With those negative, he instantly dropped to his knees and began cardiopulmonary resuscitation procedures. Alternating mouth-to-mouth breathing with the vigorous chest compressions of CPR, he lost track of time and began to fear them a pointless exercise for the sake of a corpse.

*Please, Lord, let him live.*

*You can't give up,* Paul told himself. *You've got to keep going. Don't stop. Don't slow down. Check the airway, but keep going. It's got to work. It's got to work. Keep going. Check the airway. Do it again.*

*Lord, have mercy on this, your servant.*

*What's happening? He's gagging. Get his head to the side.*

*Praise to you, O Lord.*

*Don't let him choke on his own puke. Clear the airway now.*

*Oh, praise God. He's going to make it.*

*Thanks be to God.*

Victor was barely conscious and gasping for breath, but his respiration soon regulated itself. Once Paul got him to his feet, he managed a hobbling walk while leaning heavily on Paul. Back in the bedroom Paul dumped him on the bed. Despite the heat from the open windows Victor began shivering, so Paul covered him with a blanket.

Victor was to have used the living-room sofa-bed until Paul moved out.

*Forget it, Paul. Things have changed.*

Victor rolled over and slept.

Paul monitored him a while to be sure his heart and lungs kept working. Then he started running the air conditioner with the front door and windows still open. After the gas cleared and he relit the oven pilot light, he closed the place back up. The cool air felt good, gradually drying the sweaty clothes that had formerly clung to him.

By the time Victor was stabilized, Paul realized any CPR effort on the Frenchman would be futile. A human being can hold out only so long without functional lungs or a heartbeat. This one was way past the limit.

*Everything is back to normal,* Paul thought, *except for the body on the living-room floor.*

# 51

Paul's sense of time had been distorted by the afternoon's events, but his wristwatch told him more than thirty minutes had passed since his return to the apartment. It was time to restore a little order. He thought about cleaning up what Victor had regurgitated on the landing, but decided to call for help first.

Paul took only a few minutes to go through the Frenchman's pockets, bag, and ice chest. Then he walked across the living room and picked up the telephone. He remained standing as he dialed Grogan's outside line at work. He had never called this number, but he was not surprised to find it bypassed Darlene Parker's desk and went straight to the director.

"Grogan," the answer came through.

"Paul here; you missed our man in Columbia, didn't you?"

"Barney was about thirty seconds late, but how do you know that?"

"I'm looking at him, and he isn't well."

"Is he vertical or horizontal?"

"On his back on my living-room rug. He was up to old tricks—trying to blow things up."

"How did he die?"

"Suicidal incompetence; the gas caught him before he got to the door."

"You're calling for a cleanup, aren't you?"

"I hoped you might do one for me. This definitely grew out of my last operation."

"Agreed. Are you in your old apartment?"

"Yes. I wasn't here then. I just got back in time to keep the place from going up."

"I'm glad you did. What do you need besides cleaners? Is there a car to dispose of?"

"I don't think so. No keys on the body. No accomplice in sight. He must have come by Metro, bus, or cab."

"Good. Any other special considerations?"

"One."

"Go ahead."

"Can you have a doctor come out to look at my friend Victor? That's what Otto—you remember Patroon—calls himself these days. He's staying here now and got caught up in our business with Francois. Anyway, he took a blow to the head and a near-lethal dose of gas. I gave him CPR. I think he'll be okay, but I need somebody to check him over. I'd rather not take him to an emergency room and explain how he got this way."

"Is there anything else?"

"I almost forgot. The team should be ready to pick up a piece of explosive ordnance our man brought with him."

"Is it fragile?"

"An armored box might be in order. It's a vintage concussion grenade."

"I don't think I've ever seen one of those."

"Don't try keeping it in your office. It looks like a World War II relic, so the charge may be unstable. Francois had set it to ignite the gas."

"Wasn't that wicked of him? How'd he get hold of a thing like that anyway? I hope he didn't carry it all the way across the Atlantic in his suitcase."

"At least you can tell the Nerviers it's safe to go home."

"I think I'll do that."

In just over two hours, a commercial van pulled up and parked across the street from Paul's apartment. Two men in white coveralls unloaded a medium-sized, rolled-up carpet and muscled it up the stairs to Paul's landing. Two other men followed them. One was also in coveralls and used both hands to haul what looked like a very heavy toolbox up the stairs.

The last man wore a gray, short-sleeved, open-collared work shirt tucked into slacks of the same color. Some kind of logo patch was sewn above his left, breast pocket. He was carrying a fairly large, black valise in one hand and a long, but not too heavy, blue cloth bag in the other. The shape of the blue bag suggested it might have some kind of piping in it.

Thirty minutes later, the man with the tool box came down, followed by the carpet carriers with a burden equal to the one they had taken in. They put this load carefully into the back of the van and closed the rear door. The man with the valise came down about ten minutes later without the blue bag, and they all rode away in the van.

Inside the apartment, the men with the carpet had immediately taken up Paul's old one and installed the new one, trimming a few pieces to make it fit. Paul was at first impressed at how closely someone had estimated the size that was needed. Then he realized that Barney would have included the dimensions and character of the apartment in his January surveillance report. The cleanup team had merely consulted the record.

Next, the carpet men tightly rolled up Declaire's body and effects in the old carpet and secured the ends to avoid any mischance exposure of its contents. Then they used some light instruments from the heavy tool box to cleanse the apartment of any sign the Frenchman was ever there.

The toolbox carrier very carefully took the grenade from where Paul had left it. He gingerly sealed the weapon into a well-cushioned, central compartment within the reinforced case and separate from the section where the light tools were stored. After that, he checked the stove to make sure it was safe.

While waiting for the cleaning team to arrive, Paul had first cleaned up the mess in the stairwell. After sponge-bathing the unconscious Victor and dressing him in a pair of pajama bottoms from his bag, Paul had pulled the bed covers up to keep him warm.

The man with the valise was a doctor. He looked at the dead body only long enough to be sure it was. Then he went to the bedroom to examine Victor. When Paul came in, the doctor asked him to help assemble an intravenous-injection tree he had brought with him in the blue cloth bag. While he examined Victor, the doctor continued to question Paul about what happened and how the CPR went. Victor remained groggy, which was just as well. Getting a look at the wound on the back of his head, the doctor drafted the bomb man, now with nothing to do, to help clean, shave, and dress the area.

"This shouldn't need stitches," he told Paul, "but I'll leave gauze, tape, and antiseptic in case you need to change the dressing. I'll give him an antibiotic to forestall infection and sedation to keep him still for a while."

Now that Paul had set up the IV tree, the doctor showed him how to change bags and properly adjust the drip device.

"Don't meddle with the needle. Just change the bags as they become empty. Keep them in the fridge until you need them. They'll last for three or four hours each. They are only giving him hydration, sedation, and nourishment. The last one should be finished before breakfast tomorrow. By then he'll be wide awake and ready for solid food. He will be very hungry.

"He is pretty dehydrated now, so he probably won't be running around much. Still, be alert in case he wakes up and needs to use the toilet. This IV tree has no wheels, so you'll have to carry it for him.

"I don't suppose I need to tell you, but keep your hands clean when you're fooling with any of this stuff. When the last IV bag is empty, just remove the needle from his arm, swab the area with plenty of antiseptic, and put a Band-Aid over the puncture. Make sure all medical waste goes into the plastic bags I am leaving. If you have any doubts about what's going on, tell Grogan. I'll call you back right away.

"I will come in tomorrow morning around eight to check him out and take this stuff away. Now before I go, I want to check you over too. You took some of the gas, didn't you?"

Paul's examination was cursory. It amounted to little more than checking his eyes, chest, and reflexes.

"Any questions?" the doctor finally asked.

Paul had none, but he could not help thinking the doctor must have graduated from the same school of organizational behavior as Grogan.

# 52

Whatever sedative the doctor had given Victor kept him sleeping all night. Through evening into early morning, he barely stirred, even while Paul was fooling with his IV paraphernalia. Shortly after three in the morning, the last bag ran out.

Doing this service for Victor reminded Paul of the time he spent on IVs, mostly unconscious and slowly recovering from his own injuries at the Blaskovod prison hospital. Those IV treatments had been withdrawn as soon as he regained full consciousness.

Victor was at the same place and aware of Paul's presence, but only as a nameless, faceless prisoner. Yet when he was ordered to shoot Paul, he refused and put himself at risk. That was how Paul stayed alive long enough to be repatriated through Grogan's magical maneuvering. At the same time, Victor had saved his own life by fleeing his commander's wrath.

As soon as the cleaners were out of the apartment, Paul had taken a shower and put on fresh clothes. Then he struggled to rid himself of the notion that he still smelled gas. Surely it was all gone by then. He had read somewhere that natural gas is actually odorless, but providers add a scent for safety. He definitely remembered smelling something while he searched for the igniter.

Refreshed from the shower, Paul called Petra to remind her he loved her and apologize for not coming to see her as promised that night.

"Victor and I got busy cleaning up this place, and we're both exhausted."

Paul hated lying to her, but the organization's involvement forced him to. He could not describe the Frenchman's intrusion without explaining where the body went.

Paul expected Victor's memories of the afternoon to be vague. Basically, he would know only what Paul would tell him, and Paul did not plan to say much. His new roommate would be given very few beans to spill.

"I thought the apartment was pretty neat," Petra said over the telephone. "I don't remember any mess at all."

"Take my word for it; we even replaced the old rug while we were at it. Victor was so tired he's already gone to bed."

"In the middle of your living room?"

*Oops.*

"Not really. He worked so hard I gave him the bed tonight. I thought he deserved it; I may even let him keep it. After all, I have our king-size model to look forward to—with you in it."

"How lascivious; I'm shocked," she told him, not sounding a bit so.

"Just wait 'til you know me better."

"Do you mean that in the biblical sense?"

"You might be on to something."

"How provocative," she said with a coquettish laugh.

"Hold that thought."

"I will," she said before shifting the subject. "Katya, you know, is still muttering dire threats against your French friend."

"He was no friend of mine," Paul responded, glad she brought the subject up.

"Was?"

*Impaled again.*

"I just don't believe Monsieur Declaire is still in town."

"If he is, he better keep away from Katya."

"I'm sure he will trouble her no more."

"You sound positive."

"Take it to the bank, Petra. She can forget him."

"Okay."

"Now get a good night's sleep. We have a lot to do in the next three weeks."

"And a lot more after," she announced happily.

"Bet on that too."

*Jackie Nervier,* he thought, hanging up the phone, *you've got nothing on this lady.*

Then he thought for a moment about Norman and Jackie and quietly gave thanks for their deliverance.

# 53

The doctor had been right about Victor's appetite. He woke up ravenous in the morning. This inspired Paul to make them a bacon-and-egg breakfast with toast and some French-roast coffee he had stocked after Paris. He even broke into his small hoard of blackberry jam with the seeds still in, the way his mother used to make it.

Preparing and eating the meal did not allow much time for talk. Paul was already dressed casually for the street. Victor was still in his pajama bottoms, to which he had added a clean, white tee-shirt. They had finished breakfast before Victor reached around to touch the lumpy dressing on the back of his head.

"How did I get this?" he asked.

"Something hit you," Paul said. He had not decided what to tell Victor about the previous afternoon. Before he could say more, the doorbell rang and the doctor was there. Naturally, Victor did not recognize him when Paul led him into the kitchen.

"This is your doctor, Victor. He's the one who took care of you yesterday when you were hurt. If you're hungry and happy now, it's because of what he did for you."

"I'm not hungry any more," Victor said, as if pronouncing himself recovered.

"Good," the doctor replied.

"Did you put this thing on the back of my head?" Victor asked.

"I gave you the bandage, not the bump," the doctor said, moving to the kitchen table, where Victor was still sitting. "How does it feel now?"

"It feels funny, but it isn't throbbing or anything like that."

"That's a good sign. While I think of it, do you have any allergies?"

"None I know of."

"What about penicillin? Has a doctor ever given you anything like that?"

Victor looked a bit confused. He was evidently thinking about his cover and looked over at Paul for guidance.

Paul gave him an encouraging nod.

"Once, I think—when I was in the army."

"Did you have any reaction—say, some kind of rash?"

"No."

"Good. I gave you a shot of it yesterday. If anything suspicious comes up in the next two weeks, see a doctor and tell him you think it may be a penicillin reaction. If not, forget about it. Now let me look you over."

Leaning back in his chair, Victor submitted to a cursory examination of his eyes and chest. Then the doctor stepped behind him to look at the head wound.

"Do you remember anything that happened to you yesterday afternoon?" the doctor asked.

"Not really," Victor told him. "I was in the bedroom around one o'clock. The rest is hard to put together. I can recall being on the floor with Paul somewhere. I felt awful, and he must have been trying to help me. I know I threw up. I was very sick—almost like the time I smoked too many cigarettes."

"Do you know what made you so sick this time?"

"Only about my head, but that isn't all, is it?"

"Not by a long shot, son. Now stand up and let me have a look at your ribs."

Victor stood, and the doctor began running his fingers over the chest cavity, occasionally drawing a flinch from the patient.

Now the doctor turned to Paul.

"Good news on your CPR technique. There is some bruising over the sternum, but I don't find any cracked ribs."

Next he pointed to Victor's head.

"I don't think we need to change this dressing right now. I left enough materials for you to do that every two days or so for the rest of this week. The wound ought to heal quickly. Just get it seen to if it becomes inflamed, swells, or starts to be painful. You can tell the physician you banged your head against a rafter or something. The injury is consistent with that kind of household accident."

"What really happened?" Victor asked, pointing to the back of his head.

"I have no idea," the doctor said, now addressing Victor with a smile. "You will have to ask your friend about that, but it looks rather like you backed into what police reports usually describe as a blunt instrument."

Now the doctor turned back to Paul.

"Is there anything else I can do besides get my equipment, medical waste, and self out of your way?"

"I don't think so. I stacked everything by the door. Thanks again, Doc. You did a great job."

"I just hope you will not need me back any time soon."

"That makes two of us," Paul said, as the medical man balanced his load under both arms and went out the door.

"Who is that?" Victor asked, when Paul returned from the door.

"I told you. He was your doctor yesterday."

"But what's his name?"

"It beats me. I didn't ask, and he never said."

# 54

With the doctor gone, Victor excused himself for a trip to the bathroom. Paul had already turned his spare bed back into the small sofa it normally pretended to be. Now he washed the breakfast dishes, moved back into the living room, and dropped into his comfortable chair. There he found a still-folded newspaper on the small table next to him.

*The doctor must have brought it up.*

Before Paul could start reading, Victor came back. Now he sat facing Paul on the near end of the sofa, perpendicular to Paul's chair. The square table filled the angle between them.

Victor had exchanged his pajamas for a pair of blue jeans, still wore the tee-shirt, and remained barefoot. His voice and facial expression were now very serious.

"Can you tell me what's going on, Paul? What happened to me yesterday? What happened to us both?"

Paul, unsure of his answer, gazed silently past Victor at the wall across the room.

Victor stayed as he was, quietly waiting.

Paul's adult life had been centered on keeping secrets. That was a big part of what he did and how he did it. It had kept him alive and helped him do his work, but now things were changing. He had to catch up.

His Vale experience had set Paul on a new path. He was already walking it toward something still out of sight. Other demands were crowding into his personal narrative.

He was about to marry a woman he had long loved. He deeply wanted that, but he had nearly lost it by holding on to the past—his old job and allegiances. Afraid to lose control, he had wrapped himself in the familiar chains of routine.

As he had once sealed himself away from God, he now hid from other people. No more. He must open that secret self to others, as he formerly opened himself to God. He must leave his fears behind.

With old motives gone, he faced a new danger—the real, spiritual menace of evil at work in the world. In the Vale he had learned the answer to that. It was love—God's unending love for humanity and our eternally soul-driven love for him and each other.

Paul wanted to answer Victor's question but found no simple explanation.

What happened yesterday? Was Declaire trying to kill Paul to avenge Khrabovich and the loss of his money? He might have gone after the Nerviers for that, but it would not explain his attack on Victor.

Had there been a mistaken identity? Did Declaire come to kill Paul and attack Victor in error?

Could Victor have been the target to start with? How would that add up?

*Declaire came to kill one of us. He had a grudge against me, but he nearly killed Victor instead.*

*Time's up, Paul. Stop guessing and start talking.*

"I'll try to explain what went on here," Paul said, "but I'm still not sure why it did. Yesterday, a man came here to murder one of us. I know the man, but you don't. He very nearly killed you, and he died trying."

Victor cast his eyes around the apartment, as if looking for a body.

"The apartment has been sanitized," Paul told him. "His body is gone, along with whatever he brought. No police were called, and none will be. The matter is closed. I hope you will not speak of it to anyone but me—not even to Petra."

"He did this?" Victor asked, pointing to the back of his head.

"Yes, but I'm guessing that was only to keep you quiet while he did his work."

"What work?"

"With you unconscious, he closed all the windows, extinguished the stove pilot light, and opened up the jets to fill the apartment with gas. At the same time, he rigged an ignition device to explode the gas and blow up the apartment. His timing was bad, so he was overcome by the gas before he could get away. That's how he died."

"Why blow me up?" Victor gasped. "The gas alone would have killed me. Except for your interference, it did."

"That's a good question, Victor. I suppose he wanted to destroy any evidence that your death was not accidental. He has done that before."

"Why didn't the gas explode?"

"Good luck—more probably divine intervention. I came home in time to see what was happening, turn off the gas, and disarm the ignition device. The killer was already dead on the floor."

"Then you brought me back to life?"

"I'm inclined to credit God with that too. You had stopped breathing and had no heartbeat."

Paul was puzzled to notice a wry smile flit across Victor's face before his expression again became serious.

"Why would anyone want to kill me?—someone from my country maybe?"

"I doubt that. If you went back, they would throw you in jail, but I cannot see them pursuing you this far. You're not worth that much to them. Besides, your Uncle Bill's security is pretty good. I don't believe the People's Republic knows where you are."

"If they can't find me, how—why did this other man do it?"

"I wonder about that too. That's why I suspect he was really after me. All you remember is getting hit from behind, right?"

"I really don't remember that."

"Okay. One minute you were standing in the bedroom; the next you were heaving your guts up on the landing." Paul pointed toward the front door.

Victor nodded his head.

"Like I said," Paul continued, "I know the assassin, and I knew he was tracking me. Only last week he was gathering data about me. With or without cause, I was on his list for something. If that's not what brought him here yesterday, I don't know what did."

"So why would he attack me?"

"Let's say he came here for me," Paul answered. "Maybe he hit you from behind, and thought he had the right man. He could not see your face without turning you over. Even then, he may not have known what I look like."

"Does that make sense to you?" Victor asked.

"More than the alternative does. If he was after you, why come here at all? This was not your home until yesterday. Even you could not have found it before then."

Paul paused, while Victor maintained eye contact but said nothing.

"Whatever this guy meant to do," Paul went on, "you were attacked and nearly killed while you were here. I hope that doesn't discourage you about staying on."

Victor stroked his chin, leaned back into the sofa, and lapsed into a silence Paul found audible. Paul waited in vain for him to say something.

"Do you have any ideas?" Paul asked at last.

Now Victor leaned forward, clasping the sofa arm with both hands.

*Something is going on here,* Paul thought. *I'm not the only one keeping secrets.*

# 55

"I have told you everything I know about what happened here yesterday," Victor said, speaking very carefully. "There is nothing more to tell of that, because I was gone until you revived me. I was dead until you brought me back. From then until this morning I was never fully conscious."

Paul felt the small hairs rising on the back of his neck. He needed no lie detector to tell that Victor was holding something back.

"Yes?" Paul prompted.

"Still," Victor went on, "something did happen to me—something I know about."

"What?"

"It did not happen here."

"Where then?" Paul asked, his interest rising.

"You may not know it now, but you were there with me—some of the time anyway." Victor was speaking even more deliberately than before.

"Did you have a dream?" Paul asked, his own speech growing more precise.

"I thought at first I might be dreaming, but I was wide awake for a long time."

"How long?"

"Time is not measured there, but what happened would take many hours here—a whole day or maybe more."

"Did you have an out-of-body experience?" Paul felt his facial muscles tightening beneath the skin.

"I have read of such things," Victor said. "It was not that way. Those people don't always claim to leave the earth. Sometimes, they even tell of looking down on their own bodies. It was not that way for me."

"How was it?"

"I told you, Paul. I was dead, but it was good. I felt better than ever, and I miss it now I'm back. Why did you revive me? I don't want to be here. This is not my home."

Paul's heart was racing, but he tried to keep his voice low and his face calm.

"Did you say I was there with you?" Paul could barely contain his emotion.

"Not at first, but later you came to help me understand what was happening."

"Did others visit you in the beginning, people you used to know?"

"Before you came, there was Avram, an old man who taught me about God and Jesus when I was a child. He risked a lot to do that. Next a boy named Tito visited me. He was a great friend from my school days before I was taken into the army. They both told me where I was and why."

"Where were you?"

"You may not know it here, but there you and the others called it the Vale."

The older man and the younger one stood at the same time and embraced briefly.

"Oh yes, Victor. I know that name—that place—so well."

Paul was standing away with his hands on Victor's shoulders and his eyes locked on the young man's face.

"We have a lot to talk about," Paul said, "and we will do that soon enough. I don't know what it will bring, but I think we share a future that has barely begun. I'm not sure where our partnership started, but in God's time…"

Paul hesitated briefly and dropped his hands to his sides before going on.

"Did I or one of the others talk to you in the Vale—about time where God is?"

"You mean simultaneous infinity!" Victor shouted, and Paul began laughing deep in his throat.

So much now made sense. Paul no longer faced the devil alone. He was part of a team.

Still standing in the middle of the room, Paul spoke softly.

"It hurt a lot to be torn out of the Vale, didn't it?"

"It was more than just the pain of coming back to life," Victor replied.

"I remember feeling a great emptiness," Paul told him.

"Exactly what I feel right now."

Paul bowed his head for a few seconds before lifting his face to Victor.

"I wish I could tell you it gets easier. It won't."

"But why not, Paul?"

"I've thought about that. Why did I go to the Vale, and what does it mean here?"

"Please tell me." Victor's face showed anguish, and Paul knew that feeling well.

Paul shrugged and smiled.

"I believe I know why that man came to kill us yesterday. I don't think it mattered who he got; he was supposed to take one of us out. We have a powerful enemy who does not want you and me working together."

"Again, why not?"

"God has something for us to do. Each of us has a role to play. That is why Satan—yes, the devil—sent an agent to kill at least half the team. God just used that attack to bring you into his plan for us both."

"You're way ahead of me on this, Paul."

"I've had six months to think about it. I'll bet we both have things to tell."

"I'll tell you all I know—everything."

"Good. That will make us stronger together than either could be alone. I'm starting to see why. Let's go to the window," Paul said, leading the way.

Side-by-side they stood watching the street and its traffic below. Then Paul gently rested his hand on the younger man's shoulder.

"You never knew you were coming back, did you?" Paul asked.

"No," Victor said sharply. "Everyone said I was on the way to heaven."

"It was the same for me. Back on earth I felt betrayed and abandoned. I kept my mind on other things for days. Then I had to face what happened and try to figure it out."

"My future here seems so pointless; death would be a blessing."

"Nothing God does is pointless, Victor. Your mortal body is here right now, but in God's simultaneously infinite reality you are already in heaven with him and me. You always are. Nobody lied about that."

"Is that possible?"

"Yes, and that is our life now and forever. Nothing here can ever be that way."

"But I know the truth now. I learned it in the Vale. That's what makes being here so hard."

"You're barely back now. Don't worry, you'll get through it. You will be encouraging me before long."

"Perhaps, but I'm too confused for that now."

"I know. Just don't forget what happened. Our memory of the Vale is a blessing. It gives us strength and a will we might otherwise lack."

"What kind of strength? You mentioned that before."

Paul dropped his hand and stepped back. Now they turned to face each other.

"You may not know about it, but…"

Paul was about to reveal how Victor saved his life at Blaskovod, but his oath and conditioning ran too deep. He stopped.

"Go on," Victor said.

"Look. We've already been through a lot together. You helped me find what I was looking for in Frankfurt. Now we've met again here and in the Vale. We were attacked yesterday, but we prevailed. Don't you think God has something for us to do?"

"Yes," Victor replied in a strong, level voice, "but I also think it's time you trusted me. Evasion is pointless. I know exactly what you just started to say."

"You do?"

"I know what happened to us both in Blaskovod, Paul. You told me in the Vale."

# 56

"Let's get down to the truth," Paul said. "No more holding back."

He and Victor were now seated across from each other at the kitchen table. They were sipping coffee Paul had brewed while Victor took another turn in the bathroom.

"I agree," Victor replied, smiling and raising his right hand as if taking an oath. "Should I improvise, or do you want to ask questions."

"Maybe some of both will help. You spoke of Avram, the man who introduced you to Christianity. It reminded me of my first Vale therapist. She was an academic and spiritual mentor from my youth."

"You must realize that Avram could have gotten in trouble for doing that. Being a Christian was not illegal in the People's Republic, but practicing religion was considered antisocialist. Any declaration of faith could get a person removed from public lists, like those for state-controlled employment, housing, and food rationing. I had to keep his lessons secret even from my mother. She too might have suffered for allowing me to learn those things."

"I am aware of such practices. Did Avram explain simultaneous infinity to you?"

"In the Vale you mean?"

Paul nodded.

"Not specifically. He just told me that time is different there. My old friend Tito was the one who took me through the basics of simultaneous infinity. When you came to me later, you amplified what he had said."

"I hope I was helpful."

"Obviously you were. You talked a lot about simultaneous infinity, happiness, and the life of the soul," Victor told him.

"That sounds like my third interview in the Vale, but I'm groping for something else here."

"What do you mean?"

"I may not have told you there, but soon after I returned from the Vale, I decided God had taken me away and sent me back for a purpose—a mission he wanted me to accomplish here on earth. I felt I'd been given a prophetic vision."

"That's a heavy load to bear." Victor's face now showed sympathetic concern.

"Possibly, but look at yourself. You are the only other out-of-sequence Vale visitor I know. God brought us together here and in the Vale. I'd say he has a job for us."

"I hadn't thought of that. It sounds possible, but how can we know?"

"Consider this. When I spoke to you in the Vale, I must have known what our mission is here and how it works out. Wouldn't that have been history to me there?"

"I suppose so."

"Then please comb your memory for whatever I said that might give us a hint."

Victor sat silent for a moment.

"You kept coming back to one theme. Because of simultaneous infinity, you said, the kingdom of God is as near today, tomorrow, and forever as it was when Jesus and the apostles proclaimed it so. They were telling the truth then, and it remains just as true so long as our universe lasts. We will all discover that when we die, pass through the Vale, and come before God in his simultaneously infinite now."

"I like the way you put that, Victor. Did I say anything else?"

"Of course you did, but not with the same emphasis. You hit that one several times from very different angles."

Paul's face lit up like beams flaring from a searchlight.

"Thank you, Victor. I think you just broke the code."

# 57

Victor's words took Paul back to his talk of simultaneous infinity with Brother James in the monastery graveyard. He had wondered then if spreading that message might be part of his mission.

Why had he failed to follow that up?

*Grogan got in the way.*

Within two days Grogan had dragged him back into the coils of the organization. Then one distraction followed another until yesterday, when God put the puzzle pieces back in place.

*It looks so simple now.*

"You've just told me why we went out and what we came back for," Paul said. "Now I know where to start."

"What do you mean?"

"I'm talking about a heavenly thing, Victor. You and I now call it simultaneous infinity. Don't you remember how Jesus struggled to explain 'heavenly things' to Nicodemus in the Gospel of John?"

"Of course, but what does that have to do with simultaneous infinity?"

"Isn't it one of them—a heavenly thing I mean? As soon as we knew about it, didn't it expand our perception of God? Can't it take us beyond the earthly limits that doubters claim for his power and works?"

Victor sat still and silent.

"Yesterday, Victor, God gave our operation the go-ahead and put the devil in his place with one stroke."

"You're losing me."

"I'll slow down. Let's just talk about what happened here yesterday afternoon. How did that work—here and in the Vale?"

"Do you know that?"

"I do now."

"Then tell me, Paul."

"Let's say Satan sent the man I know as Francois Declaire here yesterday to kill us. One of us would do, but both would be a homerun for hell. Are you with me so far?"

"I hope so."

"Next God took you to the Vale. You were going there anyway just for being dead from the gas."

"Okay."

"Meanwhile, God sent my simultaneously infinite person, the me who is not on earth any more, to be one of your Vale therapists."

"Huh?"

"Think of it this way, Victor. We were together in two places at once, but not really at the same time. Everything you remember from the Vale, including me, is part of God's simultaneous infinity. That's where I gave you a clue to what God wants from us here. He sent me to do that."

"That's one place. Where's the other?"

"We're in it right now. It's this apartment."

Victor's face went blank.

"Don't you see?" Paul asked. "While the devil's agent was setting you up for a visit to the Vale, God kept the earthbound me from getting in the way. Then he sent me back here just in time to pull you out of the Vale. It didn't matter how many sessions you had there, so long as I got to your mortal body in time for CPR and before the gas blew it to bits."

Now Victor's face lit up.

"Thanks to Tito's tutoring on time, I think I'm beginning to see it."

"Victor, God has given us a common bond to help us. From different earthly times and places he called us to the Vale. There he prepared each of us to fight his ancient enemy and rescue some of his children. The details are still fuzzy, but I think he's started us off and pointed the way."

"Isn't 'fuzzy' a pretty light way to describe what we've gotten into?"

"Let me speak more clearly," Paul continued. "My wording may be strong, but I would call us prophets."

"I don't like that job title much. Are you sure?"

"Yep, I expect God will give us plenty of work to do, but we are not alone. He is always with us—both of us—now and forever. He showed us that in the Vale, and he will support us here until we're done. Meantime, he sustains us with the total certainty of what comes next."

"All right, but how do we spend the rest of our lives here? Didn't you say you'd figured that out?"

"Oh, that." Paul replied playfully. "I can't know how many projects the Lord may have for us here, but now I know how to get started. Why did I fail to see it before?"

"What?"

"Don't you see? We will be looking for ways to propagate the concept of simultaneous infinity. It's not a new idea, but most people haven't thought about it. If we can promote it to ordinary people in digestible chunks, many searching souls may find reassurance, strength, and comfort."

"Why that?"

"Because it reconciles the promise that God's kingdom is at hand with the historic reality of almost two millennia since Christ emerged from the tomb."

"Is that all?" Victor asked.

"It's really quite a lot. Try looking at it the way the writer of Hebrews did."

"What do you mean?"

"Do you remember what the opening verse of chapter eleven says about faith and hope?"

"Funny you should ask. The first book I read in English after I got to Frankfurt was a Gideon Society Bible Uncle Bill dug up for me. That was one of the passages he recommended, and it gave me great confidence about my future."

"Can you quote it?"

"I know it by heart. 'Now faith is the substance of things hoped for, the evidence of things not seen.'"

"Do you get it now?" Paul asked.

"I think I do." Victor's expression brightened as he spoke. "We hope for and believe in a heaven we cannot see—at least not from here. Knowing what you and I do about simultaneous infinity makes the kingdom of God just as near as Christ and the apostles said it is. It is always like that where God always is—then, now and forever."

"And there is no true contradiction in Scripture," Paul added. "There are only lapses in our earthbound, temporal reading of it."

Now Paul stood and gently clasped Victor's left shoulder with his right hand.

"I can get started right away" Paul said firmly, "but you have to do college first."

"I suppose I must," Victor replied in a tired tone, "but I don't think they confer degrees in prophecy. All in all, I would rather be back in the Vale."

"So would I, but don't underestimate the value of what we learned there."

"What do you mean?" Victor asked, wrinkling his brow.

Paul's eyes sparkled now as they would again whenever he spoke of God's ever-present, never-ending now.

"You and I don't just hope for heaven. We are already there—and we know it."

# Epilogue

From the September edition of the St. Athanasius's parish newsletter:

We got to see something a little different in August when Father Don administered the sacrament of holy matrimony as part of the ten o'clock Eucharist. This happy event was the wedding of two well-loved parishioners. Father Don said such a sacramental mix was an ancient practice of the Church, but none of us could remember hearing about that. Maybe we are just not ancient enough. Anyway, at the end of the ceremony Father Don was able to introduce us for the first time to Mr. and Mrs. Paul Pilgrim. In case you were not there or have not heard, the new Mrs. Pilgrim is the former Petra March.